FOOLPROOF

Praise for Leigh Hays

Providence

"[O]ne of the most refreshing and sexiest romance novels I've read in a long time. The two leads had sizzling chemistry, the power dynamic between them was exciting and erotic, the romantic storyline was not formulaic in any way."—*Melina Bickard, Librarian, Waterloo Library (UK)*

"I've never stared at a book cover for so long. And Leigh Hays's writing is equally a showstopper in her debut lesbian romance *Providence*."—*Lambda Literary*

"Are we sure this is a debut book? It's Fantastic! I thoroughly enjoyed *Providence*. It was an edgy storyline with a fresh take on romance. When you start this book, you think it's going to be a romance; then you realize it's erotica with some light BDSM and then you're back to love but not before the author throws in a little drama. I was in a lesfic tailspin by the end… and completely loving it!"—*Les Rêveur*

"I liked how this was written. The settings were vivid, the chemistry well done, and their emotional journeys were a highlight…It's a solid debut book and it left me thinking for days after I finished it. I'd recommend it if you like books with tortured characters, and I'll be looking out for more from Leigh Hays in the future."—*Lesbian Review*

Too Good to Be True

"A huge part of her success in this is the characters: both Jen and Madison are complex, they're fallible in ways that make them relatable. Leigh Hays knows how to write sexy scenes, there's no doubt about that…if there's one thing Leigh Hays can write, it's chemistry. Scorching chemistry leads to a fantastic night of sex."—*Rainbow Literary Society*

"I really enjoyed it...The inevitable angst happens with enough time for things to be resolved with a satisfying end, and I felt the ending was appropriate for the pair. I'm hoping that there'll be another in the series and we'll get to see some brief glimpses of them again...Any wlw age gap romance fans should find something to enjoy in this one, as will most other romance fans."—*LGBTQ+ Reader*

"Good characters, simple plot, enough tension to keep the story interesting and to test the characters. I was rooting for them the whole way and enjoyed the supporting characters as well. If you're looking for a good, solid romance this summer, definitely check this one out."—*Kissing Backwards*

By the Author

Providence

Too Good To Be True

Foolproof

Visit us at www.boldstrokesbooks.com

FOOLPROOF

by

Leigh Hays

2022

FOOLPROOF

ISBN 13: 978-1-63679-184-5

THIS TRADE PAPERBACK ORIGINAL IS PUBLISHED BY
BOLD STROKES BOOKS, INC.
P.O. BOX 249
VALLEY FALLS, NY 12185

FIRST EDITION: OCTOBER 2022

CREDITS
EDITOR: BARBARA ANN WRIGHT
PRODUCTION DESIGN: STACIA SEAMAN
COVER DESIGN BY TAMMY SEIDICK

Acknowledgments

I wanted to thank Sandy, Radclyffe, Ruth, and the small army of people that make the books happen at BSB. I continue to learn and grow with your guidance.

This one required a lot of research. Some of it I drank, but a special shout-out goes to Maggie Campbell. Her web talks and podcast interviews were crucial in developing Martine's mindset and her distillery. And on the subject of research, a special thanks to Angie Williams for the quickest read-through ever and answering all my random Coast Guard questions.

Thanks to Barbara and her insistence that I add more feelings. With kindness and humor—lots of humor—she helps the book in my head become the book in print.

And thank you to the usual suspects: Aurora Rey for providing her own unique blend of cheerleader, task master, and mentor; my wife for finding space in our life—again—for me to write; and my son for bringing more joy and fun into my life than I thought possible.

For Clyde

Chapter One

Martine Roberts shivered as the London rain seeped under her collar. Her raincoat had been an emergency purchase in Piccadilly Circus and wasn't quite warm enough for her. She already missed the warm winter temperatures of Key West, but she couldn't miss the awards ceremony for the International Wine & Spirits Competition, even if she had begun to question its value. Her need for peer recognition had soured. After her distillery had won a Rising Star Award ten years ago, they'd never won another one at this event, though they'd been nominated seven other times. She expected this year to be no different.

At least she didn't have to wait in line too long before she entered Guildhall and followed the crowd into the reception area. She checked her coat and adjusted her tuxedo.

"Look at you." Jean-Claude Montabord strode over and hauled her off her feet in a gentle bear hug. A full head taller and twice her width, Jean-Claude towered over most of the other guests. In his early fifties, with laugh lines around his dark brown eyes, he was equal parts intimidating and approachable. His black tie tilted more toward the flamboyant with an iridescent blue waistcoat and bowtie. He made a show of looking around. "Where's your other half?"

"Someone had to mind the store." Her business partner, Ana Sofia, took the lead role in marketing and sales. She had quit her seventy-hour-a-week attorney gig in New York City before coming home to open the distillery with Martine. Award ceremonies often fell into her domain, but this year, she'd bowed out, saying, "It's your turn to listen to those pretentious assholes tell us what's wrong with our rum."

"I didn't see your name this year," she said. Last year, Jean-Claude's aged pot and column still rum took home a silver. He should have gotten the gold, but one of the bigger brands had edged him out. She'd spent two seasons working side by side with him and had a hand in the distillation of that expression. After several years maturing in port barrels, his distillery had finally bottled it last year.

He waved his hand. "I'm presenting not receiving. By the way, I tried your Cochin."

"And?" Cochin was a three-year pot and column still rum that was aged in bourbon barrels.

He paused, and she knew what he was going to say. "I'd proudly serve it at my table."

"But?" As her occasional mentor, he didn't pull his punches.

"You hit all the right notes you're going for but it's…" He motioned as if he could pluck the word he wanted out of the air.

"Bland?" she finished for him. Her professional tastings all said the same thing. A superb technical rum that lacked depth.

"I wouldn't say that. Your technique is beautiful."

A technique she'd honed through process and ingredients. She took copious notes from distillation to bottling so she could replicate or tweak her product from year to year. She sourced good ingredients because she believed in the motto, garbage in, garbage out. Starting with a subpar ingredient produced a subpar rum. But technique was only part of the equation. Distillation required a blend of science and art. An alchemy where the two met. Sometimes, the art part eluded her.

"But it's still too clinical. You need to take risks."

She curled her lip. She'd heard that before, too.

Jean-Claude clapped her on the back. "You'll get there. You've got time."

"You're not that much older than me." She nudged him in the ribs.

"A decade makes a difference."

"Whatever."

He held out his elbow. "Come on. Let's find a place to sit and watch this spectacle unfold."

They didn't make it five steps before Jean-Claude got pulled away. Martine felt his loss immediately and searched for another friendly face. The rum world was small in comparison to the international wine and spirits world. She knew, or knew of, all the rum people, a few of the bourbon folk, and virtually none of the wine group that made up two-thirds of the guests. While she could hold her own with the spirits crowd, she missed Ana Sofia's ease with strangers.

"Martine!" She glanced over and spotted her first rum mentor and old friend, Louis Rollo, heading her way.

"Louis!" He hugged her, and she looked over his shoulder, hoping his sister had not made the trip. Unfortunately, Toni was right behind him.

Toni greeted her with that "two kisses on each cheek" thing she did with strangers. A deliberate snub. "You look marvelous." She pinched the fabric of Martine's tux. "Armani?"

"No." Armani? Hardly. She couldn't afford a suit that expensive. As it was, Ana Sofia had insisted on a reputable designer with prices Martine could stomach. Although she suspected Ana Sofia had lowballed her the price and covered the rest. Something about representing the brand appropriately, and premium products required premium appearances.

"Excellent knockoff."

She chuckled. "I'm glad it meets with your approval." Did she think Martine cared what she thought?

Louis shook his head and rolled his eyes. "Yes, Toni, thank you for maintaining our standards."

"Don't be an ass, Louis." She dismissed him with a wave before bringing her focus back to Martine. "I've tried your Rooster blend. Good for an American rum."

Martine suppressed a laugh but couldn't control the smile. At least she didn't call it bland. "Thank you."

Louis scoffed. "Don't be a snob." He slung his arm across

Martine's shoulder and drew her away. "Don't listen to her. She's just jealous. In another year or two, you're going to surpass us."

Just another year? She already made a better unaged rum than they did. The Rollo family placed a higher emphasis on aged products. They had seventy years of continuous operation and had the inventory for it.

Toni pursed her lips. "Perhaps. I'll see you around."

"No doubt." Martine turned back to Louis and took a deep breath. Her chest loosened up, and her shoulders settled.

Louis squeezed her to his side. "Ignore her. She's been in a snit since Beatriz and her split up."

Beatriz had been the woman Toni had left Martine for. Both from upper class Barbadian society and both accustomed to living in the closet. Toni had been everything she'd wanted, privilege and prestige, professionally and personally. She might even have loved her, but after twenty years, she wasn't so sure. Still, her leaving had stung, making Martine feel as if she wasn't enough. For a moment, that green glow of jealousy basked in the news of the breakup before her better nature took over. "I don't want to talk about her. Tell me what's happening with that new still of yours."

She listened to him, knowing that in twelve hours, she'd be in Tampa, tired from travel, disappointed by yet another award loss, and having to suffer through Thanksgiving with her stepfamily. Hopefully, she'd duck out early and head home to Key West before the weekend.

❖

Martine took US 27 with the black smoke rising behind her and the sun on her left. Only one or two cars were out on the road as the sunrise came up over the burning sugarcane, the sky and the sun dusty and gray with the smoke and the soot coming off the fields. The horizon stretched on for miles with no signs of civilization other than the black ribbon of road in front of her. She settled back in her seat and headed south.

After enduring only one day, she'd decided that this was the last time she would ever schedule her family visit right after the awards ceremony. Every year with her mother and stepfather's family, the food got worse, and the politics got crazier. This year, she'd stayed at a hotel instead of the house, which had made the visit so much easier. But now it was done, and she didn't have to worry about them for another year.

She could also tick off seeing Toni. Even though she didn't see her every year, Toni always rattled her, even if she denied it to everyone else. But something about her and Beatriz splitting up had hit a deeper chord. Maybe because it could have been her instead of Beatriz. Would they have lasted that long? She didn't care, not really. But there was this air of what-if with her. Besides, she liked the life she led, picking up women for a night, sometimes two. She used to invest more time in her relationships, dating part-time residents for more than one season. But even that had stopped. The last few years had been a string of one-night stands and casual hookups. Low effort, no commitment worked for her.

She glanced at her speed after she zoomed past a highway patrol car. She slowed and sighed as the car switched on its lights and pulled out after her. So much for making good time. She pulled over and waited while the cop unfurled their long body from the front seat. Her eyes took in the walk and the slim hips, and a tiny spark of hope fluttered in her breast. She rolled down the window just as the officer stopped alongside her.

"Do you know why I stopped you?" The officer tipped her sunglasses down—mirrored, of course—and fixed Martine with an icy blue stare. It was so hard to tell if the cop was queer; even the straight ones were rather butch.

Martine tilted her head and offered her best "ah, shucks, ma'am" smile. "Well, I was doing about ninety-five there."

She raised an eyebrow. "It was actually one-oh-eight. That's forty-three above the speed limit. Where were you heading this early?"

Oh, that was much faster than she'd thought. Whoops. "Key West."

"Business or pleasure?"

Martine liked the way she said pleasure. A slight drawl and a pause between the words. Hints of the Deep South in those tones. "Home. Although I'm always up for a little pleasure."

The cop's jaw tightened, and any hint of warmth snapped shut. Holding out her hand, she said, "License, registration, and insurance."

Martine sighed. She'd tried. How of all places did she manage to run across the only police officer on this flat stretch of land?

She passed them through the window and admired the woman's steely professionalism. *Wonder what it would take to break that exterior?* She warmed to that idea as she watched the cop retreat in her rearview mirror. Those snug tan pants outlined a nice ass. She shifted in her seat and sighed. It was almost tourist season, and she really needed to get laid.

She picked up her phone and checked her email while she waited. The warm air blowing through her window carried the heavy humid feel that promised a hot day. She needed to be near the water and soon. That constant ocean breeze and salt spray kept the worst of the heat at bay.

She heard boots crunching the sand and shells that made up the majority of Florida roadways before the cop reappeared at her window. "Briar Rose. That's an unusual middle name."

"I'm a regular Disney princess." That joke usually got a lot of traction in the home of Walt Disney World. Briar Rose was one of the names used by Sleeping Beauty. People either got the joke or didn't. Those that did often made it into her bed. The officer's jaw twitched, and Martine was pleased to know she hit her mark.

"Where's your tiara?"

Martine grinned. "I left it at home."

The officer glanced at her license before handing it back. "Key West."

"Born and raised. You?" Since she managed to crack her exterior, there was no sense making the whole deal unpleasant. Besides, she'd liked her Briar Rose joke.

"Gulfport, Mississippi." She ripped off the ticket from her handheld and passed it over. "Along with the fine, there's a mandatory court date. You'll need to come back up here for the appearance since your speed was so high."

Martine took the ticket and held her gaze. "Any chance you'll be there?"

The cop pulled her sunglasses off, and Martine was equal parts chilled and turned on. "Are you hitting on me?"

Martine swallowed her sudden nerves. "Are you interested?"

"You should really slow down, Briar Rose." She slipped the lenses back on and walked away.

Martine slumped against the wheel and waited until the cop pulled away before turning her car on and getting back on the highway. Her brief adrenaline surge crashed as she drove home. She wanted to put her travels behind her. No more Toni, no more losing, no more family, no more hot cops. Just get home where her real life waited for her.

CHAPTER TWO

Elliot Tillman sat on the dock eating lunch and watching a gray pelican circle above the blue green water. The parmesan-crusted french fries added a salty contrast to the sweet and spicy Korean barbecue, while the tart and tangy limeade cooled the taco's gochujang sauce. Six months ashore and she still couldn't get enough of the variety of food Key West offered. She finished eating to the sound of the seagulls' caws and the slap-swish of the waves against the nearby sea wall.

"Tillman, you're up."

Elliot stuffed the last of her fries in her mouth and stood. Time to go to work. Around her, people were scrambling and picking up gear. She perked up as her lieutenant called out their orders. Propeller injury. Four miles offshore. South-southwest.

In the six months she'd been stationed in Key West, she'd seen more recreational diving accidents than in her entire career in the Coast Guard. Her other postings had less maritime recreation and more maritime commerce. Enforcing regulations, boarding ships, and searching for contraband had taken a toll on her; she almost didn't re-up. But then a position had opened up in Key West, a place filled with good childhood memories, and rescue and recovery work resonated with her need to make a difference. So, she'd extended her enlistment.

Elliot hustled out to the dock and jumped on deck. She slipped behind the wheel while the boat rocked as each member of the four-person crew hopped onboard. She finished up her final checks and looked over her shoulder. "Everybody all set?"

A chorus of affirmatives greeted her before she turned back to the helm and powered up the engine. She steered them out of the harbor and into the open ocean. The waves were relatively calm, so she could really gun it without fighting the current. Time was of the essence.

Next to her, Riviera spoke on the radio and shook his head. She half listened while she maintained speed and course. When he switched it off, she said, "Not good?"

"It's the upper thigh. Femoral artery. What's our ETA?"

"Four minutes," Elliot said without hesitation. As soon as they'd left the harbor, her mind had automatically gathered several navigational variables and kept a running calculation of speed, course, and estimated time of arrival. But four minutes was a long time when someone was bleeding out. Her mind overlaid the navigational charts on the water in front of her, and she recalculated their ETA based on a minor course correction and increased speed. She could shave off a minute and a half. She shouted over the engine's roar and the rush of water, "Everybody hold on."

She cut it closer to some shoals than was strictly regulation, but the current was on her side, pushing her away from the shallower shoals. She scanned the near water and not the horizon and didn't see the boat right away. Seconds ticked by, and she braced herself for another pass, worried that time was running out.

"There!"

Up ahead, a boat easily twice the size of their twenty-five-foot rapid-response craft bobbed on the waves. She throttled back and maneuvered into position as quickly as she could. The other two crew—Weiss and Hansford—used the boat hooks to pull them alongside. Riviera jumped across, followed by Hansford, while Elliot waited at the helm, tracking between the boat, the water, and their position. That first rush of adrenaline on the way out was beginning to dump, and she waited while others did the work.

A lot of her work was hurry up and wait. They drilled constantly and then responded to calls. As a Boatswain's Mate Second Class

Petty Officer, she'd done law enforcement, port operations, and just about every other aspect of seamanship on all kinds of boats. And she'd done it all over the world, from Alaska to Antarctica, on shore and at sea. But after Seattle, she'd actively sought assignments offshore. She'd wanted to get back to pure seamanship, but she'd also wanted to let the rumors die. Key West was her first posting onshore in three years, and so far, she didn't regret it. Perhaps the past was finally buried.

Weiss leaned in. "They're getting ready to move him."

"How's it look?" And just like that, her focus returned, and all senses were alert.

Weiss nodded. "Good. He's stable. He got lucky. An inch to the left and it would have nicked his artery. There's still a lot of blood loss." She headed back to the stern, and Elliot held the boat as steady as she could while they transferred the patient over. The cockpit sat close to the bow, and the stern was open deck. There were no fully enclosed spaces and barely enough room to move with four people aboard. The only place to sit and stand was on the open deck.

Weiss grabbed one end of the backboard while Riviera jumped across and landed on the deck. The three of them lowered the board, and Riviera sank to his knees beside his patient while Hansford and Weiss pushed off from the other boat.

She waited for the all-clear from Riviera and then pulled away. She throttled up to speed, Weiss settling in beside her to radio the ambulance waiting onshore. The return trip took slightly longer as she adjusted speed and course to keep the ride as smooth as possible. The way out was always a bit more rough-and-tumble than the way in, especially when they had passengers on board.

Weiss split her attention between the stern and Elliot. "We're going to check out this place off Duval tonight. You got plans?"

"Nope." Elliot could never quite tell if Weiss wanted something more with her. There was always this competitive undercurrent between them that felt very close to sexual tension. She loved the competition but not the sexual ambiguity. She scanned the horizon, intent on presenting a business-only exterior to discourage more conversation.

During her first posting, she'd slept with a fellow Coastie, and while it had ended amicably after they were assigned to different stations, she'd witnessed enough train wrecks to stay far away from relationships with other sailors. The one exception had been a brief fling during her last posting. She'd been assigned to the *Polar Star*, a heavy icebreaker, that regularly resupplied McMurdo Station in Antarctica, and more than a few crew members had hooked up during the long trip to the southern continent. For the most part, she used dating apps to find women and avoid messy entanglements at work.

"Then you should come." At the hopeful tone of her voice, Elliot turned and caught Weiss's smirk. The thing between them flickered.

"I'll think about it." Elliot held her look, not wanting to back down and not willing to show interest before focusing on the task at hand.

Elliot slowed on her approach to the dock, taking in the waiting ambulance. Hansford and Weiss moored the boat and helped Riviera offload the patient to the waiting EMTs. Elliot stayed on board and stowed their gear as they stood down. The initial rush wore off, and the routine monotony took over. She struggled to focus on the tasks at hand. Sometimes, a successful mission resulted in mixed feelings, pride at a job well done, letdown that it was all over, fear that she'd fail the next time. She pushed those feelings aside and went over her checklist to prep for the next crew before hopping up on the dock and heading indoors.

She sat and started filling out her paperwork; best to get it done before it piled up. She'd been there, done that.

Weiss popped her head into the small communal office just as she was finishing up. "We're getting ready. You coming?"

Despite the weird vibe between them, or maybe a little because of it, she rolled her chair back and said, "Yes." Maybe a little light flirtation would take the edge off her post-mission blues.

❖

Elliot regretted coming as soon as Weiss went straight to the bar and ordered shots for the table.

"I'm good."

"Come on, just one?" Weiss dangled it under her nose.

Elliot backed away. She was a few years older than most of her crew and a higher rank. Best to keep some distance. "Eh, me and tequila have a past."

Weiss leered at her. "Oh, really?"

She shook her head, not wanting to play this game. "Nothing exciting. Lots of vomit."

Weiss curled her lip. "Oh, okay. Never mind."

But that wasn't the end of it. Elliot spent the next two hours dodging drink offers. Her days of getting drunk and going home with a coworker were done. She played a couple rounds of darts to avoid Weiss's grabby hands before heading to the bar.

She nudged her way in and snagged a seat. The two bartenders zipped back and forth, moving around each other with ease. Elliot enjoyed the show, particularly the blond woman with a short bob and dark red lipstick. The noise, the heat, and the press of bodies beside and behind her buoyed her along, and she zoned out so completely that she lost track of where the bartender was and jumped when she came up to her.

"Sorry, didn't mean to startle you. I thought you saw me coming."

Had she seen her watching? Elliot took in her wide smile and intense energy. Was that her work persona or her real self? She wanted to know. "I must have lost track."

The bartender smiled and leaned against the bar. "Well, I'm here now. What can I get for you?"

Having spent most of her evening fending off unwanted sexual advances, Elliot had suppressed her own desires, but now they were back. She leaned in and whisper-shouted, "What do you recommend?"

"Depends. Are you looking to enjoy it or get drunk? Or both?" She broke eye contact and straightened up like something, or someone, had spooked her.

Elliot glanced over her shoulder and spotted Weiss heading her way. "How about one that makes me disappear?"

She leaned back in. "So, not a friend of yours?"

Elliot sighed. "Sort of. I work with her."

"Which branch?"

Surprised at the quick identification, she said, "Coast Guard. How can you tell?"

She chuckled. "Well, for one, we're a few blocks from both bases. And two, there's just something about you all that screams military, even when you're out of uniform."

Hard to argue that one. She opened her mouth to say more, but Weiss arrived and slipped in beside her. Elliot moved as far away as she could without getting into the lap of her neighbor. "What's taking you so long?"

The bartender leaned in and said, "That's my fault. Your friend here was telling me your drink orders, and I got confused. Is it okay if I send along a pitcher of margaritas on the house? I'll send your friend back when it's done."

Elliot doubted this woman ever got confused over a drink order. Weiss looked between them, too drunk for subtlety, and said, "Sure, but hands off. She's mine tonight."

Elliot stood, her mouth open. "Okay, Weiss. I think you've had enough for this evening."

"Are you cutting me off or just pulling rank?"

Elliot shook her head. Now she'd have to deal with Weiss's hurt feelings or worse. She'd wanted to enjoy the night, not babysit her crew. She should have known better. "Neither. I'm going to head out. And we'll leave this night here."

Weiss crossed her arms and swayed slightly. She gave the bartender a disgusted look and backed off. "Fine. Whatever. Your loss. And have someone else bring us that pitcher."

Elliot sagged forward and rubbed her forehead with both hands.

"I hope I didn't fuck things up for you."

Elliot opened her eyes and shook her head. "No. That was coming. You just got to witness it. I'm Elliot, by the way."

Wiping her hand down her apron before she touched her, the bartender said, "Brynn."

"Well, Brynn. It's nice to meet you. Maybe I'll see you around." Elliot turned to leave, and Brynn stopped her.

Sliding a card across the bar, she said, "Don't be a stranger."

She smiled and pocketed the card, a two-for-one drink coupon.

On her way out, Elliot locked eyes with Weiss and knew that she'd have to deal with her feelings sooner or later. She hoped Weiss would listen to reason. The last thing she wanted was more drama at work. She'd avoided that for six months, the longest break she'd had since Seattle. She'd almost believed that she'd outrun her past. Maybe that was too much to hope.

CHAPTER THREE

Martine opened the front doors of her distillery and paused at the edge as she always did, both impressed and pleased at the overall space. Sunlight streamed through the glass front doors and illuminated the Cejas y Roberts logo that Ana Sofia had placed in that spot for that particular effect. Visitors walked across the logo and into a cavernous room the full height of the original warehouse. But instead of up, their eyes were drawn to the glass walls across the room where Martine's steel and copper machinery worked on the rum they would be tasting. No barrels aged in the tasting room, although a few were used as decor.

A trio of ceiling fans with wide blades moved slowly enough to evoke a gentle breeze and even temperature, perfect for guests but not for how Martine liked to age rum. Pictures lined the wall, scenes of sponge divers and cigar makers, roosters, and children playing on sandy roads, all of them linked to Martine's or Ana Sofia's family history. Even the bar with its reclaimed Dade County pine had a history. It was once part of the original conch house that Martine's grandfather had grown up in.

With Jean-Claude's comments ringing in her ears and yet another loss at IWSC, she grabbed her cellar reports. Rather than discourage her, the loss had galvanized her. She didn't need to chase accolades anymore. She believed in her rum, and that was what counted. She'd continue making what she wanted. *And screw them.*

She headed back to the barrel room and pored over her inventory, trying to figure out a new taste profile. The distillery had a set number of profiles that used almost all their inventory, but there was always a barrel or two left for experimentation. Occasionally, one of their standard distillations would develop differently, but most of their experimental expressions were designed to be different. Maybe they'd distill a particular batch in a different way, longer fermentation, looser cuts. Or they'd age it in a different barrel or combined with different marks. And sometimes, it worked. Bantam, their best seller, started as a one-off that became so popular, Martine decided to replicate it. Some expressions developed a cult following, and she'd do limited releases every couple of years. But there was always one slot she kept for herself.

Her cellar reports were nothing more than several composition notebooks with weather notes, taste profiles, and a basic indexing system. Every season, Ana Sofia had one of her interns enter the data into a spreadsheet. While she appreciated the improved data mining that came with it, she preferred sitting in the barrel room, flipping through pages, where the connection between touch and taste were intimately linked. Sitting at a computer just didn't give her the same feel as being in a room with the scents surrounding her. But so far, her search had been a bust. She just couldn't get a sense of what she wanted to do next. Something sweet, something sharp. She'd land on one idea and then get distracted by another equally good one.

Totally frustrated by her indecision, she gathered the notebooks and trudged back upstairs. The heat of the cellar condensed on her arms as she entered the air-conditioned section of her distillery.

The distillery door opened just as Martine turned on the landing. Chloe came through and glanced up. "Hey, I think Ana Sofia could use your help."

Martine hurried down, passing the books off to Chloe and walked into the tasting room. A huge crowd of sunburned tourists milled around the space. Martine put on her extrovert self and jumped right in. "Are you here for a tasting?"

An hour later, the last of the crowd wandered out. A cruise ship had docked a few hours ago, and its passengers were making the rounds. Another relationship Ana Sofia had cultivated to improve their business. Martine tucked the last of the glasses into the dishwasher and turned it on.

Ana Sofia reviewed the open bottles and grabbed a few backups from the floor stock. "Sorry to pull you away from your creative time."

"*Pfft*. My time was better served out here today."

Ana Sofia grimaced. "That bad?"

Martine sighed and leaned against the bar. Ana Sofia knew that her true skills were in the back of the house. She did well in a pinch because of her passion for her rum, but sales was not her strong suit.

"Maybe this will help." Ana Sofia placed a single key on the bar and slid it across the polished hardwood.

Martine palmed it and held it up. "What's this?"

"A house key."

Three weeks ago, she'd been forced to move out of her apartment after the bank had foreclosed on it. Apparently, the out-of-state landlord was behind on his mortgage payments and still collecting rent from Martine. She drifted from cousin to cousin before "moving" into her office at the distillery. Embarrassed at being caught, she laughed it off. "I don't know. I feel like we're moving too fast. We've only known each other for twenty years."

Ana Sofia smacked her arm. "Don't be an ass. Pilar heard you were still living at the distillery. She has an open house." Ana Sofia's mother owned several houses up and down the Keys, but Ana Sofia often called her by her first name because of her tendency to go all robo-mom.

Annoyed, Martine crossed her arms. "She doesn't need to do that." She wasn't twenty-two anymore, and she didn't need anyone taking care of her. If she'd wanted help, she'd have no problem getting it. She couldn't swing a cat without hitting a Roberts or a Pinder. One call and she'd be set. She had an idea why she was so reluctant to ask for help. Over the years, she'd watched too many cousins slowly relegated to misfit status because they'd asked the family for help. She didn't want to get lumped into that group. Or maybe she was getting too old for the roommate thing. She'd liked her old place and her old roommate and didn't want something new.

"Oh, it's not charity. She expects you to pay rent. But she doesn't want you sleeping in the upstairs office. It looks bad."

That sounded more like Pilar. Even though Ana Sofia was her original investor, Pilar was the source of Ana Sofia's money. And Martine was not afraid to admit that Ana Sofia's mother intimidated her just enough for her to obey her wishes. So much for sorting it out herself.

Tucking the key into her pocket, she swallowed her pride and sighed, "Where is it?"

"Chapman Street. It's four blocks away." In the heart of Bahama Village.

"How much?" Many parts of Bahama Village, like the rest of Key West, were undergoing gentrification. The house could be one of those newly renovated jewels or a run-down bungalow with no central air. Either way, she didn't have much of a choice. Pilar had forced her hand.

The last thing she wanted was Pilar coming down and giving her a key. At least with Ana Sofia, she had the pretense of free will. Besides, the market for housing during tourist season was awful, and no matter what condition the house was in, Bahama Village was not a dangerous neighborhood.

Ana Sofia rattled off a slightly below market but still steep rent.

Martine hissed. Apparently, this house was renovated. "I can't afford that alone."

"Then get a roommate."

"Who?" Most of the people she knew already had places to live, and she wasn't interested in shopping around. Living with a stranger at this stage of her life felt kind of exhausting. Ana Sofia was the only person she knew still living at home. She leaned in and said, "You know, living at home has got to have its drawbacks. Don't you want the kind of freedom to come and go as you please?"

Ana Sofia huffed. "I have that. Thank you very much."

It had been worth a try. She didn't really want to live with Ana

Sofia; she already worked with her. She loved her, but too much togetherness would kill them. "I just don't think I can afford it."

Ana Sofia grimaced. "I can probably convince her to reduce the rent for the first month while you look for someone. But I've got to tell you, she's pretty adamant about you moving out."

Not for the first time, Martine felt the close pull of the community closing in around her. She could ignore Pilar, but the cost of defiance seemed too steep. She needed a place, and there was no way in hell she'd ask her own family. If Ana Sofia could give her the month, it would buy her time so she could find another place, something she could afford on her own.

"Fine. I'll do it. Maybe a change of scenery will get my creative juices flowing again."

"You'll figure it out. You always do." Ana Sofia didn't pull any punches with her, introspection was not her style, and that made their partnership work.

Her stomach rumbled, and she jumped at the opportunity to leave. Normally, Ana Sofia's get-things-done approach worked for her, but not today. "I'm going to get lunch. You want me to bring you something back?"

"Nah. I'm good. I have leftovers." She'd already turned back to her work.

Martine ducked into the distillery to make sure Chloe was all set before heading out into the warm afternoon. She moved through the press of bodies coming and going.

Her personal life had always been chaotic, and that didn't bother her. Keeping people close, yet at a distance, worked for her. She just needed to break out of whatever funk this was, and maybe her work could get back on track. Moving out of her office seemed like a good start.

CHAPTER FOUR

Elliot rolled out of bed and nearly tripped on a discarded strap-on harness. She stumbled into a dresser and froze as Brynn mumbled something. *Should I leave a note? Maybe she'll wake up, and I can say good-bye.* She didn't often sleep with strangers, but one thing had led to another, and here she was. Now she wanted to leave but had no idea what the protocol was, so she waited until the noise settled before collecting her clothes and leaving the room.

Afraid of getting caught, she dressed in the bathroom with the lights off. What would she say anyway? *Thanks for the sex. I don't know you, but maybe I should. I'll call you.* Or maybe she should stay. Brushing aside her doubts, she paused at the edge of the living room where another woman was pulling on her shoes beside the couch.

Something about the way this woman kept looking around made her think this was not Brynn's roommate but rather a guest of said roommate. Apparently, Elliot was not the only one in the apartment making a getaway. She hung back, trying to decide if she should wait for her to leave or commit to being seen.

But the decision was made for her when the other woman stood and turned. "Oh, I'm sorry. I didn't mean to wake you."

Elliot stepped into the dim light coming from the kitchen. She knew her, but from where?

"Oh, you're not…Elliot?" Disbelief and shock filled the other woman's voice.

That voice. The way she said her name. So familiar but not in a, "I had sex with her once" way. Had she rescued her? No, the voice reminded her of someone from long ago. Someone she'd known in Key West almost thirty years ago. Moving closer, she got a better look. It couldn't be. Here? Same age, same features, and a half-smile that had always made Elliot feel as if she was in on the joke. Her old best friend: "Martine."

Martine's half-smile turned into a full-fledged grin. "What are you doing here?"

Elliot had been low-key on the lookout for Martine since she'd arrived. But she'd stopped herself from looking too hard. Martine was special, the girl who had gotten Elliot before she'd even known who she was. What if adulthood had changed all that? She wasn't ready to see her, not like this.

Forcing a bravado she did not feel, Elliot gave Martine a once-over, stopping at her shoulder-length brown hair that was mussed in an "I just had sex" style. Her own hair probably had the short version of that look. "Same thing as you, I think."

A door opened behind them. Martine's eyes widened. Grabbing Elliot's arm, she whispered, "Come on. Let's get out of here." Martine opened the front door as Elliot scanned the room for her shoes. "Just grab them. Let's go."

Elliot scooped her shoes off the floor, and Martine practically pushed her out the door. The crushed-shell walkway cut into her bare feet, and she hissed as she walked. She paused at the edge of the sidewalk to slide on her shoes.

Martine glanced behind them. "If you're having second thoughts, I'm leaving you here. But it's going to be awkward if you stay."

Elliot stomped her feet into her shoes and squared her shoulders. She knew she should have stayed, but now that she was out of the house, she was committed. If that was Brynn following them, she'd deal with the fallout later. "My truck's over here."

They dashed across the street. The truck chirped, and they climbed in. Elliot pulled on her seat belt as she drove away. Out of the corner of her eye, she saw Martine look over her shoulder. Was someone following them? Probably not, but she still asked, "Are we clear?"

Martine rolled her eyes. "Yes, I think we shook 'em."

"Good thing." Elliot smiled, surprised at how familiar running away together felt. Almost thirty years had passed, and trouble still followed them.

"How long are you in Key West?" Martine's warm smile an invitation to share.

"I live here."

"What?"

"Well, Marathon."

Martine whistled. "That's a hell of a commute."

"Tell me about it." Ninety minutes each way.

"Well, how long have you been back?" Martine's indignant tone matched her crossed arms.

"About six months."

Martine scoffed, clearly offended. "Why didn't you look me up?"

Elliot pulled up to a red light and shifted in her seat. When she hadn't run into Martine immediately, she'd hesitated and then lost her nerve. They'd been ten when Elliot had moved away, and just because Elliot remembered her didn't mean Martine did the same. So many people must have come and gone in Martine's life. The last time Elliot had rekindled an old relationship, she'd regretted it. After Lara, she'd wanted to keep the good memories rather than replace them with bittersweet ones. She shrugged and told the truth. "I didn't know if you'd remember me. It was only two years."

Martine laughed. "Seriously? How could I forget you? You were the first friend I had that wasn't related to me."

"That's not true. Is it?" Elliot didn't have that many friends. She had grown up while being constantly on the move from deployment to deployment. She had learned independence early in life. In her twenties, she'd celebrated that experience, downplaying the loneliness and solitude, but these last few years, she'd looked back with different eyes. Something about the way Martine spoke made her wonder if she had grown up the same way, alone in her large family.

"Where am I taking you? I'm going to run out of road soon." She didn't know where they were going, so she'd picked a random direction. Now they were coming up on the Southernmost Point.

"I don't want to put you out."

"It's two in the morning, and Key West isn't that big."

"Do you know where Mallory Square is?"

"You're kidding, right? The place where all the tourists gather to watch the sunset every day? Yeah, I know where it is."

Martine held up her hands. "Well, not everyone knows how to get there while driving."

After that comment, she did end up getting turned around in the web of one-way streets, and Martine gently teased her all the way. Elliot laughed as she drove, enjoying the easy back-and-forth.

She pulled up in front of a white and red brick building but couldn't read the sign in the dark. A squat warehouse among commercial buildings. "You live here?"

Martine waggled her hand. "I'm between places. I've got a couch in my office."

Still caught up in the hint of loneliness, Elliot considered inviting Martine back to her place. But she knew nothing about her life. She'd already slept with one stranger, no need to invite another to her apartment. Besides, Elliot had slept in worse places. Who was she to judge? "Well, okay."

Martine opened the door and paused. Looking over her shoulder, she said, "It was good to see you."

"Yeah, you too."

Martine got back in the car and closed the door. "This is dumb. You want to go get breakfast? Catch up on old times?"

Not wanting to end the night, Elliot put the car back into drive and said, "Where to?"

CHAPTER FIVE

Elliot sat at the booth and finally got a good look at Martine. Her brown hair, so wild and curly in their youth, now fell past her shoulders with more of a wave to it. Her short, squat body had lengthened and become more muscular. But that smile and those dark eyes still held the sly humor and quick intelligence that had gotten them into so much trouble in the past.

"I can't believe you didn't look me up." Martine stretched her arms along the backrest, drawing Elliot's gaze to her breasts for a brief moment.

She'd spent only two years in Key West before her father had been reassigned, and most of her memories had faded, but Martine featured in the ones she did remember. She shrugged, not willing to admit her fear of being forgotten. "I don't know. People change. It was a long time ago."

Martine leaned in. "Well, not much changes here."

A server bustled over and apologized for being late. He looked like the only one working, and the diner was packed with drunk tourists. "What can I get you?"

Martine glanced at Elliot. "Do you know what you want? I come here all the time."

Elliot grabbed the menu and picked the first thing she saw, grilled cheese and ham. She heard Martine order something called chicken fried fries and a chocolate milkshake. "Can you add fries and a vanilla milkshake to mine as well?"

"With or without gravy?"

Elliot paused and looked at Martine, who mouthed, *with*. "With. Thanks." She tucked the menu back in the holder. Curious and eager to fill in the gaps, she started at the beginning. "How are your parents?"

"They're good."

Generic answer for a generic question. She'd go a little deeper. "Does your dad still run that fishing charter?"

Martine sat up and pulled her arms back to her side. "My dad died about a year after you left."

Expecting to trade mild pleasantries about their respective parents, Elliot recovered quickly. "Oh, I didn't know. I'm sorry."

Martine waved her off, avoiding eye contact. "It was a long time ago."

She wanted to ask more but got the feeling that the topic was closed. "What about your mom?"

Martine relaxed again. "She got remarried and retired to Tampa a few years back. What about yours?"

Why had Elliot brought up parents? Martine wasn't the only one with family baggage. If Elliot wanted safe, she should have talked about the weather. Their milkshakes arrived, and Elliot took a sip. The sweet smooth taste of vanilla ice cream filled her mouth, chasing her bitter thoughts away. "My dad finally retired from the Navy. I think they're in Maine these days."

"You think?" Martine stirred her chocolate shake before pulling the spoon out and tasting it.

"We had a falling-out about ten years ago. When I finally came out to them." She did not want to go into the last conversation with her parents. The anger was gone, leaving hurt and disappointment in its wake.

Martine twisted her lips. "That sucks, but I'm not surprised."

Curious, Elliot asked, "You knew that my parents were raging homophobes?"

"That you were gay. I'd wondered."

Glad that the focus was off her parents, Elliot had also wondered the same thing about Martine whenever she looked back at their friendship as two little tomboys running around.

Martine waggled a finger at her. "After I came out, I realized there were more gay people in my life than I thought. And I knew you were one of them."

Elliot laughed, delighted at the confirmation. "Happy to oblige."

Their food arrived, and they both dug in before the conversation started up again. "So what are you doing back in Key West?"

"I'm stationed here." Elliot popped a fry into her mouth.

"Navy?"

Elliot shook her head. When she decided to serve, she'd chosen the Coast Guard instead of her father's branch, the Navy. Yet another sore point between them. "Coast Guard."

"Really? Do you like it?"

No one had asked her that in many years. Everyone just assumed that since she'd stayed in, she liked it. She took a bite of grilled cheese, just the right amount of crunch to gooeyness, and considered her answer. She liked the work and the mission, but after fifteen years, the constant moving and the lack of stable relationships had begun to wear on her. "Mostly. What about you?"

Martine stood abruptly. "Excuse me."

Wondering if she'd touched a nerve, Elliot turned her head as a vaguely familiar person walked up to them. Martine hugged the newcomer and nodded to Elliot. "Cass, do you remember Elliot?"

Cass, Martine's younger cousin, who had worn pink dresses and had played with Tonka trucks. Cass held out a hand. "I'm afraid not."

Elliot half stood and shook their hand. "I think you were, like, four."

Martine nodded and sat again. "Probably. Are you just getting off work?"

Cass glanced behind them. A group wearing chef's whites waved. Elliot couldn't tell if they'd come in with Cass or not. "I don't want to interrupt…"

Martine wore a confused look, but Elliot knew exactly what they looked like: two people who'd just rolled out of bed after having sex and were looking for food. Interested in Martine's reaction, Elliot watched and waited until she picked up on the implication.

Martine blushed and stammered. "Oh, right. No, not Elliot. She…I…I was with some…I don't actually know her name."

Endeared by Martine's momentary loss of confidence, Elliot opened her mouth to defend her. Martine hadn't been the only one hoofing it in the middle of the night. But Cass spoke again before Elliot could get a word out.

Cass looked positively scandalized. "You don't know her name?"

"Well…" Martine sputtered and waved. "Don't you have someplace to be? Go be with your friends."

Cass chuckled. "I do. Nice to meet you. Again."

"You too." Elliot turned her attention back to Martine, who had recovered enough of her dignity to eat. Although they'd known each other well as kids, Elliot knew very little about her now. Was she the kind of person who slept with strangers? And what did that mean? After last night, she didn't have much room to judge. Now, if Elliot wanted to date her, she'd definitely have an opinion.

Martine paused, her eyes narrowed. "What?"

She spoke without thinking. "Do you do this often?"

"Jump into cars with old friends?" Martine's smile twitched upward, a slight tease to her voice as if she knew what Elliot was asking.

Elliot backed down. Did it matter? Not if they were friends. "You know, of all the places I thought I'd run into you, this was not one of them."

"Oh, really, and how did you figure we'd meet again?" Martine leaned in and rested her chin on her folded hands.

Elliot shrugged. "I don't know. Maybe Publix? Just not…like this."

Martine laughed again. "I can see it now."

They traded outrageous stories of how they might have met for a while. Elliot laughed so hard, her sides started to hurt. She kept the more intimate scenarios to herself, unwilling to break the growing camaraderie with her fantasies. As the night wore on, she knew a friendship with Martine would last longer than anything romantic.

Finally, Martine smiled and shook her head. "Wow. It's so good to see you."

Elliot's chest warmed as she smiled back. "I know. Me too."

Their server put the check on the table with another apology. "Can I get you two anything else?"

They shared a look, and Martine said, "No, we're all set." She handed him her card while Elliot reached for her wallet.

"Hey, I got that."

Martine waved her off. "You can get me next time."

"Absolutely." She'd already started thinking of things to do together.

They exchanged phone numbers before heading outside. The streetlights obscured the stars overhead, and a slight breeze blew in off the water. "You want me to drop you off?"

Martine shook her head. "I'll walk."

She nodded and then said, "It was really good to see you again."

"Yeah, it was."

This weird moment hung between them. Was Elliot supposed to shake her hand, hug her?

Martine looked at her for a moment before she laughed. "Come here, you." She pulled her into a half hug.

Elliot then watched her walk away, looking forward to the next time.

CHAPTER SIX

Martine managed a few hours' sleep and woke, groggy and disoriented, chased by weird childhood dreams. She hauled herself over to the bathroom and quickly washed up.

Running into Elliot had stirred up her past. She didn't keep it buried so much as she ignored it, tucked away in a box for safekeeping. Seeing Elliot had opened those boxes, leaving her unsettled but also happy to have found her again.

In her office, she stretched and cracked her back. Much better.

Ana Sofia's heels clicked across the tile floor, and Martine stepped out. "Morning."

Ana Sofia gasped and jumped back.

"Sorry. Didn't mean to scare you."

Her light brown hair was usually tucked into a messy bun when she was working the tasting room but not today. She was in full-on brand ambassador mode, elegant but approachable, dressed to impress. "Did you sleep here? I thought you'd already moved."

She headed over to the coffee machine and dropped in a pod. "Not yet. I just…" Feeling defensive, she switched subjects. "Why are you dressed up?"

"We have guests today."

"Yeah, Tuesday." The machine beeped, and she grabbed her mug.

"Today is Tuesday."

"Shit." How'd she lose a day? She didn't drink that much, and the sex hadn't exactly stopped the world from spinning. Maybe staying up half the night with Elliot had messed with her sense of time.

Ana Sofia looked her up and down. "When was the last time you showered?"

Martine glanced at her baggy shorts and V-neck T-shirt, the same outfit from yesterday. She grimaced. "Uh…"

Ana Sofia marched into her office. "If you can't remember, it's been too long."

Busted, Martine followed her, leaned against the doorjamb, and sipped her coffee. "I ran into an old friend last night."

"Anyone I know?" She wandered the office, gathering marketing materials.

"A childhood friend. Before your time."

Ana Sofia pulled three glossy folders from the file cabinet and tucked the sheets and brochures inside. "Did you hook up?"

Martine frowned, uncomfortable with the question and confused by that feeling. Not one to shy away from her casual affairs, something about adding Elliot to that mix bugged her. Ana Sofia knew about her personal life, and she didn't judge, but Martine wanted to protect her relationship with Elliot from her other affairs. "It's not like that."

"No unrequited childhood crushes?" Ana Sofia sat and pulled her keyboard toward her.

"I didn't have any childhood crushes." If she did, she didn't know it. She'd suppressed her desire for women until her late teens.

Ana Sofia didn't look up from the monitor. "I find that hard to believe."

Which didn't surprise Martine. But her friendship with Elliot had been deeper than that, a prepubescent connection between two kindred spirits. Elliot really had been her first friend outside the family, the first person who'd seen her as herself and not the family's idea of who she was. "It was never like that. Besides, we were too young."

Ana Sofia finally leveled a look at her. "I had a crush on Ms. Rodriguez when I was six."

"Well, you're just special. I'm going to unlock the front doors." She pushed away from the wall.

"At least change your shirt," Ana Sofia called after her.

Not giving her an answer, Martine headed downstairs and opened the second door leading out of the stairwell, flicking on the lights. The lingering warmth on her skin condensed in the air-conditioned hallway.

Her conversation with Ana Sofia irked her. She'd given surface details, and she'd gotten a superficial response. She usually appreciated Ana Sofia's no-nonsense truth telling, but she'd needed a gentler approach to suss out her feelings about Elliot's return. She just needed to sit with it before she tried talking again.

She paused at the start of the hallway, and all her ambiguous feelings faded as pride and satisfaction overtook her. Dubbed the Hall of Fame by Ana Sofia, the hallway held twelve years of paraphernalia: awards, media write-ups, and the labels of each expression they'd ever distilled. Martine skimmed the pictures, casually cataloging the hits and misses of each type of rum, a living history of their work together, before she entered their tasting room.

The room was more impressive, given the original state of the warehouse. When Ana Sofia had first shown the building to her twelve years ago, her heart had sunk as she'd glanced at the boarded windows, crumbling brick walls, and spots in the roof where the sun had slipped through, illuminating the dust that had swirled all around them.

"What do you think?" Ana Sofia had stopped in the middle of the warehouse and opened her arms. "It's gorgeous, isn't it?"

She had no idea what anyone could see in the disgusting and dilapidated building. She'd never be able to afford to clean it up. She had sneezed, the sting of ammonia burning her nose. "Is that pee?"

Ana Sofia had scowled. "Probably. Come on."

Unfazed by her less-than-enthusiastic response, Ana Sofia had pulled her through the building, pointing out barely discernible features while revealing her plans for the space. "There's enough room to put your still over there."

"I can't afford this."

"I'd like to finance it."

Martine's jaw had dropped. They'd talked about her dreams, but Ana Sofia had never mentioned wanting to help. "You're not serious, are you?"

"As a heart attack. You should stop working for other people and start making your own rum. With me."

She had no regrets. It had taken three years to restore the Cejas warehouse and another to get the distillery up to code, but it had been well worth the wait. Twelve years later, they were living their dream and sharing it with others.

Martine opened the front doors and headed back to the distilling room to start her day. Ana Sofia came down twenty minutes later. She nudged her and pointed toward a trio peeking through the door. "Looks like they're here. Let's show them around."

Martine braced herself for a day of extroverting and headed out to greet them. Ana Sofia gave their guests a general rundown of the tasting room and the way she ran it. Martine tuned her out. She'd heard it before. Both their reputation as a quality distiller and their longevity—not long compared to the centuries behind the Caribbean, South American, and Central American distilleries—meant they often played host to newer distilleries.

Martine was seeing more and more people getting into the business as the craft distilling industry turned toward different spirits. Rum, in particular, was seeing a rise in popularity similar to bourbon's reemergence. She'd begun to guard her time to avoid working with fly-by-night operations. The Sawgrass team took their business seriously, and she had made time for them. They had been in operation for a few years, barely enough time to get a good quality aged rum on the market but long enough to have established a brand.

The questions they asked were more in-depth and homed in on the logistics of running tastings. Martine picked up the tour near the fermentation tanks, where the bready smell already permeated the room. "We use grade A molasses and open tanks for the fermentation process..." She rattled off times, temperatures, and pH balances while she moved toward the two stills they used.

One of her early mentors had sworn that she could tell the flavor of the rum by the shape of the still, and Martine had believed her. She had toured several distilleries and had sampled it all, designing the bright and full-bodied rum she wanted. She'd started with a column still, getting those clean and intense notes. Still not satisfied, she'd searched for depth, switching out components in her still and changing her fermentation time and temperature. Nothing was sacred to her. She tinkered with everything until Ernie had arrived, her pot still. Ernie brought the depth she'd searched for, and blended together with the column still rum, she'd found her style. Her patience and perseverance had paid off.

"Have you considered making an agricole?" Daniela asked. She'd been hanging in the background while Luiza and James had done most of the talking.

"I'd love to, but fresh cane juice takes too long to get here." At least, the kind of fresh cane juice she wanted, not the stuff they sold in stores. Martinique had cornered the market on that particular style, partly because of their strict labeling laws and because of the availability of sugar cane, but she'd had a few good ones from Hawaii and Louisiana. She enjoyed the grassy bite of a good agricole.

Daniela continued, "We're working with a couple local growers. I think we can get a steady supply."

"Then you should do it. There are very few craft distillers who can. Anything to set yourselves apart is a win." She envied them a little bit. They were at the beginning of the journey that she'd already taken. The joy of discovery and the thrill of putting it all together still lay ahead of them. Not that she'd want to go back. She'd worked hard to get where she was, but part of the reason she liked helping other distilleries was seeing the different paths people took to get their product made.

Martine circled her still, rattling off the way it worked and the parts she used. Each part she described evoked a taste mnemonic for her. The toasty notes she'd gotten from burning the yeast on the bottom had disappeared when she'd installed an agitator, but the resulting cane flavor had turned out to be what she was looking for.

Chloe, her assistant distiller, wandered in and out of the space and the conversation. Since Chloe did more of the hands-on distillation, Martine let her field the day-to-day questions. Her background in chemistry paired nicely with Martine's practical experience and intuitive touch. Chloe had shown up three years ago, running from a lucrative but soul-sucking corporate chemist position. She'd wanted to do something, anything. Martine had recognized a kindred spirit and had hired her immediately.

Martine took them into the barrel room, and that distinct smell of wood and spirits washed over her. She gave them a rundown of their aging process, pointing out the lack of air-conditioning and open-air slants in the roof as stylistic choices and not a lack of funding. "We do lose more alcohol to evaporation with these conditions, but the mix of salt air, heat, and wood bring that extra wow to our rum."

She spent the next hour going through their inventory, sampling her marques, and sharing her blending process. She didn't hold back like she'd seen other distillers do. So much alchemy existed in creating good rum that sharing a recipe or secrets wasn't commercial suicide. She eventually cut them off when everyone started flagging in the growing heat. Collecting a box of labeled bottles, she said, "Let's go inside and sample these in the air-conditioning."

Ana Sofia poured from their current stock, and Martine talked about their next expression. After twelve years, Ana Sofia could talk about esters and flavors almost as well as Martine, but only Martine could sample distillate and project what those tastes and smells would be like in six months, two years, and longer. By the time they were done, the tasting room staff had arrived, along with the midmorning crowd. They made plans for dinner and drinks before they were alone again upstairs.

❖

Elliot drove back to Marathon, tired and wired from her late-night breakfast with Martine. Of all the places to run into her. Seeing her again felt a little like coming home, if she had a home. Growing up, all the bases had the same look and feel. Even the people blended together. Key West had been different. In every memory, Martine had been different:

"Elliot peed her pants. Elliot peed her pants."

Elliot tried to protest—the chair had been wet before she'd sat down—but the older kids didn't care. They started to move away until she was left alone, trapped in her humiliation until the bell rang. A tray slammed down next to her belonging to Martine Roberts, who sat two desks in front of her and had never said anything but hi. "Francis Robert Pinder," she bellowed.

A few titters and catcalls of "Francis" stopped Elliot's bully in his tracks. But the words "At least she didn't shart her pants during Thanksgiving and pretend the dog messed on the couch" shut him up.

Laughter erupted, and Bobby's face went red, but he backed down.

Martine sat next to her and started eating her fries.

Elliot wanted someone to listen to her. "I really didn't pee my pants. There was water there."

"I know. He's just being mean." Martine put a hand on her arm. "He can dish it out, but he can't take it."

Elliot didn't know quite what that meant but was relieved that Martine believed her. "I'm Elliot."

She smiled. "I know." She pointed to herself. "I'm Martine. Francis is my cousin, and he's not going to bother you again."

Moving from place to place, she'd always been the butt of the joke, the outsider of the group. No one had ever stood up for her like Martine had that day. Martine had earned her gratitude and loyalty in that moment, and the friendship that grew out of that meeting cemented Martine's specialness in her past.

She parked behind her apartment complex just as the sun rose.

Someone called her name, and Weiss jogged over, either coming or going on a morning run. "Do you got a minute?"

She suppressed a yawn. She didn't have the energy to deal with Weiss hitting on her. "Can it wait until work?"

Weiss fidgeted with her earbuds and stared at the ground. Her tone went from casual to serious. "I don't want to do this at work."

Steeling herself, Elliot said, "Okay. What's up?"

"I...I wanted to apologize for the other night. I was drunk, and I crossed a line."

Relieved at the admission, Elliot made a choice to let her down easy. Their night at the bar had been off-duty, and although she could reprimand Weiss, she wanted to put it behind them so they could move on. "Apology accepted, and look, I'm flattered. But we work together. It gets too complicated."

Weiss tilted her head, a half-smile on her face. "Thanks."

Reassured by her response, Elliot nodded toward the stairs. "Well, I need to get some sleep."

"Right, sure." Weiss stepped away, but when Elliot made the landing, Weiss called, "You know, I heard a rumor about you."

A tiny knot formed in Elliot's stomach, but she forced a nonchalance she didn't feel. She was too far up to get a good read on Weiss's expression. "Is that so?"

"I heard that your testimony took down David Shaw."

Elliot waited for the other shoe to drop. The one accusing her of turning on one of their own. It always found her no matter where she was stationed. The Coast Guard wasn't that big. "Well, don't believe everything you hear."

"But you were in Seattle at the same time, weren't you?"

"I knew David. Everyone did." And that was what made his black-market business so successful. When Grace Blackwell had approached her to be an informant, she'd done her duty. She hated being caught in the middle, but she couldn't ignore it either. Despite the fact that her testimony was sealed, the rumors persisted, and Shaw's popularity meant she faced subtle and sometimes overt backlash at her subsequent postings. She chafed at her unfair treatment while Shaw's legacy lived on, untarnished. Six whole months had passed at this station before someone had brought it up. She'd hoped that reprieve meant that maybe his misdeeds had finally caught up to his reputation, but now she wasn't so sure.

Elliot didn't bother to hide her yawn and nodded toward her apartment. "I've got to go."

"Oh, right. Yes. See you later."

She headed up another flight, unlocked her door, and shivered at the extra cold air-conditioning. Fully furnished with the hint of stale cigarette smoke, her small one-bedroom apartment had a tiny galley kitchen and a barely-there hallway between bedroom and bathroom. While not the worst place she'd ever lived, it ranked toward the bottom. At least it had a washer and dryer, even if they were stuffed inside the bathroom. The rent had been reasonable but not if she'd have to put up with the rumors again.

She crawled into bed and woke up in the early afternoon. She listened to a couple podcasts while she did laundry and cleaned the apartment. When she got to the kitchen, she paused and took out her earbuds. Her appliances were at least twenty years old, and no amount of scrubbing had ever made them look any better. If she'd known how bad the kitchen was, she wouldn't have rented the place. She hated using her prized All-Clad on it. But she'd been so desperate to be onshore again after nine months on the *Polar Star* that she'd picked the apartment with the densest Coast Guard population. She'd thought the familiarity would be comfortable, but perhaps that had been a mistake.

Convinced that this time, she'd get those stains off the stove, she pulled apart the burners and started cleaning. She stopped twenty minutes later after little effect on the caked-on, baked-on grime. She literally threw in the towel and showered instead.

Drying off, she watched a cockroach saunter across the bathroom sink and sighed. She'd really thought she'd be at a different point in her life after fifteen years in the service. She didn't want to leave the Coast Guard. It was her career, and she was good at it. But after so many years in, she had aged out of the party life of the much younger members, but she didn't quite fit with the older married enlisted, either. With her nine months on the

Polar Star and these six months in off-base housing, she had social claustrophobia. Running into Martine only reinforced the obvious: she craved new people and new perspectives. And she was going to start with Martine. They'd been friends before, she wanted to be that again.

CHAPTER SEVEN

Two full weeks passed before Martine saw Elliot again. She kept meaning to text her, but work consumed her every waking moment. Her new fermenter arrived, and she spent all that time getting it installed and running test batches before she linked it into production. She barely managed to get the rest of her furniture over to the Bahama Village bungalow.

Throughout the years, she'd thought about Elliot, and she'd looked for her on and off. She'd go a few years without a passing thought, then something would remind her, and she'd think about her again, wondering if two queer kids had seen something in each other that they hadn't seen in themselves. But the last place she'd expected to find her was leaving someone else's house in the middle of the night.

Gone was the gangly little kid who had a hard time expressing her feelings with words. The Elliot she'd spoken to clearly knew who she was and what she wanted. Her quiet confidence had impressed Martine, and how often did people get a second chance at a friendship?

When she spotted Elliot in the lunch line at Garbo's, she debated if she should interrupt, but if Elliot saw her and she didn't say hi, it would be weirder. Besides, she hadn't blown Elliot off; she'd been busy. And if Elliot was one of those friends who needed constant reassurance, best to know now before they got much closer.

She walked over and tapped her on the shoulder. "Mind if I join you?"

Elliot turned, and her smile erased any doubts. She gestured beside her. "Of course."

"I've been meaning to text you for the past two weeks."

"Ugh. It's been two weeks?" Elliot asked.

Martine smiled, pleased that she didn't seem bothered. "Well, at least it's not just me." Elliot looked confused, so she added, "Busy. I've been busy."

Elliot nodded. "Yeah. Me too." She gestured at the food truck. "Have you eaten here before?"

"Oh yes. It's all about the shrimp tacos for me. Totally addictive." Her mouth watered just thinking about the tangy meat on a bed of crunchy red cabbage, spicy jalapenos, and ripe mango.

"They're good, but the Korean barbecue is what I'm after."

They kept it light, extolling the virtues of the short menu. Apparently, Elliot had become enough of a regular that she'd tried everything. Martine hadn't veered away from the seafood tacos. Why stray? Once she found something she loved, she was all in.

While they waited for their food, Martine scoped out the seating options. Several chickens milled around the dining area, and she sought a table away from them. "Want to sit together?"

Elliot handed Martine's tacos over and grabbed her own, tucking their drinks under her arm. "Sure."

Sidestepping a brown and white hen, Martine led them to a black metal table tucked under leafy palms.

"What's with all these chickens?"

Surprised Elliot didn't remember them, Martine gave her a brief background. Like most Key West people, she had a love-hate relationship with them. Along with the Hemingway cats and the wild iguanas, the chicken and rooster populations were part of the local landscape. "Whatever you do, don't feed them." She took a bite of her taco and sighed. Just what she wanted. Taking a swig of Coke, she nodded toward Elliot's Korean barbecue. "Well?"

Elliot swallowed and picked up a piece of the beef. "Mmm. Do you want to try?"

She didn't want to dilute her tasty shrimp. "I'm good."

"Suit yourself." With a wink and a smile, Elliot tipped her head and popped the morsel into her mouth.

Martine laughed at the less-than-subtle flirt, not exactly immune to Elliot's charm but not falling for it either.

"What?" Elliot looked at her shirt, brushing her chest. "Did I get something on me?"

Martine caught herself staring at Elliot's hands. Would they be rough from her work? Steady and sure or tender and tentative? She mentally slapped herself and focused on something, anything else. Her clothes—casual shorts, light blue T-shirt, and sandals—not work clothes. "Is this a lunch break for you?"

She shook her head. "My day off. What about you?"

"Lunch break. What do you do in the Coast Guard?"

Elliot sipped her drink. "I'm a coxswain." She said it quickly, like *cock sin*.

That couldn't be right. "The what?"

Elliot smiled and spelled it. "I'm in charge when we're on a small boat."

"What's small?" For Martine, small meant a rowboat, but she suspected that the Coast Guard had a different definition.

"Anything less than sixty-five feet. Basically, yacht size and smaller."

Not small at all. "So you're a captain, then." Captains were always in charge of the boat.

Elliot smiled and shook her head. "No, that's an officer rank. I'm enlisted. I'm a petty officer second class."

"I don't know what that means."

"Right. I'm like a sergeant with a bit more technical experience."

That didn't clear it up, but she didn't need precise to understand. "Huh. That's pretty cool. What kind of work does that involve? Like, day-to-day?"

Elliot shrugged. "Everything. We're like a blend of road service assistance, law enforcement, and first responder, all on water."

Martine laughed, and Elliot smiled. "I've never heard the Coast

Guard described that way, but that makes sense. I was asking what you did in particular."

"Oh, on smaller boats, I pilot and direct operations. On bigger boats, I'll have a copilot to help."

"You're mostly onshore, then."

"Not always. Before Key West, I was stationed on an icebreaker to Antarctica."

"No way." Martine shivered. She'd had no idea that the Coast Guard went so far abroad. "That's amazing. What was it like? Antarctica, I mean. Well, you could tell me about the ship, too. Did you pilot that?"

Elliot shrugged and took another bite. "Sort of. I was the helmsman."

"That makes sense. Same job, bigger boat. Now, why Antarctica? Is it something you earn, or something you get stuck with?"

"I volunteered."

"Why? Not that I wouldn't have jumped at the chance, too. Well, minus the cold."

Elliot shrugged. "I wanted to get away."

From what? She wanted to ask but didn't. Their easy connection had no comparison in Martine's current life. Elliot was both a stranger and an old friend, so finding the boundaries of their relationship was tricky.

Elliot leaned forward. "And what about you? What do you do for work?"

Martine thought she'd told her about the business, but maybe that was because Elliot had dropped her off at the distillery that first night. "I'm the head distiller at Cejas y Roberts. I make rum."

"Really? How'd you get into that?"

Martine grinned and trotted out the same story she always told to receptive audiences. "There was this woman."

Elliot laughed. "There always is."

Martine opened her arms, palms up, enjoying Elliot's playfulness. "That's what I say, and no one believes me."

"I believe you." Elliot's deadpan sincerity was offset by her crooked smile.

Martine made a show of looking gratified. "Thank you. Anyway, her family made rum in Barbados. I went to visit her for winter break and fell in love." She paused, a quick beat. "With rum, not her."

Elliot took the bait. "How'd she take it?"

Martine almost missed her cue. Talking about Toni had brought up all her old feelings. "Not bad."

"That's good." Elliot popped the last of her taco into her mouth.

Martine looked at her own food and pushed it away, her appetite gone. Sitting with Elliot, swapping stories, she didn't have the courage to tell her the truth. She had delivered the story of how she'd gotten into rum so many times that she'd almost forgotten the truth. That she had fallen in love with Toni as well as the rum. That making rum had healed her broken heart when Toni had left her.

Overcome by an urge to get away, she stood. "I hate to dine and dash…"

"Oh, sure." Was that disappointment? Had she been too abrupt? Elliot started to get up and nearly tripped over the chicken lurking behind her.

Martine steadied her and quickly entangled them. She was inches from Elliot's face. So close, she saw the golden flecks in her brown eyes. A little closer and she could kiss her.

What was she doing? This was Elliot.

Ignoring her inner turmoil, Martine stepped back. "We should get a drink sometime. Hang out. Talk. If you want."

Elliot grinned. "Totally. Text?"

Relieved that Elliot hadn't noticed her mini-freak-out, she nodded and headed back to work.

Thinking about Toni had stirred up feelings she didn't know what to do with. She only thought about her once a year—at the awards dinner—and that was it. Why, all of a sudden, was she coming up now? Martine had practically run away from Elliot because of her. By the time she opened the door to the distillery, she'd stuffed all her Toni feelings into a box.

Ana Sofia was working the bar, chatting with a couple of customers while making one of their signature cocktails. She caught

Martine's eye and nodded, then waved her over and introduced her to their guests. Martine answered a few distilling questions before the customers settled down with their cocktails, and she moved away.

Ana Sofia came up beside her. "How was lunch?"

Martine ducked under the bar and handed her another bottle of Bantam. Annoyed that Toni had gotten mixed into her lunch, she focused on the rest of the meal. Elliot's laugh, their easy banter, the way she'd felt in her arms.

"What are you smiling about?"

Martine pushed off the bar and crossed her arms. "Nothing. I just had lunch with a friend."

Ana Sofia lowered her voice. "Some friend. You know they can be both, right?"

"Huh?"

"A friend and a lover. They can be the same person."

"Like friends with benefits?" Sadly, she didn't think that would work with Elliot.

Ana Sofia rolled her eyes. "No. Like a girlfriend. Someone you date."

She shook her head, thinking about the last time she'd tried that. After all this time, she had another chance with Elliot, and she wasn't about to fuck it up with sex. She didn't want to risk losing her. She'd rather keep her as a friend. "Elliot's not like that. We're just friends."

❖

Elliot's reception at work had definitely gotten a little frosty, and she suspected it had something to do with Weiss. Leaving work, she had no desire to go home to Marathon, but she didn't want to be alone. She considered texting Martine. Instead, she went to Publix and wandered the aisles, looking for something exciting to make for dinner. But everything she picked up reminded her how truly horrible her kitchen was and how little she wanted to go home. She finally walked out with a packaged salad, a bag of chips, and a bottle of seltzer. She sat in the parking lot and ate her dinner while she stared across the water at the naval base.

If she took Sigsbee Road, she'd could probably find the house she'd lived in, but she didn't feel like reliving that part of her time in Key West. In fact, the only part of her past she wanted to connect with was Martine, who'd more than lived up to her memories. Funny and vibrant, she commanded her space with ease. And she loved good food. *Wonder if she'd be up for something to drink?*

She pulled out her phone and texted, *Are you up for a drink tonight?*

Martine replied instantly and sent her an address. Excitement bubbled inside Elliot as she clicked on it.

A few minutes later, she pulled into the half-empty parking lot, the crushed shells crunching under her tires. Looking like little more than a weathered fishing shack that had been added on to through the years, the bar leaned into that aesthetic with hand-painted signs and loops of netting hanging from the roof. Music poured out the open windows, a mix of bass and guitar neither pop nor country but something vaguely in between. She opened the door to an interior that matched the exterior, down to the rustic plank bar, mismatched chairs, and plastic cups.

She stopped at the bar, and a quick survey of the high-end labels told the true story behind the run-down look. Trashiness had become trendy. A cocktail chalkboard boasted a list of reimagined classics with significantly higher prices. The bartender drifted over and asked, "What can I get you?"

She smiled at the familiar face. "Cass."

Cass returned her warmth. "Elliot, right?"

She nodded. "What do you have on tap?"

Elliot picked a pilsner and looked around for Martine. She spotted her at the back of the bar, leaning over the pool table and lining up a shot. The cue careened off the red ball and drifted to a stop at the other end of the table. Picking up her pint, Elliot thanked Cass and drifted closer.

"Better luck next time." A white man in his early forties and wearing a baseball cap that probably hadn't left his head since his early twenties picked up a cue and took a shot. He didn't do any better, which made Elliot smile.

A woman on the sidelines stepped up, and Martine leaned into her, whispering in her ear. She blushed and giggled. Her shot went wide. The way they touched bothered Elliot, an intimacy that she didn't share. Maybe she shouldn't have come. Did Martine want her here or was she interrupting?

Another white guy followed and managed to get the ball in but couldn't deliver past the single. He complained about his cue and furiously rubbed chalk on it.

Still uncertain, Elliot moved closer, and Martine spotted her. "Hey, I see you found the place. Let me finish up here." She winked. Then, with an almost casual air, she walked over to the table, nodded toward the corner pocket, and sunk the first ball.

Elliot's mouth opened as Martine systematically cleared the table, calling shot after shot.

"What the fuck?"

"That's not fair."

Martine shrugged and held out her hand. "If you can't stand the heat, get out of the kitchen."

One of them slapped a few bills in her hand, and they huffed off.

Martine's pool partner wrapped a hand around Martine's bicep. "I had no idea you knew how to play."

Elliot walked up to her and said, "Me neither."

The woman shot her a look that clearly said, "This one's mine, not yours." Elliot sent her back one that she hoped said, "I don't need your permission for anything." Judging from her less-than-impressed expression, Elliot's message was not received. She didn't care. She wasn't looking to hook up with Martine, but she wasn't going to back away from a turf fight. She'd spent her entire career carving her place in a man's world. She didn't back down.

Martine squeezed the woman's hand. "Do you mind if I check in with you later? I didn't know I'd run into you tonight. Elliot and I were going to get a drink."

"Of course." She headed back to a crowd of similar-looking

women. Not related by blood but like the two bros from earlier, she was of a type. Attractive and uptight. A little too put together for Elliot's taste. Probably a pillow princess. Elliot liked women a bit less polished and a lot more assertive in bed.

"She doesn't like me." Elliot chuckled, not at all concerned about the opinion, merely making an observation.

Martine slung an arm over her shoulder. "She doesn't know you."

Elliot rolled her eyes. "She thinks I'm competition."

"Well, you are."

Elliot paused, and the arm around her felt more intimate than she was expecting. Was that how Martine viewed her? Had she worked herself toward building a friendship for no reason? Was Martine going to be another hookup, albeit with personal history between them? Her stomach dropped. She didn't want that. She wanted, no, needed a friend.

Martine gently tugged her. "Come on."

The physical touch, the offer to go out, the whole evening shifted, and the nice warm feeling of friendship flip-flopped into something more. Something pleasant but not entirely welcome. She didn't want to be another fling.

Martine bumped her shoulder. "What's up?"

Pushing past the lead weight in her chest, Elliot asked, "Is this a date?"

Martine laughed and then stopped herself. "No." After a beat, she pulled her arm away. "Oh, is that what you thought?"

Although she should have been offended at how easily Martine dismissed her as a dating partner, the tension in Elliot's shoulders relaxed, and she exhaled. Martine's obvious discomfort at the idea made her smile. "I thought you thought that."

Martine's head tilted. "Why?"

"You just called me competition." Best to get it all out at once.

"Oh, that. I meant for time." Martine gave her a once-over and shrugged. "Although I could do worse."

Elliot stared at her and caught the sly smile. She snorted and gently pushed Martine to the bar.

Martine slapped the twenty down and nodded toward the guys she'd just taken down at the pool table. "Cass, find out what they're drinking and spend this on them."

Cass palmed the twenty. "I don't know why you bother taking their cash. You just buy them drinks afterward."

"It's not about the money. Besides, if they're too drunk, they can't punch."

Elliot questioned that logic, having seen more than one very drunk person do well in a fight. But she didn't argue.

"Elliot, you remember Cass?"

Elliot smiled. "Yes. We've already said hi. How many cousins do you have?"

"Too many to count." She leaned in and ruffled Cass's hair. She ordered a beer and added, "The Robertses and the Pinders took the lessons of 'be fruitful and multiply' to heart."

"Ain't that the gospel truth." Cass set the bottle in front of her and moved down the bar to help the next customers.

Martine cut Elliot a look. "And that's why I date tourists. Anyone local and I feel like I should have a DNA test before we have sex."

Elliot laughed. Glad that she didn't fall into either category and yet a little disappointed. She squashed that thought. She wanted a friend, not a lover.

CHAPTER EIGHT

Elliot arrived at the Eaton Street Seafood Market and bought two orders of stone crab claws and key lime mustard before heading outside. Work had been busy and emotionally difficult as the rumors had spread. She looked forward to spending time with someone who wasn't judging her.

The late afternoon sunlight reflected off the white concrete, and by May, the outdoor sitting area would be unbearable, but right now, the warm breeze and mild temperatures messed with Elliot's perception of time. She still couldn't believe it was almost Christmas.

She scanned the crowd and couldn't find Martine. Was she too early? It took her a week to find time in her schedule, and she didn't want to miss her. Finally, she spotted her tucked under a red umbrella in the far corner of the yard. Martine waved her over, and Elliot's anxiety disappeared.

A couple of roosters wandered past. Elliot avoided them as she sat opposite and cracked open a claw. The succulent meat, steamed to perfect tenderness, melted in her mouth and she relaxed for the first time in days.

"So good."

Martine dipped her meat in the key lime mustard and took a bite. Licking the sauce off her fingers, she said, "So why the Coast Guard?"

"Well, the Navy was out of the question." Throughout her

childhood, her father had told her she'd never make it in the Navy, so when she'd decided to enlist, she didn't even bother. She now knew that her dad never would have made it in the Coast Guard, and she would have survived whatever military branch she'd wanted to join.

She looked up at Martine, wondering how much more she wanted to say. So far, she'd shared surface stuff, things she'd divulge to a stranger, but now she had to decide if she wanted to trust her with the truth. Three years was a long time, and she was tired of holding on to it. The words came out before she could stop them. "I was running away." She cracked one of the claws with more force than she meant.

Martine leaned back and held up her hands. "Oh, sorry. I didn't mean to touch a nerve."

She sighed. "You didn't."

"What were you running away from?" Martine looked right at her, and Elliot felt the weight of her look. The moment stretched for a fraction too long until Martine added, "Or who?"

She looked across the street, not wanting to see the pity in Martine's eyes. But now that it was out there, she couldn't stop. No more hiding behind "we wanted different things" or "I wasn't ready to settle down." Time to face the truth. "Her name was Lara, and we were high school sweethearts. I wanted her to come away with me, and she didn't."

"That sucks."

She shook her head. "Oh, it gets worse. We had this on-again, off-again thing for many years whenever I was back in town. Then a few years ago, I decided it was time to make a go of it, and I was ready to resign, and she…well, she wanted something else, and we broke up. For good."

Martine covered her hand. "I'm sorry."

Elliot stared at their hands before she looked up and locked eyes with Martine. No pity, just understanding. Her initial surprise turned to relief as she let her guard down and opened up. "And that's how I ended up going to Antarctica. I accepted a posting as far away from her as I could get and then kept picking ones farther and farther away until I was standing in McMurdo Station a few days after Christmas wondering what the fuck I was doing there."

Martine whistled. "Wow."

"I know." How did this conversation get so serious so quick? But hadn't that always been the way with them? No pretense, the frank honesty of kids from day one. And with only that history between them, the need to hide herself seemed silly. Was this what having lifelong friends felt like?

"And now?"

Elliot shrugged and smiled, pulling her hand back. Lara had been part of this other life she'd planned that had never materialized. And once she went back to work, it had been easy to compartmentalize and tuck it away. No one needed to know what had happened, and so they didn't. But two years of constant moving and nine months on the *Polar Star* had taken its toll, and that was why she'd finally accepted a position onshore again. "And now I'm here."

Martine grinned. "Yes, you are."

"Enough about me. What about you? Any soul-sucking relationship woes?"

Martine laughed and ducked her head. "Nah. I live light on the land."

There was a story there, but she'd get it later if Martine wanted to share. She didn't need to rush their friendship. She wasn't going anywhere. "Good for you."

Martine waggled her hand. "Not always. You witnessed a particularly poor showing the other night."

"Well, if you remember, you weren't the only one abandoning ship."

"True. But still." Martine's embarrassment was written on her face and in her gestures.

Elliot nudged her foot. "Hey, your secrets are safe with me."

Martine tilted her head, something darker crossing her face.

"What?"

"Do you remember that time I broke my grandmother's vase?"

"And I took the blame?"

Martine shook her head. "She knew it was me. She told me that years later."

Stuck in the memory, Elliot smiled. "She scared the shit out of me. Is she…" She didn't know how to ask, and the thought that the short, stout, slightly stern matriarch might be gone picked at a hollow place inside her.

Martine sighed. "About nine years ago."

"I'm sorry." Elliot regretted bringing it up. More than twenty-five years had passed since she'd been in Key West with Martine. Her own grandfather had died in that same time frame.

Martine waved her off. "She went in her sleep. Do you remember what my gram used to call us?"

Elliot heard her voice in her head. "Two peas in a pod."

Martine crumbled her napkin and gathered up the remains of their meal onto her tray. "I looked for you, you know? Once I finally came out. I'd do an online search every now and then. Could never really nail you down."

"I thought about you, too. We moved around a lot." She'd had other friends but no one quite like Martine, her first real friend. Not her first love, no, that had been Lara. But the first friend who'd known who she was without her having to say a word and who had liked her for that alone.

Martine seemed to be waiting for something, but before Elliot could respond, she scooped up the tray and said, "I've got this."

Somehow, Elliot had missed the moment when the conversation had changed, and dinner was over. She scrambled to her feet and met Martine at the edge of the sitting area. Tucking her hands in her pockets, she said the first thing that came to mind. "This is so weird."

"What part?" Martine gave her an odd look.

"Seeing you again, talking, it feels so familiar and yet…" She opened her hands, unable to come up with the word.

"Completely different," Martine finished.

She looked over and smiled. "Right, but good different."

Martine grinned, seeming to find her footing again. "Totally."

Elliot glanced at her watch and yawned. She'd been up for work since four in the morning.

Martine chuckled. "Well, there goes my plan."

"Hmm?"

"I was going to see if you wanted to go get a drink…" She let it hang there.

Elliot smiled, warm and content at both the food and invitation. "I'd love to, but I've got a long drive and another early morning."

"Marathon, right? What the hell are you doing up there?"

She shrugged. "Well, there's no base housing. And rent here is astronomical."

Martine groaned. "Tell me about it. I've had the roommates to prove it. You're always welcome to crash on my couch in town."

"I might take you up on that." Although touched by the invite, she didn't think she'd take her up on it. She felt comfortable with her, but not that comfortable yet.

"Please do."

Martine walked her to her truck, and they talked for a few more minutes before she climbed into the cab. Martine leaned in the window. "Look. A couple of my friends are coming over to play poker next week. You should come."

Elliot adjusted her seat belt and smiled. "Poker, huh? High stakes?"

She chuckled. "Hardly. But there's usually a bottle of expensive liquor involved."

"What time?"

"About eight."

"Can I bring anything?"

"Something you want to eat. There'll be other food there. I'll text you the address."

Elliot drove home, mulling over their conversation. Moving from place to place had made her adept at creating fast connections with different people. She'd almost said yes to another night out, but calls had been up for the past two weeks, and she couldn't afford to be tired on the water. And talking about Lara had taken more out of her than she'd expected.

Most of her off-duty relationships had been with other Coasties. That left a very small circle of confidants, and she didn't want to share all her business with them. Three years of isolating assignments had left her with very few social outlets. Maybe that was why she'd opened up about Lara. Not only because she'd needed to get it out but because she'd wanted to share, and Martine had always understood her. And now that she had, she wanted more of it.

CHAPTER NINE

Elliot's week dragged on. Each day brought more of the same. She spent too many hours on her phone, looking for the right food to bring to Martine's poker game. She didn't want to pick up chips and salsa, but she also didn't want to overdo it. She finally settled on a warm artichoke dip, a cheese board, and fresh bread from the local bakery. But once she got to the store, she doubted her decision and tossed in a few bags of pretzels and candy.

Martine lived in the heart of Key West on a quiet street a couple of blocks from Duval. Tucked away from all the tourists, the green and white single-story shotgun bungalow held on to its turn-of-the-century charm. Ropy vine trees and short spiky ferns shaded the covered porch, welcoming visitors with bright white blooms.

On her way up the porch stairs, she touched the banister and imagined all the other hands slowly smoothing it down. The wood creaked under her feet as she knocked on the edge of the open door and called through the screen, "Hello?"

Martine called, "Come on in. Down the hall."

She walked down the long hallway that gave the house its name. She had lived most of her life in prefab houses and industrial dorms, cold and empty places. This house called to her with its old-world beauty and loving craftsmanship. How much of Martine lived in this house?

On her left were large windows where sunlight peeked through the foliage, splashed on the tile, and reflected off the white walls. On her right sat two rooms, the first filled with boxes and the second one with its door closed. Elliot stopped at the back of the house where the whole width opened up on the living room, and water shadows danced on the ceiling from some backyard source. She'd love to live here.

Martine came up beside her and took the artichoke dip. "Here, let me help you. Ooh, what did you bring?"

Putting aside her house envy, Elliot set her bags on the counter and started unloading. "Just some snacks. Pretzels, M&M's. But I wasn't sure if we'd want something a little more substantial, so I made artichoke dip and brought stuff for a cheese plate. The dip needs to be heated up. I thought I could use your oven."

She finally looked at the kitchen and accidentally moaned. Brand-new cabinets, stainless-steel appliances, subway-tile backsplash, brushed-nickel hardware. She sighed and ran her hands along the countertops. Her envy turned to lust. She wanted this kitchen.

Martine leaned in and whispered, "Are you okay?"

She touched the pristine knobs of the five-burner gas range and forced herself to move away. "Your kitchen. It's so…gorgeous."

Martine cocked her eyebrow at her. "Thanks?"

Elliot laughed and shook her head. It was just a house. She couldn't help it if Martine's kitchen made her swoon. "It's just…my apartment has the worst kitchen. And I like to cook."

"I'm afraid its features are lost on me. If I was staying long-term, I'd say you're welcome to it."

Elliot couldn't believe she would willingly leave this house. "You're leaving? Why? This place is perfect. And in a great location."

"I can't afford it."

"Couldn't you get a roommate?" Elliot looked around. If she could get out of her lease, she'd do it.

"I've been there and done that. Most of my friends have coupled up. I don't know anyone looking, and I'm kind of done living with strangers."

"How about me?" Once she said it, she knew she didn't want

to take it back. And now that it was out there, the idea of leaving the tight-knit off-base housing sounded like a relief. She didn't really know the adult Martine all that well, but the child Martine had been her best friend. And nothing she'd learned yet had changed that feeling of childhood closeness.

"Really? You'd do that?"

Elliot heard the hope in her voice, saw the boxes lined along the wall, and decided. "Yes. I need time to get out of my lease. And to know how much."

Martine threw out a number, and Elliot did a quick budget in her head. It was a bit more, but she'd save on gas and with the added bonus of getting home in fifteen minutes instead of ninety. "I can do that."

She was already thinking of a couple Coasties she could offer her apartment to. Worst-case scenario, she might have to pay double rent for one month. But with any luck, she could be out of that lease and living in town in a few weeks.

Martine showed her around the rest of the house. It had a central hallway leading from the front door and straight out a set of double doors in the back. The bedrooms and bathrooms were on the opposite side of the hallway. Martine led her to the front bedroom. "This would be your room. Private bath. In fact, it's my one quibble with the place. You have to go through a bedroom to get to a bathroom."

Elliot peeked into the bathroom—walk-in shower, sink, and toilet. Bright white tiles and pale green accents mixed with nickel fixtures and a cherry vanity. All new and shiny. The bedroom had space for a queen if that was all that was in it. The closet would just hold her suitcase and her uniforms. She'd need to buy a dresser and a mattress. Even though the dollar signs were adding up, she wasn't worried. She'd known that coming to Key West might bring back memories, but she'd never anticipated that she'd feel at home so quickly. Running into Martine had been the best thing she'd done in a few years.

Martine led her out the French doors to a tile veranda and a small swimming pool tucked among the tropical bushes, vines, and palm trees that covered the rest of the yard. A wild space in the midst of civilization. "Wow."

Martine crossed her arms and said, "I know. Welcome to tourist housing."

"I'll take it."

Martine grinned, and Elliot knew she'd done the right thing.

She heard the screen door open and shut before a voice called, "Hello?"

"Out here," Martine called.

Cass walked in carrying a brown paper bag. "What are y'all doing in here?"

"I might have a roommate after all." Martine grinned and clapped a hand on Elliot's shoulder. Elliot reached up and held her hand for a minute. Martine squeezed, and something tight that had been burrowing inside her for the past few years started to let loose.

CHAPTER TEN

Martine woke up to the uneasy feeling that she wasn't alone in the house. After picking up the bat tucked in her closet, she snuck down the hallway and quickly swung into the kitchen, ready to kick the shit out of whoever was in her house.

"Whoa," Elliot yelped and splashed coffee on her black T-shirt.

Oh, shit. She'd forgotten. Elliot had moved in yesterday. Martine put the bat down and grabbed a handful of paper towels. "I'm so sorry. I thought you were breaking in."

Elliot took the paper towels and blotted the growing stain. "Do criminals in Key West make coffee before they rob you?"

She laughed, a little embarrassed at her overreaction. "The better sort do. What are you doing?"

Elliot paused, a playful quirk to her lips. "Making coffee."

Still flustered, Martine backed out of the room. "Well, then, carry on."

She scooped up her bat and headed to her bedroom. Leaning the bat against the wall and grabbing her cell phone, she paused at her distorted reflection. Her hair stuck up in the back, her shirt was on backwards, and the sleep shorts just barely covered her ass. She raised her voice slightly so Elliot could hear her in the kitchen. "Why didn't you tell me I looked like this?"

"You had a weapon," Elliot called back.

She chuckled, enjoying the back-and-forth, and moved into her bathroom. "Good point. I'm going to shower."

"Do you want coffee?"

She popped her head back around the corner. "Is there any left?"

Elliot walked to the counter and hefted a French press that Martine didn't recognize. "My carafe cracked in the move, so I used your French press."

"That's mine?" Maybe Ana Sofia must have snuck it into her cupboards. Not the first time she'd acquired a new kitchen appliance without noticing.

Elliot narrowed her eyes. "You don't have a coffee maker, do you?"

This time, Martine was embarrassed. "No, I buy it on the way to work."

Elliot tutted and pulled a mug down, pouring her a cup. "Then you're in for a treat. I grind my own. It's my one expensive habit."

Abandoning the shower, Martine stepped fully into the kitchen. She took the mug, cradled it, and inhaled. A slight nuttiness underlay the pungent coffee scent. She took a tentative sip and held it in her mouth, letting it coat her tongue. A slight pepper taste with a flash of brown sugar and then a soft finish with a lingering note of dark chocolate and maybe cherries. She took another sip and closed her eyes. No, it was more of a raspberry.

"It's good, isn't it?"

She opened her eyes and hesitated under Elliot's intense stare. She forced herself to concentrate on the words. "It is, but it would be even better with steamed milk."

"I've got half-and-half." Elliot opened the fridge, bending over so that her pants pulled tight against her ass.

A warmth that had nothing to do with the coffee crept up Martine's face. She shook her head, ridding herself of that flare of attraction and replacing it with the comfort of routine. "That'll work."

The cold dairy cut the edges of the bitterness and added a touch of sweetness that punched up the finish. She hummed. "Perfect."

"What are your plans today? It's a workday, right?" Elliot put the half-and-half back and started pulling other stuff out.

Martine sat, not quite ready to face her responsibilities. "It's always a workday this time of year."

"You want some breakfast?"

She leaned forward. "Are you cooking?"

Elliot smiled. "Don't sound so shocked."

She didn't doubt Elliot's ability. Anyone who owned those kinds of pots was serious. Her tone had more to do with the fact that no one ever cooked for her. Her mother had never been the cooking type. "I'm not. I just…yes, I'll eat whatever you're making."

Elliot twirled a pan and grinned. "I feel like crepes. What about you?"

Martine's stomach rumbled in agreement.

"I guess that's my answer." Elliot smiled and glanced in the pantry. Whatever she saw there passed inspection. She grabbed a few measuring cups from the drawers and started scooping out flour.

Martine watched her work, her attention captured by her quiet competence. "No recipe, huh? Do you make crepes often?"

Elliot shrugged. "Often enough."

None of her other roommates had ever cooked for her. They'd eaten meals together and sometimes shared the kitchen while cooking. Perhaps this was the difference between roommates and roommates who were also friends. After all, Ana Sofia cooked for her.

"You don't do a lot of cooking, do you?"

Blissed out by good caffeine, she sipped her coffee, savoring the smooth bitterness and roasted cocoa. "A little. Why do you ask?"

Elliot swung the fridge wide and gestured at the meager contents by way of answering. A few takeout containers and some condiments sat beside a fresh gallon of milk, two packs of butter, and a carton of eggs. None of which Martine remembered buying. Had Elliot already gone shopping?

She pulled the new stuff out of the fridge and started whisking flour and milk. "This is going to take a bit. You can shower if you want."

Unwilling to relinquish her prize, Martine brought her coffee into the bathroom and got ready for work. She ran through her list while she showered. So much to do. She should just skip breakfast and head into work. But if Elliot's crepes tasted half as good as the coffee, there was no way in hell she was missing that.

On her return, Elliot presented her with a perfectly plated crepe.

"Thank you." She took a bite and moaned. The sugar and butter notes mixed with the tangy sweetness of the mangoes and hazelnut filling.

Elliot chuckled. "That good?"

Martine stuffed another bite in her mouth and nodded. If breakfast was any indication of Elliot's cooking skills, they needed to talk. She was willing to trade other chores for food like this.

Elliot turned back to the stove. "Well, there's more where that came from."

She hoped so. She polished off two more crepes before calling it quits. "Thank you, that was wonderful. I owe you a meal."

Elliot shrugged. "Don't worry about it. It's fun to cook for other people."

She could work with that. She put her plate in the dishwasher. "Leave the dishes. I'll take care of them tonight."

The domesticity of the moment struck her, and she leaned into that sense of belonging and home. And if she happened to want something more for a fleeting moment, then she'd be happy to dismiss it as a half-awake, half-baked, half-caffeinated response to an attractive woman in her kitchen. Nothing more, nothing less.

Elliot spent the rest of December settling into the apartment. The day after Martine had marched out of her bedroom with a baseball bat in hand and her hair sticking up in the most adorable way, Martine had called on her network of family and friends and had found Elliot a bed.

She had expected a slightly used mattress, not one still wrapped in plastic. "How much do I owe you?"

"Nothing."

"This is brand-new." She almost refused, not used to being helped.

Martine shrugged, unmoved. "My aunt owns a bed-and-breakfast. They shipped her the wrong size. Another year in her shed and it'd be full of bugs."

Still not comfortable with charity, Elliot said, "Well, then, at least let me pay your aunt."

Martine laughed. "Fat chance. Once I told her how little furniture you brought, she wanted to decorate your whole room. She has this white wicker thing going on. Be thankful you got away with a mattress and a box spring."

But Elliot couldn't let it lie, so she'd bought a fancy coffee thermos—the kind that kept coffee hot for hours—and left it on the counter with a note: "Since you won't let me pay for the mattress… enjoy. Please bring back for refills."

She'd come home late and found the thermos in the dish drainer, a note taped to the fridge: "Thank you. I'd like another."

Most mornings, she woke up and left for work before Martine got out of bed. But on her days off, she'd drink a second cup of coffee and make breakfast. Sometimes, Martine would join her, shuffling out completely nonverbal and with her hair askew.

At first, she gave Martine a wide berth, filling a mug before talking to her. And even then, she'd get one- or two-word answers to any questions or comments. For a week, she worried that she'd upset her, wondering if Martine regretted living with her.

Then one morning, Martine came out, and Elliot handed her a cup without a word. Turning back to her batter, Elliot risked a question. "Do you like waffles?"

Martine grunted. Elliot couldn't tell if that was a yes or a no, so she kept cooking. A few minutes later, Martine cleared her throat. "Yes."

Elliot froze, totally confused. "Yes?"

"Yes, I like waffles." Martine yawned. "I'm sorry I've been so grumpy this week. I'm not a morning person."

Happy that Martine's mood had nothing to do with her, she turned away and smiled. "I hadn't noticed."

"Bullshit," she grumbled.

"Well, okay, I did. But it's all right." She liked this grumpy version of her. They got quiet for a minute while Elliot racked her brains for something else to say. Something casual but engaging. Maybe she'd spent too much time in the service. Maybe she didn't know how to do small talk that didn't revolve around work. Maybe…

Martine saved her. "What are you doing for Christmas?"

A tiny knot formed in Elliot's stomach. Christmas always brought up mixed feelings. Everyone put such an emphasis on it, but it was just another day. She should care, but she didn't. So she pretended. "I'm on duty. What about you? Are you heading to Tampa?"

Martine laughed. "Oh no. I saw them at Thanksgiving. It's high season, so I need to be nearby. I do have an open invite to at least five different gatherings. But I'm not sure I want to go to any of them."

"Then don't." Maybe she'd have an out this year with someone who understood. Since she avoided her own family, she had no home to go, to nor did she care. The few times she'd gone to another Coastie's family gatherings had been awkward, so every year, she volunteered for Thanksgiving and Christmas. If her coworkers felt particularly guilty, they'd bring her leftovers. It was a win-win.

"It doesn't work like that. You see this place." Martine waved around. "I didn't find it on my own. Pilar owns it. She didn't want me sleeping at work anymore. So she offered it up."

"Pilar?" She recognized the name from the lease.

"Ana Sofia's mother."

She knew Ana Sofia was Martine's business partner but hadn't met her yet. "Why does it matter what she thinks?"

Martine cocked her head. "Well…hmm. Take out the tourists, and Key West is a tiny town. There's this whole network of friends and family. Pilar is a part of that for me."

"She's family?"

Martine shrugged. "Close enough. It's just easier to go along. Besides, it turned out okay."

Although Elliot agreed, she couldn't imagine living in a

community that close-knit. The Coast Guard was small enough, and she chafed at the constant togetherness. But she understood duty and obligation. "Then you can't duck out of it."

"Not so much." She grinned and leaned forward. "Wanna come?"

"Uh…" No.

Martine laughed and gathered her dishes. "You should see your face. Don't worry. I won't make you."

"It's not that I don't want to go," she lied. She definitely didn't want to.

Martine held out a hand, and Elliot passed her more dishes. "Uh-huh."

But maybe it wouldn't be so bad. Martine's family weren't complete strangers. It would probably still be awkward. Fortunately, she'd already committed to working. "No, really. It's just that I work."

Martine took the dishes to the sink and turned on the water. She looked over her shoulder as she washed. "Then you're definitely coming to New Year's for the fireworks. You'll be my plus-one."

Check and mate. She'd walked right into that. She didn't have the heart to say she'd already signed up to work that day as well.

CHAPTER ELEVEN

"Martine?" An insistent knock pulled her out of a deep sleep. Why was Elliot knocking on her door? Had she made breakfast again? Not that she minded, but this was the first time she'd woken her up for it.

She rolled over and opened her eyes. "Yeah?"

"We're late." Ana Sofia, not Elliot, answered, her impatient tone curt and clipped.

Adrenaline shot through her as she sat up and swore. She scrambled for her phone. Dead. "What time is it?"

"Eight thirty. We need to be there in half an hour," Ana Sofia said through the door. "Get dressed."

"Okay, okay. Give me five." She rushed through the bathroom, wetting her hair and brushing her teeth. Ana Sofia hated to be late.

Bracing for the busy day ahead, Martine stepped into the hallway and heard Ana Sofia in the kitchen. "...primarily wine, but the past two years, they've added other spirits. We have a tasting booth. This year, we auctioned off a private expression."

"A what?"

Martine answered as she grabbed her keys. "It's like a mini-barrel-pick. Oh, right, barrel pick is when you let the customer come and taste all your barrels and then buy one for you to bottle. It's really big in whiskey right now. Exclusive and one of a kind."

"And expensive. One barrel yields about one hundred and fifty bottles. If we bottled straight from that barrel at forty dollars, it's six thousand. But we actually blend so that one barrel could go into several different expressions…bottles." Ana Sofia rubbed her fingers together to signify more money before nudging Martine toward the door.

Still talking, Martine moved down the hall, Ana Sofia practically pulling her along. "We give them a taste of a few barrels and blend them together. Give them a case—twelve bottles—and an experience."

Elliot followed. "Sounds fun."

Martine jumped at the chance to show off. "Anytime you want to come down, I'll do it with you."

"I'll keep that in mind." Elliot paused halfway down the hall.

"See you tonight?" Martine called over her shoulder. In her peripheral vision, Ana Sofia rolled her eyes.

"If you're up after midnight, maybe."

She doubted she'd be awake after working all day at the festival. She waved and said, "Maybe."

Outside, Ana Sofia waited with the car idling. Martine slid in, and Ana Sofia started to pull away as Elliot ran out carrying a familiar silver mug. "You forgot this!"

Touched by the thoughtfulness, she smiled and reached through the open window. "Thank you, I'm going to need this."

Elliot nodded and trotted back into the house. Ana Sofia didn't pull away.

"What? What are you waiting for? Go." She'd rushed her through the last fifteen minutes, and now she just sat here?

Ana Sofia tapped her fingers on the wheel. "That was very domestic. Does she always get you coffee?"

"Yes." No way was she admitting that Elliot had bought the mug, too. She already didn't like this line of questioning.

"Hmm." Ana Sofia drove away.

"Say what you're thinking. I'm not going to do this all day." If she didn't get it out now, Ana Sofia would poke and prod at her.

"What's going on with you two?"

"What do you mean?" She ignored the defensiveness creeping into her voice.

Ana Sofia nodded at the mug. "The coffee, the...back-and-forth. Are you sleeping with her?"

Warmth spread from her neck to her ears. She'd successfully ignored any lingering attraction in the weeks that they'd lived together, content to enjoy Elliot's companionship. "No."

Ana Sofia cut her a look that said, "I don't believe you."

Better to go with a partial truth. "Well, I'm not blind. I see what you're seeing. This thing between us, but we're just friends. What's your point?"

Ana Sofia held up her hands. "Whoa, hold on. It's just different. That's all I'm saying. She's different. You're different with her."

And so what? She didn't have to sleep with someone to be close to them. What was Ana Sofia getting at anyway? "I guess I've never lived with a friend before. It's different."

Ana Sofia dropped it, and when Martine came home that night, too tired to make dinner, Elliot had taped a note to the fridge: "Leftovers. Enjoy."

Ana Sofia was right. Elliot was different; Martine was different with her. But she liked that difference, and she wasn't going to dwell on it.

❖

Elliot glanced up from her tablet as Martine sauntered past in a one-piece bathing suit, her toned arms on full display. She forced herself to look away. Nothing wrong with admiring her roommate's upper body strength. She went back to reading and heard a splash.

Almost immediately, she heard a scream, and Martine dashed back into the house, soaking wet and shaking. Elliot scrambled off the couch. "What happened?"

Martine locked the door and jumped from foot to foot. "Snake." She pointed. "Snake in the pool."

Her high alert dropped, but Martine's reaction warned her not to make fun. "Oh, right."

"I can't." Martine shook her head, closing her eyes and hugging herself.

Elliot inched closer and slid into her Coast Guard persona. *Semper Paradus. Always Prepared.* "Do you want me to take care of it?"

Martine looked at her, her eyes wide. "I don't think you should."

"It's just a snake." She'd dealt with snakes before. How bad could it be? She unlocked the door and walked onto the deck. A long black snake drifted through the blue-green pool. She'd expected something a little less than three feet, but the snake looked closer to six.

Her calm cracked, and she said, "Holy shit."

Martine popped her head out. "I told you."

She looked around and spotted the pool skimmer. Maybe she could dip it out with that. She grabbed hold and picked the far side of the pool. Inching slightly closer, she tapped the snake's tail with it. It folded in on itself and darted toward her. She yipped and swatted at it, but it just kept coming.

"Fuck this." She dropped the skimmer and ran back to the house. Martine danced out of the way, and they shut the door, turning the lock together. The black snake slithered toward them and slid half its body up the glass.

Martine pounded on the glass with her bare hand. "Shoo. Go away. Go on, get out."

The snake slithered away, and they watched it slide off the deck. Elliot opened the door.

Martine grabbed her hand. "What are you doing?"

"Seeing where it went. I want to make sure it's gone."

"Why?"

She didn't answer. Judging from Martine's slightly high voice, it was a rhetorical question. She tiptoed after it, but it was already gone. She made a circuit of the pool, picking up the skimmer along the way.

Martine poked her head out. "Is it all clear?"

"I think so." She scooped up Martine's towel and went inside. Averting her eyes, she held it out and looked up after Martine wrapped herself in it.

"I can't believe I jumped in the water with that."

Elliot chuckled. "I can't believe you told it to shoo."

Martine smiled. "And locked the door."

Then Elliot started to laugh. "Right."

"Like it could open the door with its body."

Elliot laughed harder. "Or flick it open with its tongue." They laughed for a bit until wiping her tears away, Elliot said, "Do you still want to swim?"

Martine looked horrified. "Not in that."

"Nah. I was thinking about an ocean picnic."

"A what?" Her confusion was obvious in her expression.

"A picnic on the water." She already knew where to rent a boat and pick up some food. She'd take them out to Waltz Key Basin and its clear waters, anchor near one of the unnamed mangrove islands, and swim. Maybe snorkel along the sandbars.

Martine grew quiet and spoke with a distant look in her eye. "My dad and I used to do that." She hadn't brought up her father's death, other than a fleeting reference that he'd passed away shortly after Elliot had moved away. Elliot hadn't wanted to pry, but she'd been curious how he'd died so young. "This is dumb." Martine shook her head and moved to the couch.

Realizing that they were no longer talking about the picnic, Elliot followed and sat next to her. "I'm listening."

"He's been dead for most of my life. I should just get over it."

Elliot wasn't so sure she'd just get over it, even if her father and she had been on speaking terms. Both Martine's parents had worked while she and Elliot had been children. Elliot had more memories of Martine's grandmother than either of them. But she remembered how close Martine had been to her dad.

Martine sighed. "No, it's...sometimes, he'd go out with a skeleton crew to scout out new spots. One morning, he packed my lunch, walked me to school, and went to work. That was the last time I saw him. He never came back." Her voice had changed timbre and gone flat, as if by keeping it in neutral, it would keep the feelings at bay.

"How old were you?" Something told her that saying "I'm sorry" wouldn't be welcome.

"Twelve."

Four years after they'd met. Her father had been gone for almost thirty years. That was a long time, and this was an old pain. "Shit. So no one ever found anything?"

"They found a cooler with his name on it. Floating in the ocean."

"Wow." She wasn't surprised by the details. The ocean held on to her mysteries, and boats often disappeared without a trace. Hell, the *Titanic* had sunk in five minutes.

"Yeah, it was weird not to have a body. Or a boat." She looked over her shoulder. "For years, I'd see him in a crowd or expect him to come home."

Thirty years ago, a lot of boats had gone missing—hijacked— their owners killed, and the boats confiscated to run drugs in the Caribbean. But saying that wouldn't help. Better to let her think the ocean took him. It was part and parcel of life on the sea. So much of the sea lay unexplored. It was still possible to lose something out there and never find it.

And to lose someone while so young with so little closure, no wonder she lived life so unattached. Children did not see the world the same way, but that didn't stop their perceptions from lasting long into adulthood. She mourned her lost childhood with Martine and regretted not growing up with her.

Lost in thought, she missed any further reaction until Martine tried to pull her hand away.

"See? Stupid."

Elliot stood and pulled her into her arms. Martine had trusted her, and she didn't want her to hide from it now. "No, not stupid."

Martine stiffened but did not try to pull away. She squeezed her as if hugging would make up for the lost time and pull all the bad memories out. Elliot held her longer than she'd ever held a friend, and as she started to pull back, Martine relaxed and rested her head on Elliot's shoulder. Well, if Elliot couldn't be there then, she could be here now. And someday soon, they'd go for that ocean picnic together. For the first time in her life, she wasn't going anywhere.

CHAPTER TWELVE

Martine handed over a paper basket of conch fritters and key-lime iced tea. She loved Mallory Square, despite and sometimes because of the tourists. All of Key West's oddities and eccentricities were on display. Sunburned snowbirds, families of all shapes and sizes; young couples both straight and queer watched contortionists, street artists, tightrope walkers, and musicians ply their wares, a sunset carnival every night. A cellist played "Smells Like Teen Spirit" with blistering speed at one end while a magician worked the other.

Elliot looked this way and that. "I don't remember Key West being so queer."

Martine laughed. "You were eight. You missed it." They walked by the cellist, and she tossed a dollar into the hat. The woman winked at her without missing a beat.

The press of bodies pushed them away from each other, and she lost Elliot for a moment. Worried that she'd never find her in the crowd, she spotted a concrete barrier a few feet away and jumped on it to get a better view. She'd been spending more of her downtime with Elliot than anyone else. Partly because they lived together. During high season, all she did was work, eat, and sleep. Two out of three of those activities happened in their shared space. Partly because Martine liked spending time with her. She felt more authentic with her than anyone else, even Ana Sofia. There was no pretense with her. Their friendship had existed before puberty and predated all the baggage that had accumulated from then on out. When talking about her dad, she'd felt a weight lift by giving it voice. No one had ever understood her loss like Elliot did.

She scanned the crowd and spotted Elliot near the beer truck, but she was not alone. She had an arm around a woman who leaned into her side and nuzzled her neck. Martine's blood boiled. Why was Elliot chatting up some woman while here with her? Then she scolded herself. *She's your roommate, not your lover. You don't have that hold on her.* Still, they were hanging out together not cruising together. The violation stood. Time to nip this in the bud.

She pushed her way through the crowd and overheard them.

"I ran into an old friend," Elliot said.

"In my apartment?" The other woman's disbelief came through loud and clear.

"Actually, yes. She was with your roommate."

Oh, was this the woman from the night they'd met? Awkward.

"Kristen? With a woman? Huh."

Something about her voice sounded familiar. She moved closer and got a good look. "Brynn?"

"Martine!" Brynn pulled away from Elliot and hugged her.

Okay, this was even weirder. Once again, Key West proved to be too small. She looked directly at Elliot, trying to gauge her reaction while she talked to Brynn. "I didn't know you were back in town. Got tired of the princess gig?"

"And the constant back-and-forth." Brynn stole one of Martine's fritters.

"Hey, buy your own." She curled her hand around to protect them from further theft.

Elliot frowned. "Are you two…have you two ever…"

Brynn made a face and she said, "Ew. No."

Was Elliot jealous? Of her? Or Brynn? "Brynn's my second or…maybe third cousin. Her dad was my mother's nephew."

"Oh." Elliot's frown lessened, but she still looked confused.

"I wasn't kidding about my family being everywhere." She popped another fritter into her mouth.

Brynn narrowed her eyes at them. "Wait. Am I interrupting something?"

"No, we're roommates." Something about Elliot's rapid response hurt her. Was it the way she'd said it? Or how quickly she'd dismissed the idea of something more? And why would that bother Martine? She didn't want Elliot that way, did she? Their intimacy had grown since they'd moved in together, but that didn't translate into more, did it? If she was confused about her feelings or lack thereof, it was because she'd never had a relationship like Elliot.

Brynn stared at her. She and Brynn often chased the same women. "Well, if you're sure."

Not wanting her cousin to get the wrong idea, she answered, "Quite sure."

"Excuse us." Brynn pulled Elliot to the side, and Martine did her best not to stare. Elliot sleeping with Brynn stirred up a weird possessiveness. It didn't matter that it had already happened. They pulled out their phones and exchanged numbers. Martine looked away. *Time to get a grip and let this nonsense die down.* She needed a distraction and quick. She glanced through the crowd and locked eyes with the cellist. The smile she got was all invitation. Not tonight but soon.

She turned in time to see Brynn kiss Elliot on the cheek and whisper something in her ear. Annoyed, she moved away, looking for an open spot facing the water.

A few minutes later, Elliot slid beside her, their shoulders brushing. Martine leaned into the contact, enjoying the closeness while she settled her thoughts. Brynn's familiarity with Elliot bothered her, not that it should. They'd obviously slept together, and she had no hold on Elliot. But she couldn't ignore the tiny pinprick of jealousy scratching at the edges of her emotions.

"You okay?"

"I'm fine." Martine stared at the boats, the horizon turning sunset red.

Elliot nudged her. "You don't seem fine."

Plastering a smile on her face, she tilted her head. Elliot's open expression tore at her heart. Elliot had no idea what she was doing to her. Martine knew she should just rip the bandage off and get it over with. "You could have gone home with Brynn, you know?"

"Really? You wouldn't have minded?" Elliot's earnestness killed her.

Of course she'd mind. But it wasn't like they were dating. She wiped those thoughts and turned. "Of course not. Why would I?"

Elliot looked relieved, and that made Martine feel worse. "I'm so glad we met again."

Martine stared at the shadows along the water and injected joy she did not feel. "Me too." On their way home, she pretended to forget something at work and left Elliot to walk alone. She needed a little space and maybe another woman to fix this longing. Then she'd be good to go.

CHAPTER THIRTEEN

O h yes."

The breathy sounds coming from Elliot's room slowly woke Martine from a sound sleep. The moaning alternated with a rhythmic *thud, thud, thud*. Great. Elliot had company. Rolling over, Martine shoved a pillow over her head and fell back asleep.

A hand ghosted up her leg, feather light touches at the edge of her consciousness. She tried to turn over, but she couldn't move. "Shh," Elliot whispered in her ear, kissing down her spine. She arched into her touch. "Is this what you wanted?"

Martine moaned. How did she know? "Yes."

Elliot rolled her over and kissed her stomach before dipping lower. She gasped as Elliot licked past her clit. Another swipe this time, touching her directly. Martine groaned and gripped her hair.

She needed more.

Without words, Elliot increased the pressure, alternating licks and sucks, bringing her closer and closer until she came and woke up totally wet and all alone.

Shit. What was that? Was her subconscious trying to tell her something? Like she wanted Elliot, or maybe she just needed to get laid, or maybe her roommate having sex next door meant her mind substituted her.

Martine got dressed with the smell of coffee coming through her door. That meant Elliot was up. She wasn't sure about seeing her after that dream. Taking a deep breath, she walked into the kitchen, prepared for anything but the sight that greeted her.

Brynn leaned against the kitchen counter fixing a cup of coffee in a USCG T-shirt and not much else. "Morning."

So much for awkward conversation with Elliot. Martine just wanted that coffee and was in no mood for chitchat. "Make yourself comfortable."

Brynn grinned and sipped her coffee. "Oh, I did."

"Mmm." She raised an eyebrow. Seeing her cousin lounging in her kitchen irked her.

Elliot strolled in and kissed Brynn on the cheek. She smiled before reaching around Brynn to make her own coffee. She glanced over her shoulder at Martine. "Do you want one to go?"

Brynn giggled and cuddled into her. "That's so cute. You make her coffee?"

Martine folded her arms. "And?"

"Oh, someone woke up grumpy." Brynn plopped on a chair.

"Hey." Elliot frowned at Brynn and handed Martine a cup. She leaned in, and Martine's dream-Elliot overrode her senses. She backed into the counter. Elliot reached out a steadying hand, which was worse. "Careful. I'm sorry about the noise last night."

"What noise?" She did not want to have this conversation at all. Good thing she couldn't form words.

"Okay. I was worried. I'm working late, so you're on your own for dinner." Elliot pulled back and handed her the thermos. The domesticity of the moment clashed with the booty call behind her.

Martine left the house without tripping over her feet or running into walls. But their conversation did nothing to improve her mood, and Ana Sofia confronted her about it a few hours later. "What's got your panties in a twist?"

"Nothing." She didn't look away from the still. She needed to make cuts soon, and she didn't want to miss her window.

"*Pfft.* Bullshit. You've been banging around here all morning."

"What?" She smelled it as she made the first cut. Not yet. She'd hoped distilling would settle her turbulent emotions; instead, Ana Sofia had stirred them up. "Can we talk about this later?"

Ana Sofia took in her work. "We'll grab lunch when you're done."

She nodded without listening and made another cut. Too late. Damn it. Not ruined but not what she wanted. She'd have to distill another batch and put this batch into a barrel. Not a total disaster but not ideal. She'd need to move their inventory schedule around to adjust for the addition. She'd changed the fermentation process to create a particular distillate, and now she'd have to start again. This was why she didn't do relationships; they screwed up her work.

She stopped working when Ana Sofia returned with lunch— seafood paella and salad. Ana Sofia left the food in the upstairs office, and their staff wandered in and out, helping themselves while Martine and Ana Sofia talked in the office. "We should eat outside."

Ana Sofia wrinkled her nose. "Next to the dumpsters?"

She smiled. "You got a point."

"Now, if we put a patio out there…"

"That would be nice. We could do events and outdoor tastings. Maybe some food." She played with the idea and her Elliot-sized distraction subsided.

"We'd need more money. Maybe we could do a partnership." They bounced ideas off one another until they ran out of steam.

Ana Sofia sighed. "We can dream."

In a slightly better mood and full of food and future ideas, Martine told Ana Sofia about Elliot's guest.

"Really? Your cousin? How'd that happen?"

"Coincidence. You know the Pinders. They're everywhere."

"So what's bothering you about it?"

"You don't bring people home." She had strict rules about bringing her lovers home. She didn't. She valued her privacy, and if any drama occurred, she could walk away.

Ana Sofia wiped her hands and set her lunch plate aside. "That's kind of an odd rule."

"Is it? Home is where you relax."

"And sex isn't?" She gave her the lawyer look. The one that said, "We're about to debate this topic, and you are already on shaky ground."

"It is, but I like to keep them separate." Apparently, Elliot did not.

"You know that's fucked-up, right?"

"No, it's not. I don't want people getting attached. Bringing them home…" Implied intimacy and she did not want that. Apparently, Elliot didn't mind getting close to people. She stopped talking. "Okay, it's fucked-up."

Ana Sofia opened her arms. "I rest my case."

Martine balled up a napkin and threw it at her.

Ana Sofia swatted it away. "Well, if it keeps bugging you, you need to talk with her."

Martine hated when Ana Sofia was right. She needed to get over herself. What Elliot did was her business, and she had no right to interfere. They were roommates who happened to be friends. And if there was a little something else between them, then she needed to set that aside.

Martine came home and poured herself a bowl of cereal for dinner. She sat on the couch, careful to avoid the cushion that sucked everyone in, and turned on the TV. She watched the local news out of Miami before switching channels and landing on an old *Law & Order*. She slowly numbed out on the TV and was just putting a bag of popcorn in the microwave when the front door opened. She poked her head around the corner as Elliot locked the door, still in her blue uniform.

Martine had never had a military fetish, but the way Elliot filled out that uniform, the cut defining those broad shoulders and long legs, Martine could almost feel the muscles under the fabric.

"Hey."

Feeling flushed, Martine forced herself to look up and smile. "Hey. How was work?"

Elliot yawned and rolled her eyes. "Long. I didn't get much sleep."

"Yeah, I heard." The words left her mouth before she thought about it.

Elliot's mouth opened. "Oh no. I thought you said you couldn't hear. I'm so sorry."

She shrugged, trying to look more casual than she felt. "Well, it did give me interesting dreams."

Elliot grinned, a slow, simmering look that did nothing to quell Martine's growing desire. She sauntered down the hall. "Did it now?"

Martine moved closer, eager to meet her head-on. "Absolutely."

"Do tell."

The microwave timer went off, and Martine moved away before she did something stupid. She called over her shoulder, "Saved by the bell."

Elliot's laugh followed her, and then her door closed. A minute later, the shower came on, and Martine sat back down to finish her show.

Elliot joined her a bit later, and she passed the popcorn.

"I'm not wedded to watching this."

"It's okay."

Their legs touched—damn couch—and Elliot's citrusy shampoo surrounded her. The bowl of popcorn sat between them, and they brushed hands grabbing a handful. Martine lost count of how many times, but each touch set her nerves on fire. She didn't want to move away, nor did she want to address it, so she threw water on the proverbial fire.

"So, you and Brynn?" Nothing like bringing up another woman to dampen the desire.

"Yes?"

"Is it serious?"

Elliot laughed. "No. How well do you know your cousin?"

She curled her lip. "In that way? Not at all."

Elliot shook her head. "That's not what I meant. She's not into long-term."

"Huh."

"What?"

"Guess it runs in the family."

"No long-term relationships for you?"

Martine opened her mouth and closed it. She didn't want to talk about Toni. "Um. I guess not."

"Not even one?"

She smiled with slight wistfulness as she thought about a couple. "There have been long-term seasonal residents."

"But no more than a few months?"

"Over a few years. I've had a couple that lasted a few seasons. But only when they were in town. What about you? Short-term hookups or are you looking for Ms. or Mr. Right?" She didn't know how exclusively Elliot dated women and didn't want to presume.

"I've had a few longer term. You know, Lara. But she was special. Nothing longer than five years. And nothing steady since Seattle."

Martine knew Seattle had been a few years ago, and whenever Elliot mentioned it, her body language tightened. Something had happened out there. "Bad breakup?"

Elliot chuckled but with an edge to it. "You could say that. I turned in a fellow Coastie for corruption."

Martine whistled. "Holy shit. Were you dating them?"

Elliot shook her head. "Oh no. Nothing like that. But he was very popular, and not many people realized what he had done. The atmosphere got a little chilly. It was hard to think about dating and working at the same time. Yet another reason I went to Antarctica."

"I can only imagine." *Talk about workplace drama.* Ana Sofia and her got into an occasional argument, but nothing like that.

"Is it weird for you that I brought Brynn home?"

In so many ways. "A little."

"I can stop seeing her."

"You'd do that for me?" Why would she do that? Did she really not care about her relationships?

"Of course. You're my friend."

"Bros before hoes?" How did those words ever come out of her mouth? She cringed.

Elliot smiled. "Exactly. But with less misogyny. Like I said, it's casual."

"It's not my place. You should do what you want." Even if what she wanted was different from what Elliot wanted.

"I hear a but in that statement. Tell me."

In her head, she saw Ana Sofia roll her eyes as she confessed. "It is weird to have overnight hookups here."

"Oh, I thought you said it was okay."

The Ana Sofia in her head said, "So fucked-up." But she said to Elliot, "To see Brynn, yes. But I didn't mean here. I meant in general."

"Oh okay. Sorry."

"It's fine." Now she felt silly and weird.

"So you're not bringing dates home?" Elliot asked, looking genuinely confused.

Not that she'd slept with anyone since that night in November. Something she planned to fix. "No."

"Then I won't either."

She hid her surprise at how easily Elliot complied with her wishes. She felt like she was taking advantage, but she needed to stop thinking about Elliot and sex, and the quickest way to do that was to have it happen somewhere else. That stupid dream.

CHAPTER FOURTEEN

Elliot stared at the array of dark blue and black T-shirts before shutting the drawer. She opened the closet and ran her hand along the same color scheme in short-sleeve shirts. Nothing brighter than a pale gray. When did her off-duty clothes start to mimic her on-duty clothes? She liked to blend in, but tonight, she wanted to stand out just a little bit.

She'd asked Brynn out on an actual date, and she wanted to make a good impression. She liked Brynn, but other than sex and Martine, they didn't have a lot in common. She hoped tonight would move their relationship forward. But she wished she'd looked at her clothing choices before now. The sun had already set, and the likelihood of finding something other than a tourist T-shirt was low. There were a couple boutique shops along Duval, but she had her doubts about finding something that would fit.

She stepped into the hall as someone inserted a key into the lock and opened the door. Martine walked in, her hair plastered to her head and wrapped in a USCG-issue blanket. Her shoes squished and squeaked as she toed them off by the door.

"What happened?" She knew that blanket. She'd offered hundreds of them to people throughout the years. Seeing Martine wearing one scared her.

Martine barely looked at her. "My boat sank."

"What? What were you doing on the water? Are you okay?"

She hurried down the hall, needing to do something, anything. She hated feeling helpless.

Martine gave a half-smile. "Booze cruise. And yes, I'm fine. Some very nice Coast Guard people bailed us out."

A protective urge rushed through her, and her training kicked in. "Let's get you out of those wet clothes."

She led the way to Martine's bedroom. She ignored the unmade bed and clothes scattered on every surface. Ushering her into the bathroom, Elliot stepped back as Martine stripped off her shirt and bra in one move, the shorts and underwear next. Her clothing landed with a loud slap on the tile floor.

Shocked into a stupor by Martine's sudden nudity, Elliot lingered for a moment, taking in the curve of Martine's breasts and the dip of her ass. She hid a beautiful body behind baggy clothes and work outfits. Elliot wanted to run her palm along her lower back and follow that curve with her hands. What was she doing? She was going out with another woman tonight.

"Elliot?" Martine turned, completely naked.

Shit. *Don't look down, don't look down.* But she couldn't help noticing the tattoo at the edge of Martine's pubic area. She needed to get out of here before Martine called her on her staring. She didn't want things to get weird between them, especially right now. Martine needed someone to take care of her, not come on to her. She stammered. "Uh…yeah." Looking down, she scooped up the wet clothes. "I'll take these. Get them in the washer."

She called Brynn and told her the situation. She couldn't leave. Going out on a date felt callous after Martine's near miss in the water.

Rather than be mad at their canceled plans, Brynn asked, "Is she okay?"

The joy of dating your roommate's cousin. "Yeah. I think so, but I don't want to leave her alone, you know?"

"Should I come over?"

She panicked, thinking about negotiating both of them in the same space. "No, I'm good. It's good. Let's reschedule."

While Martine showered, Elliot made a fresh pot of coffee and tried not to think about how she'd ogled her roommate. That sort of thing had to happen sometimes, especially in queer households. Or maybe it didn't, and she'd violated some unwritten rule. Shit. What if Martine was in there trying to decide how to tell her to move out?

Enough. Martine wasn't getting ready to kick her out. Her concern for Martine was wreaking havoc on her rational mind. She needed to pull herself together if she wanted to help.

Martine padded into the kitchen, dressed for significantly colder weather than the mid-70s outside: plaid lounge pants, a Worthy Park sweatshirt, dark green socks. She needed slippers to complete the look.

"Feel better?"

Martine nodded. "Much."

Elliot pushed a mug toward her along with the half-and-half. "Can I get you anything else?"

"My dignity." Martine took a sip.

"If it helps, we're a no-dignity-required kind of operation."

Martine laughed. "Ain't that the truth. I don't know why I'm so cold. The ocean was like bathwater."

"Shock. How long were you in the water?" She couldn't help asking. She needed to assess Martine's mental and emotional state.

"Not long. The boat didn't really sink. I fell in getting rescued."

"Ouch. I'm sorry." She knew how vulnerable that felt.

Martine sat. "Yeah. They were very kind."

"Do you know what happened?"

"Engine fire. It was still burning when we left."

Elliot glanced around the kitchen, trying to appear casual. She knew exactly how wrong things could have gone, and how quickly it could happen. Time to change the subject. Keep it light. "Are you hungry?"

"Starved."

What could she make that would be warm? She looked around the kitchen and opened the fridge. She could make grilled cheese. Did they have tomato soup? Nothing in a can and she didn't have enough tomatoes to make it from scratch. Something else, something simple yet warm, rich, and filling. She spied the Arborio rice and double-checked the rest of the ingredients. Yep, risotto.

"You don't have to make something. We could order in."

Elliot dropped the bag of rice on the counter. "I've got this."

"I could go get it."

She set the pan on the stove and faced her. "Do you really want to go back out?"

Martine's shoulders sagged. "No, not really."

"Then it's settled. You can stay here and watch me work, or you can cuddle up on that couch."

"You don't need any help?" Martine cradled her mug to her chest.

Elliot grabbed an onion, sliced it in half, and peeled it. "I've got this."

Martine took her mug and wrapped herself in a blanket.

Elliot kept an eye on her while she prepped the ingredients, wondering how to truly check in with her. So far, Martine had shared surface emotions, but Elliot knew how events hit people differently. She'd watch over her for the next few days.

In the meantime, she'd keep things light. "Do you want to listen to music?"

"What do you listen to?"

Elliot poured oil into the pan and waited for it to heat while she grabbed her phone and shuffled her playlist. "I'm kind of stuck in the nineties. Is that okay?"

"Depends. Are we talking Justin Bieber or Beyoncé?"

After hitting play, she tossed the onions in and stirred. "Beyoncé, of course."

Martine laughed. "I sort of thought you'd be into Coldplay."

Wondering what about her said Coldplay, she shrugged. "I have them, too."

While they talked and Elliot cooked, Martine's mood seemed to lift, and she laughed more as they compared notes on music and movies.

"But I was totally obsessed with *Titanic*," Elliot admitted as the rice sizzled when it hit the pan.

Martine shrugged out of her blanket and came back to the kitchen. "No. Why?"

She grinned. "I was a sucker for Leonardo. I watched everything with him in it. But looking back, I think I wanted to be him, not be with him." Elliot didn't share these parts of herself very often. The chain of command limited her work relationships, and her constant moving impacted her long-term friendships. But with Martine, there were no barriers.

Martine shuddered. "Oh, I hated *Titanic*. All that drowning. But Kate Winslet…"

She hummed her appreciation. "Yeah, I know what you mean."

"Have you seen her in *Mare of Easttown*?"

"No." She had never heard of it.

Martine moved closer. "You have to watch it." She went on a semi-rant.

Elliot smiled as she listened, pleased to have taken Martine's mind off her rescue. "I'll have to watch it then."

"Yeah, you will." Martine tilted her head. "Are you making risotto?"

Shifting to the side, Elliot gave her an unobstructed view. "Yes."

"Why's it yellow?" Martine moved closer and leaned against her shoulder.

Wanting to give her physical as well as emotional comfort, Elliot wrapped an arm around her waist, and Martine relaxed into her. She held up a jar. "Saffron makes it yellow."

"Oh. Cool. I've never had homemade risotto."

"It's much easier than it sounds. Here. I'll show you." She handed Martine the spoon.

"Whoa, wait." Martine held the spoon away from her body as if it might bite her.

Undeterred by Martine's reluctance, Elliot smiled and held out a hand. "Come on."

With a skeptical look, Martine put a hand in hers. Elliot pulled her forward and spun her around. Martine leaned back into her.

Elliot closed her eyes, enjoying the way Martine felt against her a little too much, and forced herself to take a step back. "It's okay." Reaching around Martine, she flipped the spoon, and together, they stirred, their fingers entwined.

Elliot's gaze swept over Martine's features, her strong hands, sinewy arms, and delicate neck. The rough texture of her hands, the tight squeeze of her fingers, Elliot struggled to focus. Impressed by how good she sounded amid her growing desire, Elliot grabbed the ladle and poured it in. "See how it's got that whitish center? You want to keep adding broth until it disappears but not so much that it boils."

The broth hissed, and Martine gasped.

Alarmed, Elliot swung to the side. "Are you okay? Did you get burned?"

Martine kept her head down, her cheeks red. "No, I'm good. Just startled me."

Was she embarrassed? Maybe Elliot had pushed her too hard. She stepped away and reached out. "I can do this if you don't want to."

Martine pulled the spoon away, indignation written all over her face. "I've got it."

"Okay." Elliot moved in again but kept a slight distance. Teaching her how to make risotto had become far more intimate than Elliot intended. She slipped into her instructor role and walked her through a few more times. "Good. Like that."

Martine's forehead crinkled in concentration, and she moved more surely. Elliot wanted to smooth that crinkle and kiss her worries away.

"Like this?" Martine turned, her expression so eager to please that Elliot's desire surged.

What the fuck was she thinking? She needed some space and choked out, "I'll be right back."

"You can't leave me. Where are you going?" Martine's voice sounded both amused and alarmed.

"The bathroom." She hustled down the hallway, stumbling into the wall. She called out, hoping her own voice didn't betray her. "You're doing great. Keep stirring until it's absorbed, and then add more."

❖

Martine had no idea what she was doing. Did she put broth in now? Elliot had said to do so when it started to absorb. How much did it need to absorb? She'd only half listened; she'd been so distracted by Elliot's closeness. How hard could it be? She spent her days calculating the influence of time and temperature on fermentation. She could do this. She stirred while the rice soaked up the broth.

She closed her eyes and breathed in the scent of onions and butter. Underneath that delicious smell lingered a faint hint of sea salt and citrus. Elliot's scent. When had she started to notice her smell? Before the sex dream or after? Shit. The way Elliot had held her, turning her toward the stove and directing her with sure and steady motions, reminded her of the dream again. A flush of arousal had made her gasp, and worse, Elliot had heard it. If Martine had moved back a few inches, she'd have been resting against her chest.

Elliot came back and leaned in, apparently unaffected by the closeness. "Looks good. More broth."

Martine suppressed the urge to lean into her again and ladled more. "How do you know it's ready?"

"Mostly by taste, but here. You see that white line there? You want that to get smaller, and when you drag a spoon through it, the rice should fill slowly." She plucked one out of the pan and bit into it. "A little too much crunch. Not yet. Keep going."

She kept stirring while Elliot opened the fridge and came back with something wrapped in butcher paper. She set a colander in the sink and dumped out a mass of shrimp. Martine breathed a bit easier with a few feet between them.

They worked quietly for a few minutes while Elliot cleaned the shrimp, and Martine continued to stir. Elliot finished and washed her hands. "Do you mind if I put something more mellow on?"

"Sure." She'd been mildly surprised by Eminem, but the rest of her music meshed with Martine's tastes. Something classical started playing next. Huh. She wasn't sure she'd peg Elliot for cellos and violins.

"What?" Elliot put her hands on her hips.

"Nothing. I was expecting...something else." Less romantic.

Elliot shrugged. "I like loud, too, but this relaxes me."

"I don't think I've ever seen you stressed. At least not as an adult." In fact, Elliot's adult calm contrasted with the energetic and serious kid she remembered. Knowing that person once existed added depth to Martine's perception of her.

"Yes, well, fifteen years in the Coast Guard knocks that out of you." She pulled out a head of broccoli. "I'd normally make a salad with this, but I think we're looking for warm."

"Yes. Warm." She wanted to know more about Elliot's relationship to her job. "What do you like about the Coast Guard?"

She washed it and started cutting it into florets. "What do I like?"

"Is this done yet?"

Elliot tucked the broccoli into a steamer basket, then reached over and scooped out a couple pieces of rice. She blew on them for a second before tasting. "One more."

Martine poured more broth and kept stirring. "Yes, what do you like?"

Elliot fitted a steamer basket inside a pan and put it on the back burner. "I like the water. I like the travel. I like the work. Most of the time. And I like helping people. What about you? What do you like about making rum?"

Martine almost went with something flip and generic, but it felt wrong. Elliot deserved the truth. "I like the challenge. You're taking three basic ingredients—yeast, water, and molasses, sometimes sugarcane juice—and adding heat and time. And even though you can do the same exact thing every time, some slight variable changes, and the taste is different. I like trying to replicate that mix of magic and science."

But there was more to it than that. No other job appealed to her like distilling. Distilling grounded her like nothing else in her life ever did. Distilling narrowed her focus, pulling her away from her personal life and sprawling family networks. Distilling gave her an emotional outlet with almost no risk. While she hungered for recognition, at the end of the day, she knew she didn't need it.

"How do you keep it consistent?"

She shrugged. "You blend. The aggregate taste of several fermentations often adds up to a consistent flavor profile." A process she made sound easier than it was. She'd worked years to perfect her blending skills.

"Wow. I never knew that." Elliot grabbed another pan and switched on the gas. Pouring a bit of olive oil in, she swirled it around and then added the shrimp in an even layer.

Dinner came together quickly after that. The shrimp were ready first, then Elliot stepped in to finish the risotto before checking on the broccoli. She handed Martine a wide bowl with the shrimp and broccoli tucked on top and a curl of parmesan cheese. "Where do you want to eat?"

Martine nodded toward the couch. Settling in, she took the first bite and moaned.

Elliot chuckled beside her. "That good?"

She rolled her head to the side. "That good. How did you get into cooking?"

"My aunt encouraged me. And then I got tired of ship food, so I watched cooking shows."

Impressed by her drive, she took another bite. "Well, it's amazing. I feel almost normal."

Elliot shut off the music and picked up the remote. "Do you mind?"

"Allow me." Martine scrolled through the channels, finding the on-demand station for *Mare of Easttown*, and hit play.

Elliot turned, eyebrow raised. "Are you sure?"

Martine smiled at her thoughtfulness. While falling into the water had sucked, she didn't think she'd have any lasting trauma from it. "Oh, yeah. I'm good."

Halfway through the second episode, Elliot stood.

Martine hit pause. Maybe she didn't like it. A little disappointed, she asked, "Is this okay? It's not too dark for you?"

Elliot laughed. "No, it's dark, but I'm good. I should put away the food." She held out her hand, and Martine passed over her empty bowl.

"Let me help." She didn't need Elliot waiting on her hand and foot, no matter how good it felt.

Elliot stopped her. "Sit."

The warm touch and full belly convinced her to stay. She'd always taken care of herself, but Elliot's attentiveness reminded her of what she was missing. She drifted off, her thoughts unspooling, her body relaxed.

Elliot wrapped a blanket around her and pulled her closer. Her breath caught, and a burst of warmth washed through her. The dinner, the cooking, the conversation; she'd fall into the water a hundred times to have Elliot take care of her like this. Fuck her independence. Where did cuddling with your roommate rank on the platonic scale? Not that she cared. She could get used to this. Too bad it wasn't a date. It was perfect. She closed her eyes and fell asleep.

CHAPTER FIFTEEN

Elliot stayed close to home for the first few days after Martine's rescue to keep an eye on her. After Martine had fallen asleep, she'd held her for a bit, enjoying the physical closeness that added to their emotional intimacy. She'd never had a friend like Martine, and she'd wondered if all close friendships felt like this, or was this something different? Whatever it was, she'd take it.

She'd tucked her into bed and stood at the door for far longer than she'd meant to before heading to her own bed.

As the weeks flew by, they spent more time together, and Elliot learned more about Martine than anyone else in her life. At first, it was the small things. Little nuggets that she shared and Elliot collected. Martine preferred a light breakfast and a big lunch. She hated ketchup on french fries but loved mayonnaise. She loved the chickens but hated the roosters. The iguanas freaked her out, but the snakes scared her more. She had a soft spot for cupcakes but didn't care for chocolate.

Elliot saw other things that went unsaid. When Martine laughed, she sometimes snorted. When playing poker, she had a tell: she talked too much. When she was stressed, she cleaned. When she was sad, she barked in anger. When she was happy, she sang and not very well. And so many other details that drew Elliot closer to her.

Brynn texted her to reschedule, but something always came up, and eventually, Brynn stopped texting. Elliot didn't care. But even as she and Martine grew closer, she kept a physical distance, afraid to accidentally step over that line and move them into something more than friendship. She craved Martine's presence and didn't want to lose it by acting on her fleeting desires. Which they had to be. She was not going to be the person who brought it up. If Martine wanted that kind of relationship, she'd have said something by now.

The week before Memorial Day, she waited until Martine had poured her second cup of coffee before she said, "I want you to come out on the water with me."

Martine put her cup down. "Today?"

"If you're willing, yes."

"Where are you thinking?"

"Waltz Key Basin." She took it as positive sign that Martine didn't dismiss her idea immediately. She didn't seem to have had any lasting reaction to the rescue. Perhaps she could persuade her to go.

"I've been there."

Suddenly nervous, Elliot grabbed that opening. "I won't take you into open ocean. I just want to get you out on the water with me. Maybe swim. Bring a picnic lunch. Chill out."

Martine tilted her head with a look Elliot was starting to recognize: intrigued with a touch of calculation. "This means a lot to you, doesn't it?"

Elliot nodded, swallowing her nerves. "I want you to see the ocean the way I do."

Martine's smile started slow and didn't bloom until she said, "Okay."

Elliot kept them to the shallows while coasting along the edge of the unnamed keys. Martine didn't say much on the way. She hung back behind Elliot, who took the boat slow so that their movement barely stirred a breeze. A few fluffy white clouds skated across the pale blue sky, and the sun bounced off the bay with a bright intensity that made sunglasses necessary. Surrounding the bay were loose clusters of mangroves and the sandy islands they built through their roots.

"How are you feeling? You're not seasick, are you?"

"No, just…nervous?" Martine laughed at herself.

Elliot half turned and held out a hand. Martine grabbed it. "You've got me. You're safe." She caught the smile before she let go and brought her full attention back to the boat. The slight breeze picked up as they moved away from the shallows. The boat started handling odd, and she realized they'd gotten snagged on a sandbar. Turning the engine off, she moved toward the bow.

"What's wrong? What do you need?" Martine asked.

Elliot grabbed a boat hook and looked over the starboard side. She slid it into the water until it hit bottom. Half the pole was submerged. "We're a little stuck."

Martine came up beside her. "What?"

Elliot pushed, but the pole slid along the sand, moving the boat in the opposite direction. She shifted her grip and tried again. The boat started a slow pivot. She dashed to the helm and put the boat into reverse, but the current pulled them back in place. She needed help.

Why had she hugged the shore? Martine didn't need to be coddled, and now she'd gotten them stuck on a sandbar. She handed Martine the pole and locked eyes with her, pouring all her confidence into her look. "I need your help."

"Okay." Her voice came out strong and confident.

With Martine on the pole and Elliot at the helm, they pushed out of the sandbar and back into open water. She'd misjudged the depth, and the shallow channels around these islands shifted with the tide. To avoid another mishap, she'd have to stay in deeper water.

"How are you doing? Are you okay?"

Martine glanced at her. "I'm fine. Just freaked out for a second."

"Well, the water doesn't get much deeper than nine feet out here. But these shorelines are a bit too shallow. I need to go farther out, or we'll be scraping bottom for most of this trip."

"How far?"

She pointed to a calm area halfway between the island astern and another mangrove bunch ahead. "About there."

Martine shaded her eyes and scoped it out. "Fine."

She eased the throttle, taking it slow. Martine sat beside her, scanning the horizon. Eliot slowed down and then killed the engine before dropping anchor. The waves slip-slapped against the boat, barely rocking it. "Are you ready?"

"For what?"

Elliot tossed off her T-shirt and shorts, revealing the bathing suit underneath. Going to the stern, she sat on the outboard and dropped into the ocean. The warm water sluiced over her head, and her feet didn't touch bottom before she popped back up. "In that bag, there are a couple masks. Toss me one."

Martine handed her the equipment, and she slipped it on. Adjusting it one last time, she dove down and swam along the bottom. She glided past rocks and coral, watching tiny fish dart in and out. But that wasn't what she was interested in. Near a sand-covered rock outcropping, she spotted the long antennae of a spiny lobster. She counted at least two, maybe three. She moved on before surfacing a few yards from the starboard side.

She waved and swam back. Excited, she hauled herself up and grinned. "You should come down here. There's so much to see." And she couldn't wait to show her.

Martine sat beside Elliot and dangled her feet off the edge. She stared at the watery depths, so clear she could see straight to the bottom. A few fish darted below but nothing bigger than a loaf of bread. Getting stuck on the sandbar had ramped up her anxiety from that stupid booze cruise. "You're sure there are no sharks in there?"

"I'm not going to lie to you. There could be. But other than us, there's no food for them here right now. And we're a lot of trouble to eat when there's a whole lot of food out there." She waved beyond their boat.

Martine stared out at the water as Elliot's words calmed her. This wasn't the ocean. This was the bay, and the bay was protected by lots of islands. She could do this. She used to love the ocean. She still loved the ocean. Ana Sofia and her family took her out on their yacht at least twice a year. She'd forgotten the ocean's power until she'd been stranded on the damn boat as it slowly sank. And now everything was so much harder.

She glanced at Elliot one last time, remembering her words and the feeling behind them. "I just wanted to show you a part of myself." They'd been slowly opening up to each other since they'd moved in together, but the last two months had been more intense and more intimate than she'd been expecting. Rather than pull away like she normally did, Martine had stayed with her and continued to share. That was why she'd said yes. She could do this for herself and for Elliot.

Reaching behind her, Martine pulled the mask closer and lowered herself into the water. The warmth enveloped her, and she ducked her head under. While she put her mask on, Elliot crawled up on deck and affixed a diving flag to the back of the boat.

Together, they dove to the bottom. Martine let the currents take her, only putting effort into swimming when she moved too far from Elliot. They talked through gestures and touches, communicating directions and mood. A careful dance with eye contact and no words.

Whenever they came up for air, Elliot would ask, "Did you see that..." some fish or bit of fauna that Martine had heard of but hadn't seen. Then they'd go back down, and Elliot pointed them all out again. During one dive, Elliot stretched her arm in front to slow Martine down, and she watched a gray-speckled stingray scuttle along the bottom, kicking up sand dust behind it.

Back on the boat, Elliot opened a cooler and handed her a tomato and mozzarella sandwich on a fresh baguette. The salt water on her lips added the right amount of seasoning. She ate chips and water and then chocolate chip cookies. Such a simple lunch, and yet everything tasted so much better out here on the water. When she said this, Elliot nodded.

"That's because it's an ocean picnic." As they finished, Elliot said, "Are you ready to explore topside for a bit?"

Full and totally relaxed, Martine nodded.

"Good. Come up here, and I'll show you how it's done."

"You want me to drive?"

Elliot nodded. "You should know how to operate a boat. The basics."

She got behind the wheel, and Elliot leaned over her, showing her the throttle and wheel and how to read the instruments, most of which she forgot as she got lost in Elliot's nearness. Elliot had kept her distance after that night of cuddling on the couch. Had she realized how aroused Martine had been when she'd leaned in during the risotto? And now Martine leaned into the same warm feeling as Elliot recreated the same set of circumstances.

"Are you even listening?"

Martine turned toward her and laughed. "Not really."

Elliot smiled, her eyes twinkling with suppressed laughter. "I think I can forgive you."

But their physical closeness returned. Out here, Elliot became lighter, and her inhibitions diminished. Sitting on the bench, side by side, Martine yawned and stretched. Elliot opened her arms, a clear invitation.

Martine hesitated before giving in and resting her head in Elliot's lap. Her touch drained all the tension out of her, and she relaxed. She stared at the wisps of clouds floating past the clear blue sky and listened to the pelicans whirl overhead. "You know, my dad used to take me out on his boat, and we'd go swimming just like this."

Elliot's fingers combed through her hair. "You miss him."

She looked up at her, a dark shadow against the sun. "All the time, and sometimes not at all. But being here with you, I feel… okay." Like someday, she might let it all go.

Elliot laughed, sitting so close that she shook Martine with her laughter.

Martine had no experience with intimacy like this. Was Elliot interested, or was this how a close friendship worked? Asking could ruin what they already had. She pulled her hand away, singed by the burn of possibility.

Elliot stopped laughing and stared for a moment before she shook her head. "You got a little sun. Right here."

Martine stood before Elliot touched her. "Great."

"I've got aloe at the house."

Martine stood and started picking up. "We should head in. Are you hungry? I know a place."

They moored at the Hogfish Bar and Grill on Stock Island and enjoyed a couple of beers and fried grouper. The conversation petered out and settled into a comfortable silence. Martine's mind stilled, and her body relaxed.

Back at the house, they went their separate ways, but before Martine could walk into her bedroom, Elliot called out to her. "Thank you for today."

She lingered at her bedroom door. "I feel like I should be thanking you."

Elliot smiled, a shy, almost embarrassed set to her shoulders. "I'm glad I could share it with you."

"Anytime." The word came out without thought, and she almost corrected herself. But if asked, she would head back out on the water with Elliot again. Before she exposed any more of her feelings, Martine pointed behind her. "I'm going to take a shower and pass out."

Elliot chuckled. "Me too. Good night."

She closed the door and leaned against it. She really needed to find someone to fuck away this tension before she did something with her roommate she'd regret.

CHAPTER SIXTEEN

"Do you have any toilet paper?" Martine closed the cabinets under her sink and walked into the hallway.

"Check under my sink," Elliot called from the living room.

Elliot's bathroom smelled like her—citrus and salt—and Martine bent over to open the doors but not before she spotted the large blue dildo resting on the counter. Shaped like a traditional dildo on one end, the other side curved and ended in an oval. She'd never seen one quite like it, and she picked it up without thinking.

"Did you find it?"

She spun around still holding the dildo.

"Oh." Elliot scratched the back of her neck. "I forgot about that."

Flustered at being caught, she quickly put it down and said, "I haven't looked yet." *Because I found this fascinating dildo and couldn't resist touching it.*

Elliot brushed past, pressing into her from behind. Her belt buckle touched Martine's ass, and she closed her eyes, imagining her picking up that dildo, bending her over the sink.

"Here."

She opened her eyes and a roll of toilet paper sat in front of her. Elliot stared at her in the mirror and gently plucked the sex toy from her nerveless fingers. "I didn't mean for you to find this."

"It's okay." Why did her voice sound so weird? She coughed to clear the dryness.

"Just to be clear, that wasn't from here. I mean…I never used it." Elliot tripped over her words, the only clue that Martine wasn't the only one having trouble with this conversation. "On someone else. Uh, I mean…I didn't bring anyone home."

That thought hadn't even crossed Martine's mind. She'd been too preoccupied with its use on her. But now that Elliot mentioned it, Martine visualized Brynn on the receiving end. Okay, no. That image cut through her desire-laced brain fog, and she heard the defensive undertone. Elliot didn't have her weirdness about hookups and home, but she'd agreed to her terms. What had Elliot gotten in return?

"Oh, yeah, about that. This is your house, too. You should bring home who you want."

"Are you sure?"

No. She could still hear Ana Sofia saying, "you know that's fucked-up" and silently acknowledged her point. "I was wrong to ask you."

Elliot exhaled, her relief visible. "Thanks."

That relief brought home how one-sided her request had been. Maybe loosening it up a bit wouldn't be so bad.

Elliot winked. "It's been harder than I thought, carrying around a bag of toys."

Martine hoped her face didn't show the blush creeping through her body. She really wanted to know what else was in that bag. "I bet. Well, now you don't have to." Somehow, she made a graceful escape from her bathroom and practically snuck out of the house to go get a drink.

When she sat at the bar, Cass wandered over. "You're out late tonight."

"I couldn't stay at home anymore."

"Trouble in paradise already?"

"More like frustrated in paradise."

"Frustrated? I thought you were just roommates."

"We were. We are. My libido is just all fucked-up. I need to get laid." She took a sip and surveyed the room. A couple women appealed to her, mainly because they looked different from Elliot. No need to confuse that issue with look-alikes.

"Well, you've come to right place. Are you sure you don't want to talk about it?"

"What about?" She played dumb. If she wanted to avoid talking about it, she wouldn't have come to Cass's bar.

"Your childhood crush."

Martine laughed. "It wasn't like that. We were too young."

"I've had a crush on Ana Sofia since I was sixteen."

"Well, you're just special." And maybe so was Elliot.

❖

Elliot woke up as a loud crash came from Martine's bedroom. Jumping out of bed, she burst into the hallway as Martine's door swung open, and a shrill voice demanded, "Who the fuck is Elliot?"

A blond woman stomped down the hallway while straightening her dress and putting on her heels. Apparently, giving Elliot permission to bring people home had opened the way for Martine to do the same. Elliot just hadn't expected it to happen so soon.

"Shh…baby. Come back." Martine followed her, clutching a sheet that did not conceal so much as highlight the fact that she was naked.

"What are you looking at?" the woman shouted at Elliot, and she held up her hands. Maybe this was why Martine didn't bring "dates" home. Elliot backed into her room, leaving the door open just a crack. She climbed back into bed, grabbed her phone, and scrolled through her Instagram feeds, trying to tune out the conversation but keeping an ear out if Martine needed help. Finally, the front door closed, and she heard a timid knock on her door.

The nearby streetlight turned her bedroom into pockets of light and shadow. Martine hung by the door with that blue sheet wrapped more securely around her. "El, are you sleeping?"

The shortened name and easy familiarity made her feel warm and cozy inside. "No, are you okay?"

Groaning, Martine shuffled in and perched on the mattress. "I'm fine. I'm sorry if I woke you with...that."

"Well, it wasn't you shouting." She inched over and patted the bed beside her.

"This is why I don't bring people home." Martine flopped on the bed. The movement pulled the sheet tight against her curves.

Elliot balled her hands into a fist to keep from touching those curves. She focused on their conversation instead. "Are they always so...volatile?"

Martine laughed, and the whole bed shook. "No, she was a mistake. I'm usually more selective."

"I see." Even though she didn't. Her lovers often chose her, so she had a hard time imagining herself deliberately choosing someone who wasn't right for her. "Do you have a lot of mistakes?"

"Recently, that's all I seem to have."

"That's too bad." She didn't understand how. Martine could have anyone she wanted. Shit, even she was better than them. Why did Martine keep picking the wrong ones?

"Tell me about it." She rolled over and propped her head on her elbow. "At least you have Brynn."

"Not anymore." Brynn had stopped answering her texts, and Elliot hadn't pursued her. Nothing in their relationship had said permanent anyway.

"Oh, I just assumed. I mean, that dildo."

She smiled. She'd bought it a few days ago and had been dying to try it out. "I know, right? It's brand-new."

Martine traced along the bedspread with a finger and spoke without looking at her. "So you've never used it on anyone?"

Was that a question or a statement? Where was this conversation going? The undercurrent between them flared to life as that blond woman's words came back to her. *Who the fuck is Elliot?* What had happened in that room while they were having sex? "Martine, why was she asking about me?"

Martine stilled and finally looked at her. "I accidentally called your name."

She didn't need any more details. She just needed to know, "Why?"

"I can't stop thinking about you." Her tone held none of the charged undertones between them. She could have been saying almost anything. But the implications remained. An intangible ball of want and desire.

How long had she been feeling this?

"Okay. I officially had too much to drink and overshared." Martine slowly stood.

Stuck in her own head, Elliot had waited too long to respond. "Wait."

Martine sat on the edge of the bed with her back to her.

"I'm not sure…" Elliot shifted toward her.

Martine held up her hand and pushed off the bed. "You know what, let's just pretend I never said anything, okay? Good night."

Elliot threw off the covers to go after her but didn't get up. Too much was at stake to chase after Martine in the middle of the night. Besides, she'd mentioned drinking. What if she had regrets in the morning? Better to leave it at words spoken while half-drunk and totally horny. Didn't everyone have the hots for someone they shouldn't want? Fantasy was one thing, reality another. She'd let Martine sleep it off and see what the morning brought. And if the morning brought her to her bed while she was sober, well, then she'd have her answer.

But one thing was certain. She couldn't stop thinking about Martine, either.

CHAPTER SEVENTEEN

Martine dreaded the gentle letdown that no doubt waited for her in the kitchen. She'd woken up mortified by her late-night confession, both relieved and disappointed that Elliot had turned her down. Had she ruined their housing situation by bringing it up? Was it going to be weird from now on? Unable to delay any longer, she walked into the kitchen and went straight for the coffee.

Fully dressed, Elliot glanced up from her phone and said, "Good morning."

"Morning." Same tone, same routine, but Martine couldn't face her.

"How are you feeling?" Again, nothing but courteous consideration. Typical roommate-Elliot.

"Good." She sat at the table and took a tiny sip, avoiding eye contact. "Better."

"No hangover?" Would she stop with these questions and just get it over with?

"No. I didn't really drink that much." She paused as her admission blew her cover from last night. Maybe Elliot wouldn't notice.

"I see." Elliot set her phone down.

Oh, she'd noticed. Well, okay. Martine didn't dare hope that Elliot would respond in kind. Looking up, she put her mug down, folded her hands, and braced herself for disappointment.

Elliot slowly turned her cup before focusing in on her. "Then, everything you said…"

Martine swallowed her doubt, and went all in. "I meant." She squirmed under Elliot's look as the silence stretched between them.

Elliot put on a better poker face now than she did when they actually played. And then Elliot let just the hint of a smile show through, the only indication that this attraction wasn't one-sided. Martine's heart skipped a beat. "Are you sure?"

"Yes," she said without hesitation. Fuck the consequences.

Elliot pushed away from the table and said in a low, sexy rumble, "Come here."

The authority in her voice short-circuited Martine's brain and turned her knees to jelly. Where had that come from? She'd seen Elliot's confidence before, but this directness was new. A good new.

Elliot seemed to read her hesitation as something else. "If you're not sure, we can stop."

"No. I'm good." She stood, placing her hand on the table to steady her nerves. She trusted Elliot's lead. Wherever this was going, she would follow.

"Then come here." She paused. "Please."

She loved that word coming from her lovers' lips. Such power in that one word, to please, to tease, to control. Hearing it from Elliot made Martine wetter than any fantasy she'd been harboring for the past twelve hours. But to be on the other side of it turned her on even more. She stepped into the V of Elliot's legs and draped her arms around her neck.

Elliot rested her hands on Martine's hips and looked up at her, eyes and expression intense and direct. "I won't do anything you don't want. Just tell me to stop, and I will. Do you understand?"

Martine chuckled on hearing the words she'd used on other lovers said to her for once.

Elliot tilted her head. "What?"

"That's usually my line."

Elliot's smile slowly morphed into a grin. "Then let me take care of you. For once."

A heavy weight lifted off Martine's shoulders, and she exhaled, closed her eyes. She could still back out. After some awkwardness, they would go back to being friends. But she wasn't sure that this connection between them had ever been strictly friend territory. The little touches, the caring, the cuddling, all of it had been leading up to this moment. If that was the case, why fight it? And if she was wrong, she'd deal with the fallout later. "Okay."

Elliot cupped her face, and she opened her eyes just as Elliot pulled her into a gentle kiss. She moaned as Elliot's tongue tasted along the edge of her lips. Wanting more, she opened her mouth, and the kiss deepened, still slow and building, a growing fire instead of a burning blaze. But that fire ignited, and her arousal took control of her senses. Reaching down, she palmed Elliot's crotch and gasped when she touched the dildo Elliot was packing.

She stepped back and looked at the unmistakable bulge.

Elliot covered her hand and joined her in stroking its length. "I wore this for you. Hoping you'd still want it."

Martine traced the contours of the dildo with her fingertips. Oh, she still wanted it. She licked her lips, and her thighs clenched in anticipation.

"Normally, I'd ask you what you like…" She trailed off, but Martine knew what she meant. Last night, she'd practically begged for it. "Do you still want it?" Elliot's eyes darkened.

"Yes."

She spread her legs. "Then take it out."

Martine unbuckled her belt, flicked open the button, and unzipped her pants. She pulled the dildo out, and Elliot groaned as her hand wrapped around it. But the little nub was nowhere to be seen. "Is it inside you?"

Elliot nodded, biting her lip and sucking in a breath as Martine applied pressure.

This dildo was the gift that kept on giving. She smiled as an idea formed in her head, and she sank to her knees. "Let me get it wet for you." She took the tip of it into her mouth, and Elliot gasped. Martine moved back. "Did you feel that?"

Elliot shook her head. "No, it's just you. There."

Martine knew what she meant. Seeing a woman on her knees always turned her on. But that wasn't the only thing she was going for. Licking along its length, she used her hands to stroke it in and out.

Elliot grabbed her, fingers digging into her shoulder.

"Do you feel it now?"

"Yes," she hissed.

"Good." Elliot's fingers tangled in her hair while she licked and sucked. She moved closer and inched Elliot's pants farther down her hips, exposing black boxers. She kissed the skin at the top of the boxers and dipped a hand behind the fabric. She delved through Elliot's hair and touched the dildo sticking out of her. She gathered her wetness, moving toward her clit.

Elliot clamped a hand around her wrist and slowly dragged her up from the floor.

"Oh, I'm sorry. I didn't ask."

"It's okay. If you touch me, I'm going to come." She stood and slipped out of her pants, kicking them to the side.

"That's a bad thing?" Martine ran a finger down Elliot's chest.

Elliot lifted her onto the table and helped take off her shorts. "It is when I want to fuck you."

Shuddering, Martine shifted her hands back and knocked into a mug. She twisted around and handed the mugs to Elliot, who moved them off the table. Coming back to her, Elliot moved between her legs and toyed with the edges of her underwear, a question in the tilt of her head. Martine leaned back on her elbows and lifted her hips. Elliot pulled her underwear off and ran her hands down Martine's bare legs.

"Ready?"

Opening her legs, Martine reached down and drew her hand through her inner lips, her fingers coming out drenched. "What do you think?"

Elliot caught her hand and brought it to her mouth. Martine closed her eyes while Elliot sucked on her fingers, and she imagined what that mouth could do to other parts of her body. Maybe she should tell her. Elliot released her fingers with a loud pop. "I think you are."

Are? What was she saying? She couldn't think through the fog of arousal. Elliot pushed the tip against her opening and brought her right back to the present. "Oh."

"Mmm." Elliot slowly sank into her, opening her up.

"Yes." Martine hooked her heels into Elliot's back and arched into her, the feeling of fullness sending tremors throughout her body. Those tremors continued beyond her and into the table. It shimmied beneath her, followed by a loud crack, and she scrambled up and into Elliot's arms.

"Oof." Elliot caught her. Luckily, the dildo managed to fall out without hurting her.

Martine looked over her shoulder and gasped. Two of the four legs splayed at odd angles, leaving the table half collapsed. "Oh, shit. You broke the table."

Elliot chuckled. "No. We broke the table."

Martine stepped away and circled the mess. She squatted and picked up a leg. The shaft had split down the middle. No wood glue was going to fix that.

Elliot chuckled again, and Martine looked up. "What?"

"You. This." She glanced at the table and considered how she looked, crouched on the floor while naked below the waist. Elliot didn't fare any better with her hands on her hips and a dildo jutting out in front of her. A dildo that was jumping up and down with her suppressed laughter. Martine burst out laughing, and Elliot joined her.

In between bouts, Elliot choked out, "I hope...I hope that wasn't an heirloom."

"No...no...Target..." Martine sat her bare ass on the floor, careful to avoid the splinters.

"I've never broken furniture before."

Martine snickered. "Well, there's always a first time." They laughed even harder and finally stopped, sneaking looks at each other as they wound down.

Inching closer, Martine tugged at Elliot's shirt. "You have too many clothes on."

Elliot looked at her, eyes half-lidded and her voice all husky. "Is that so?"

"Yes." She undid the first button.

"Should we do this in another location?"

"Yes." Another button.

Elliot moved toward the living room.

"Not the couch. My room." Martine took her hand and walked backward, undoing another button with each step until Elliot's shirt hung open. Martine kissed the bare skin at the base of her throat, pushing the shirt down her arms and letting it float to the floor.

Martine shoved Elliot backward, and she grabbed Elliot's hands, pulling them both onto the bed. "Come here."

Martine crawled up and straddled her waist, the position spreading her labia.

Elliot reached up and slowly played with the top of Martine's vulva, circular movements brushing near but never touching her clit. She leaned forward, her body pressing the dildo between them.

Elliot gasped, the shift in angle obviously moving it inside her.

"Do you like that?" Martine angled her hips again, loving the way Elliot responded.

Elliot nodded, her voice low and hoarse. "I want to see you take it inside you."

Those low tones and strangled words made Martine even wetter. More comfortable being in control, she sat up and positioned herself over the tip. "Like this?"

Elliot steadied her while she sank down, feeling the stretch in a deeper way. Elliot's tenderness pierced her heart, almost overwhelming her lust, but that fullness was exactly what she'd been fantasizing about since picking that dildo up off the bathroom sink. "So good."

She rolled her hips, and Elliot moved with her, slow at first, and then her need overtook her. Their bodies slammed together, wet smacking sounds that made her hotter. The pace was too much to keep upright, and she fell forward. Elliot held her, and the tight hold combined with the furious pace pushed her to the edge. But there was still something missing. She squirmed and Elliot loosened her grip.

"Am I hurting you?" Her gentleness and care amplified Martine's desire.

"Need...more..." She panted and braced her hands against Elliot's shoulders. Reaching down, she touched her clit.

Elliot moved her hand away, and Martine's legs trembled as she took over, rubbing back and forth, up and around, and then finally settling into a fast rhythm that took her up and over the edge. She threw her shoulders back as her orgasm rushed through her and slammed her hips down, eliciting a startled gasp from below. Her whole body let go, and the tension leached right out of her. She managed to move off the dildo before falling flat on the mattress.

"Fuck, I needed that."

Elliot caught her, ever attentive to her needs.

Little warning bells rang in Martine's head. She shouldn't get used to this. They were friends first, and this might be a one-time deal. But she'd been walking on an emotional tightrope for almost twenty-four hours and needed release. Did it matter who helped her out? Besides, if she hadn't broached the subject, she'd have no idea what a fantastic lover Elliot was. Knowing that couldn't be all bad.

❖

"I had no idea." Martine's words bounced around in Elliot's head before she fully acknowledged them.

"Hmm?" Elliot's heart raced, and her muscles clenched tight around the dildo still inside her. On the edge of coming, she almost missed Martine's comment. No idea? Desire turned her thoughts to mush. What were they talking about?

"That you were so good in bed." Her praise barely registered beneath the fog of desire.

Martine shifted and threaded their legs together, her body pressed close, and her damp curls brushed against Elliot's thigh. Whatever focus she had disappeared. She turned and trapped

Martine's leg between them. She kissed her hard, no dueling tongues or playful nips, all raw want and desperate need. She clutched her closer and gasped as Martine bumped against her dildo.

Martine pulled back and stared at her, her voice silky smooth. "Can I touch you?"

Wasn't she already doing that? She gasped as Martine rested her hand on her dildo. Oh. "Yes."

She tilted her head and closed her eyes as Martine slowly fucked her with the double dildo. Martine kissed her neck and moved lower, trailing her fingers down Elliot's bare stomach and inching her way behind the harness. Her muscles tightened and she twitched when Martine finally touched her clit.

Martine stilled and whispered, "Is that too much?"

Yes. No. Don't stop. "A little."

Martine switched directions and circled it. "And this?"

She moaned. "Yes."

Martine moved closer and rubbed harder. "I want to hear you come."

Those words spoken so close to her ear gave her the final push, and her orgasm punched through her, hard and heavy. Tightening all her muscles at once and then letting them go. She groaned long and loud.

Coming back to herself, she almost repeated Martine's words: *I needed that.* She had no idea how much sexual tension had built up between them. Had it been in the last twenty-four hours, or had this been a slow burn that she hadn't noticed until Martine had stood in her bathroom, holding the dildo now lodged in her vagina? Rolling over, she pulled it out and dropped it on the floor. She didn't bother with the harness.

Martine sighed. "Why didn't we do this earlier?"

Elliot glanced at her sideways. Was she serious? She couldn't tell, so she answered truthfully. "Because we live together."

The afterglow faded as the elephant in the room showed up. "Oh, yeah, that."

Elliot sighed and flung an arm across her eyes. As much as she hated to admit it, she figured she should give Martine the out. "This can be a one-time deal."

"Are you kidding?" Martine sounded either appalled or offended or both and pushed upright.

Elliot looked at her from under her arm. "No?"

Martine folded her arms. "Is that a statement or a question?"

The way her breasts settled over her folded arms distracted Elliot from the whole conversation. "Maybe."

"Eyes up here."

She looked away. "Right, sorry."

Martine grabbed the covers and tucked herself in. "I guess that answers one question."

Elliot lifted her arm and turned on her side. "Which is?"

"If you still want me." Martine broke eye contact and smoothed a wrinkle in the sheets between them, the only sign of her nervousness.

Elliot leaned in and whispered, "After what we just did, how could you doubt that?"

Martine met her stare. "Because you immediately went to the regret stage."

Oh. Good point. She sighed. "I was just doing that so you didn't have to."

Martine brushed her hand along Elliot's cheek. "No regrets, then?"

"No." And she didn't. She wouldn't mind doing it again.

"Me neither."

But now they had another awkward problem. Elliot stared, trying to figure out their next step. "Where do we go from here?"

Martine gave her a smile that promised more of what they just did. "Well, we're consenting adults. We can do anything we want."

Maybe she didn't need to overthink it. She'd been completely comfortable with Martine from day one. That thirty-year-old intimacy had returned immediately. No surprise that sex turned out to be just as easy. And while she'd never had sex with someone she was so personally close with, it actually felt better, safer, to do it.

She knew Martine, and she knew how to talk to her. If something came up that they didn't like or needed to change, they'd talk about it. Like adults. She could get the best of both worlds, sex on demand with someone she cared about but with no strings attached.

"I'd like that."

"Good, because I've been dying to see what you have in your bag of sex toys."

CHAPTER EIGHTEEN

Martine woke up as the mattress dipped, and someone kissed her cheek. "Morning. I'm going into work. Want breakfast?"

Elliot. What was she doing in her…oh, right. Was it morning? Did they lose a whole day? Not that she minded. She'd lose another day if she could. "What's today?"

"Monday."

She rolled on to her stomach and groaned. Elliot rubbed her back. She closed her eyes at the gentle touch and snuggled deeper as the circular movement pulled her into that half-dream state. Nonsensical images and thoughts drifted through her head.

"Are you going back to sleep?"

She sighed. "I will if you keep doing that."

Elliot chuckled and broke the spell by getting up. "Well, you have another half hour if you change your mind."

She lay in bed for a few more minutes, trying to recapture that blissful state, but the moment was over. Her whole body sluggish and slow, she sighed, totally spent. She'd explored every inch of Elliot's body in their sex marathon, always searching, never getting enough. Just in case this was the only time. Without words, they acted on an unspoken agreement to explore and enjoy, deal with reality later. Now reality had come, and she didn't want to face it. What if this was all they had?

She threw the blankets off, padded into the bathroom, and ran her hands across her face. Elliot's scent lingered on her fingertips.

She should shower, but she wanted breakfast more. She washed her hands instead.

Elliot stood at the counter cracking eggs into a bowl. "I don't have a lot of time this morning. Scrambled eggs work?"

"Yes." She poured herself a cup of coffee and stared at the mess of their table. She nudged it with her bare foot and shook her head. "There's no fixing this."

Elliot glanced over her shoulder and smiled. "Nope."

Martine turned a chair around and sat, folding her arms along its back. Like so many times before, she sipped her coffee and watched Elliot cook. A part of her worried that they'd ruined this part of their friendship by sleeping together. But the routine of their morning ritual remained. Relieved by the normalcy, she openly stared at Elliot.

She knew what those hands could do and how those hips moved. She'd been in the circle of those arms and had whispered in that ear all the filthy things she'd wanted to do. Still wanted. Putting her coffee on the floor, she stood and came up behind her. Wrapping her hands around Elliot's waist, she said, "I can't stop thinking about yesterday."

Elliot leaned back and covered her hands. "What part?"

Martine kissed up her neck and toward her ear. "All of the parts. Especially your parts." She slid her hands inside Elliot's shirt and along her stomach. Elliot turned and kissed her until the smell of burning eggs overpowered her.

"Shit." Elliot pulled away and took the pan off the burner. Glancing at her watch, she said, "Well, that's it for breakfast."

"Sorry." Not that Martine wanted to take back kissing her, but she had distracted her.

Elliot tossed the eggs into the garbage and set the pan on the stove. "I'll do the dishes when I get home."

"I've got them." Martine rummaged in the cabinets, pulled out a protein bar, and handed it to Elliot. "Breakfast?"

She laughed. "Make that two."

"Sure." She handed her a second one, wished her a good day,

and kissed her cheek. And then totally froze. A simple kiss really—so chaste and domestic—yet nothing like they'd ever done before. Their familiarity mixing with their newfound intimacy creating a third relationship between them. Had Elliot sensed it? What was happening between them?

"This is weird, isn't it?" Elliot looked at her with an open and direct expression.

Relief poured through Martine. "I'm so glad you said that."

"Maybe we should have some rules." Elliot said the last word almost like a question.

Knowing what lines to cross and what lines to keep might be a good idea, especially if they wanted to keep sleeping together. And Martine did want that. She really wanted that. Hopefully, Elliot did, too. "Yeah. We should talk."

"How about tonight? I'll bring home takeout."

Elliot left a few minutes later with no hug and no kiss, but Martine's thermos was filled and ready to go, just like before. At least that hadn't changed.

After everything that had happened in the past few days, Martine welcomed her normal workday. She spent most of the day bottling the Pride blend that she had put the finishing touches on a few weeks ago. Working took her mind off the conversation waiting for her at home. She didn't want to think about the ramifications just yet.

Martine checked in with Chloe before getting the wash ready for fermentation. She waited for it to come up to temp before connecting the hoses and pumping it into the fermenter. So far, their standard batches from the new fermenter had lived up to her expectations, but now, she was going to test another yeast blend. She got to the top of the ladder before she remembered the yeast at the bottom. She groaned, not wanting to climb back down. She was sore in places she hadn't even known existed. "Chloe, can you hand me that bag?"

Chloe came over and passed it up. "You look a little stiff. You okay?"

"Yeah. I've been doing more work around the house lately." Like her roommate. For the past twenty-four hours.

She had to think long-term with Elliot. She didn't want to wreck their friendship. Maybe they could still sleep with other people and each other? Like friends with benefits. It had a certain appeal. She'd had intimate relationships with people without sex, and she'd had sexual relationships without intimacy. So what if she blended the two? How hard could it be? But if she saw other people, so did Elliot, and she didn't like that.

Lost in thought, she accidentally doubled the yeast mixture. "Shit."

"You okay?" Chloe called out.

"Fine. I doubled the mix."

"Want to dump it out?"

"No." She couldn't justify the waste. Besides, she could blend or age any mistake, and then this batch would end up in her experimental inventory. She clambered down the ladder and made a note in the logbook in case she wanted to replicate it. Replication had become a cornerstone to consistency in her fermentation process.

In the early years, she'd learned the hard way that experimentation also required copious note-taking. Several of her earlier distillates had been lost to poor documentation. Distilling took patience and foresight. While some rum came off the still ready to drink, most of them required time in a barrel to smooth them out. She'd never had the focus to concentrate on relationships the way she did with her rum. Maybe that was why they'd flamed out like the rums straight off the still, potent and young.

Martine wrapped up with Chloe before heading home.

The more she thought about it, the better friends with benefits sounded. That way, if Elliot wanted out before Martine did or vice versa, they could just stop the sex and keep the friendship. Martine trusted her and knew that if it got hard or too much, Elliot would say something. They'd always been able to tell each other the truth. No reason to doubt that now.

❖

Elliot finished with her reports and started closing out the day. She'd filled the hours with busywork between calls, all to keep her mind off the evening. She'd spent hours wrapped up in Martine, literally and figuratively. As the day wore on, her doubts slowly seeped in. She didn't regret the last few days. She'd repeat them in a heartbeat, but what if Martine wanted something more? Or something less? She hardly knew what she wanted except to feel Martine under her again. Her nerves made her snappy, and her crew finally gave her a wide berth.

Finishing up the last check-in, she walked past the radio room and doubled back as her CO called out to her. Ducking into his tiny office, she pushed away her impatience and stood at attention while he shuffled papers. Personable and professional, Harriman's office reflected his personality. On the wall hung certificates and charts. A picture of his wife and kids sat on one corner of his desk and a brass astrolabe on the other.

"Tillman, I'm glad I caught you. Did you have a good time off?"

"Yes, sir." *Not nearly enough. I just want to go home and finish what Martine started this morning.* Home. How quickly she'd started to think about it like that.

He waved at her. "Have a seat." He put on a pair of reading glasses and glanced at the paper in his hand. "I want to send you to Camp Lejeune for tactical training."

Her heart sank. She didn't want the tactical rating. She'd had enough of port security and law enforcement in Seattle. Going for this training put her on the wrong career path. "Sir, with all due respect, I'm looking for heavy weather certification. Maybe even to qualify for Surfmen."

He held up a hand. "I know, I know, but there's only a certain number of billets for the First Class rank. I think the tactical rating will give you a leg up this year. We need more tactical folks on-site."

She'd topped out at Second Class two years ago and had avoided promotion through shifting assignments. So much of the Coast Guard's mission was law enforcement, and Key West's location made it a perfect place to intercept drugs and human trafficking. If she wanted to stay in Key West, she couldn't say no.

"There's a spot open tomorrow. You leave at 0500 from the naval air station."

"How long?"

"Seven days." And with that, he dismissed her.

Irritated at the timing and the training itself, she swung by her locker room, and all conversation stopped as she walked in. Weiss pulled away from her group and folded her arms. By moving in with Martine, Elliot had kept a careful distance from Weiss and her cronies. But every time Elliot had seen her, there'd been this friction between them. Nothing overt after Elliot had put a lid on it almost six months ago. More low-grade insolence than outright insubordination.

"I heard you got picked for tactical training. Think you're going to get First Class?"

Ah. So that was Weiss's beef. They'd both been up for it, and Harriman had picked her. *Minimal engagement, don't encourage her.* She opened her locker and started gathering her gear. "I go where I'm told."

"Or maybe Blackwell pulled some strings."

And there it was again. The whole Shaw case thrown in her face whenever anyone had a conflict with her. So much for minimal engagement. But if she wanted to rumble, Elliot was tired and tense enough to have a go. "Do you have a problem with me, Petty Officer Weiss?

One of Weiss's followers stood. "Weiss, let it go."

Weiss didn't fight the pull on her arm. "Watch yourself," she muttered as she stormed out of the room.

George Cowles stayed behind. "Hey, she's just jealous. And that Shaw bullshit?" He snorted. "Everyone who knew him knew what he was doing. It took balls to stand up to him."

She slammed her locker and sighed. The last thing she wanted was a work confrontation. "Thanks."

She'd been nervous all day about her upcoming conversation with Martine, and to end the day with Weiss sucked. The more she thought about it, the angrier she got. How long was she going to have to defend her actions? More and more people like Cowles were coming out of the woodwork, but Shaw had been a respected and popular Coastie. Not all his behaviors were corrupt. He'd helped and mentored many people, including Elliot herself. But those connections had built his empire, and he'd abused his position for profit. When Blackwell had asked her to help bring him down, she'd had no choice but to say yes.

Elliot fumed the entire ride home. By the time she pulled into the driveway, she had a full head of steam. She needed to calm down before she could even begin to discuss her future with Martine.

CHAPTER NINETEEN

Elliot went straight to her bedroom to collect herself. Unfortunately, Martine came to her.

"Anything I can help with?" Martine leaned against the door, her arms crossed, and her face concerned. She wore a tight T-shirt and low-slung sleep pants, so the curve of her stomach peeked out above her waistband. Elliot wanted to pin her to the wall and mark that perfect patch of skin, but she was in too foul a mood to pick up where they'd left off yesterday.

Forcing herself to look away, Elliot slammed a drawer closed. "Not unless you want to fuck or fight." As the force of those words seemed to hit Martine, Elliot regretted them. "I'm so sorry. I didn't mean…"

Martine pushed off the door. Elliot searched her face for some clue as to what she was thinking. Had she gone too far? They still hadn't talked through what they were doing. Then Martine stepped into the room. "Well, I won't fight you…" She left the second half unspoken.

Elliot froze, her thoughts crashing together. Did she trust herself with the way she was feeling? Was she too angry to do this?

Fuck this, she'd had enough overthinking for the day.

Crossing the room in two steps, she poured all of her pent-up anger and frustration into a kiss.

Martine matched her intensity before wrenching aside and taking a deep breath. "Wow. I'm glad we're not fighting."

Elliot laughed, delighted that Martine wasn't deterred by her anger. If her flushed face and quick breathing were anything to go by, she found that anger arousing.

Martine shoved her backward, and Elliot grabbed her hands, pulling them both onto the bed. Elliot scrambled back, but Martine pinned her down. "What do you need?"

Elliot dislodged her and reversed their positions. "Control."

"I don't give that up so easily." Martine's eyes narrowed, and she captured Elliot's lips in another searing kiss. Her tongue demanded entry, and Elliot opened up. Sharp sparks shot down her arms and curled her toes while she struggled to regain control. While they fought for dominance in their kiss, Elliot managed to slide a hand between them and brushed along that very skin that had tantalized her just a few minutes ago.

Martine gasped and grabbed her hand. "Sneaky."

Elliot leaned in and nipped behind her ear, inching her hand under Martine's waistband. "You have no idea."

Martine shifted and slipped a knee between Elliot's legs. "Then maybe you should show me."

Elliot ground on her and groaned, letting her grip loosen. Martine took advantage of that, grabbed her ass, and moved that knee at the same time. Elliot moaned at the increased pressure and toppled forward, catching herself with both hands. They were so close, she had to pull back to focus.

"Now who's sneaky?" She knew what Martine was doing, and she wasn't about to let her get away with it. "Do I need to tie you up?"

Martine smirked and cocked an eyebrow. "I told you, I don't give in easily."

Elliot growled. Maybe this was a bad idea. They were too alike for this to work. She flopped beside her and flung an arm across her eyes. "This was a mistake."

"Whoa, I wouldn't say that."

Elliot looked at her from under her arm. Martine was propped up on her elbow with a gentle smile on her face. She leaned in and nudged Elliot's arm away, brushing a soft kiss on her cheek. Her other hand slid under Elliot's shirt and traced lazy patterns on her stomach.

Elliot closed her eyes and sighed, the edges of her anger beginning to fray.

"You're just going about this all wrong," Martine said.

The question irked her, but Martine's continual rubbing softened her immediate response. "How so?"

"You can't control anger. Channeling it only derails you." Martine sat up without losing contact.

"I've done it before," Elliot said defensively.

Martine straddled her thighs and moved both hands along her skin. "And how'd it go?"

"Fine." She spit the word without really thinking about it.

"I see." Martine's expression said it all. She didn't believe any of it. And now her hands were moving more purposefully, brushing up along the edge of Elliot's sports bra and back to her stomach, then moving lower toward her waistband. Somehow, Martine had shifted their bright burst of passion into a smoldering burn.

She tugged on Elliot's pants, and Elliot let her pull them off. Her breath hitched when Martine leaned down and kissed her lower stomach. What had they been talking about? Oh, right, anger and fucking. Looking up and locking eyes with her, Martine moved lower, and Elliot spread her legs.

She moaned at the first touch of lips along her labia and gasped at the first swipe across her clit. She opened wider when Martine hooked Elliot's legs over her shoulders. She took her time, tasting and sucking softly. Going so slowly that Elliot's anger faded, and the overwhelming loss she'd smothered earlier bubbled up. She shoved her fist in her mouth to stop the sob and bit her knuckles, the pain forcing her to stay in the moment and focus on those lovely lips sucking her off. She should have stopped this or found someone else to fuck it out with. There was too much tenderness, and she couldn't cope.

She gritted her teeth, and her words tumbled out, strangled by her own emotions. "Bite me. Please."

Martine paused and looked up, her chin wet, and smiled. Flipping her hair to one side, she ducked down again, and this time, all pretense of slow and lingering vanished. There were sharp flicks and harsh nips. Elliot's thoughts coalesced on those lips attacking her and nothing else. Martine's tongue danced around her opening and slid down her perineum, lapping at her anus. That touch pulled another groan from Elliot, one that brought Martine back to that spot again and again. She shuddered when two fingers slipped inside her, corkscrewing along her G-spot before one was shoved up her ass, and she came so hard that she snapped her legs closed on Martine's head.

Martine laughed and moved out of range.

Elliot looked down. "Oh shit, I'm sorry."

Martine chuckled, wiping her chin with the back of her hand. "No need to apologize. But if sex with you is going to be this dangerous, I might need to reconsider."

"You are a free agent in this arrangement." Still blissed out, she meant to tease, but they needed to have this conversation.

Martine smiled and wiggled up beside her. "Well, that's what we should talk about."

"Right." Her stomach knotted. Work had consumed so much of her day that she'd avoided thinking about what she wanted. But after this last time, she didn't want to give it up. The sex, the intimacy, she wanted whatever Martine would give her.

"This feels natural." Martine motioned between them.

The knot loosened. "Yeah. More than natural."

Martine tilted her head and smiled. "You know I don't sleep with my friends."

Had Elliot said the wrong thing? Had she given away too much? Where was this going? "I figured."

"This feels...different. Good different." And yet it still felt like Martine was looking for the words to let her down easy. Her next words only contributed to that gently breaking-up feeling. "I care about you. I enjoy spending time with you in and out of bed."

"If you want to call this off, I'd rather keep our friendship than have sex." Even if the sex had been fucking incredible.

Martine sat up abruptly. "What? No. I mean, unless that's what you want."

Elliot had no business hoping for something more. After Lara, she still had trust issues. But she propped herself up so she could see Martine's expression. "No. Not unless you do."

Martine rolled her eyes and flopped beside her again. "We're like two butches holding the door open for the other. No, you go first. No, you."

Elliot snorted. "Okay, then. We keep having sex."

"Yeah. But not at the expense of our friendship." Martine tapped her on the chest.

"Agreed." Elliot held her hand.

Martine tucked under her shoulder. "If you need space…"

"If someone else comes along…" But she really didn't want to hear Martine fucking someone else next door.

CHAPTER TWENTY

K nock, knock," Cass called.

"In here," Martine shouted from her kitchen as she put the dishes in the dishwasher.

Cass strolled into the kitchen and stared at the empty space. "What happened to your table?"

"It broke." She washed her hands, careful not to drip on her outfit.

Cass cocked their head to the side. "How?"

"The legs snapped." Martine kept her answers deliberately vague. She didn't want to open the door to the teasing she'd get from breaking a table while having sex on it.

Yet, with the unerring accuracy of close family, Cass zeroed in on it. "So how's Elliot working out?"

"Good. Are you ready?"

"You don't sound so sure." They ducked out of the house as Martine locked up.

"Seriously, Cass. It's fine. She's awesome. Best roommate ever." Which wasn't a lie, even without the sex. Elliot cooked and cleaned. There was no chore chart. She actually was the best roommate Martine had ever had. But she'd overplayed her hand with her enthusiasm.

Cass followed her down the street. "Okay, now I know something's up. Are you still nursing a crush?"

Martine stopped walking, knowing it was a mistake but unable to stop herself. "A crush? Who said anything about a crush?" But protesting was her second mistake.

Cass smiled, and Martine shook her head.

"There was never a crush. I didn't even know I liked girls that way when I knew her."

"But you know now."

She continued walking. "I know now. Yes. But it's not like that. We're just friends." She didn't even have a name for what they were or the weird mix of emotions it stirred up. She knew she liked it, and she wanted to keep it just between them while they sorted it out.

She gave Cass a look that said "end of subject." But as she said it aloud, her internal conviction wavered. Something she hadn't voiced with Elliot but thought about now. What if they could have something more? She had no idea what she was doing, and not knowing worried her. She didn't like to take risks with her heart, but she could manage short-term. And that was all she ever committed to, even with Elliot.

"I swung by the distillery yesterday and tasted the Pride blend."

"And?" She jumped at the change in topic.

"It's good, but there's a depth missing." Cass worked as a professional bartender and had a solid reputation around town. With their skills, Cass could go anywhere, but they'd chosen to stay close to home. In the past few years, they'd branched out and had started to do guest stints in Miami and New Orleans. Every time Cass left, they came back a little more restless. Martine ignored the signs, hoping they'd settle, but deep down, she knew she'd lose Cass to the wider world. For now, she'd take what she could get.

"I know what you mean. Now last year's…"

Cass kissed their fingers. "Perfection. It's part of the reason I won."

She wouldn't go that far, but Cass did win the annual bartender competition at Bourbon Street Pub with a stunning riff on the El Presidente using the Cejas y Roberts Pride blend as its rum component. "It's a good thing you're not competing this year, then."

Cass shrugged. "I would have used another rum."

Martine faked shock. "Oh no, what would the family say?"

Cass looked at her. "Make a better rum."

Martine laughed harder than the joke warranted because it was the truth. Her family wasn't known for extensive praise and had no qualms about criticizing in the interest of making something better. She'd developed a pretty thick skin when it came to her creative projects, and that included her rum. "Well, with that attitude, you're all set to judge this year."

"About that. Thanks for coming. I know how you feel about the whole bar scene."

She didn't really have an issue with the bar scene so much as the tourist bar scene. And the Bourbon Street Pub with its outside pool and decadent party ambiance of queers on vacation epitomized that scene. She tended to avoid it. "At least there'll be eye candy."

Unfortunately for her, most of that candy was male. But among the droves of men, she spotted a few women. Cass and she split at the bar. She made her rounds, checking in with the local people and working her magic on the tourists. Ana Sofia wasn't the only one with a gift for selling. When she was on, Martine held her own, but Ana Sofia drew energy from the networking. Martine poured hers into it.

By the end of the night, another winner had been crowned, Cass had been sucked into rounds of shots, and Martine had turned down no less than three propositions, two from tourists and one a local repeat. The last one, Jessica, she'd seriously considered when the pounding music, the press of bodies, and the alcohol had made her hornier than normal, but her memories of their last time together paled next to Elliot.

When Cass headed to an afterparty in Old Town, Martine ducked out.

"Leaving so soon?" A hand stopped her by the open doors, and Jessica pulled her back inside.

"Yes. It's getting late."

"I'll walk you home." There it was, another invitation, and in the relative darkness and warmth of a late summer evening, she almost succumbed to temptation. Jessica clearly ranked above average, but something was off. Maybe the last-minute change of plans had distracted Martine and kept her from being fully present. Or maybe Jessica just wasn't Elliot. And even though they'd said they weren't mutually exclusive, she hated the idea of Elliot seeing other people. She just couldn't do it.

"Thanks, but not tonight." Or really, ever.

❖

"Tillman!"

Elliot stopped short. She turned and spotted Grace Blackwell running across the parking lot to stop in front of her. Surprised to see her, Elliot snapped off a salute. "Sir."

"At ease." Grace reached out, and Elliot hesitated. Grace was one of the few Coasties Elliot considered a friend, but after Seattle, they'd drifted apart. She wasn't sure where they stood, and she'd didn't want any more work drama than she already had.

Grace grabbed her hand and pulled her into a tight hug. "How've you been?"

Reassured, Elliot returned the embrace, then spotted the gold leaf on Grace's lapel. Feeling guilty that she'd missed her promotion, she said, "Congratulations, Lieutenant Commander."

Grace glanced down with a slight shrug. "Oh yeah. I got them a year ago. What have you been up to? Are you stationed here?"

Grace's casual questions and easy manner reminded Elliot why she liked her. Being her friend was effortless. And she needed that right now. "No, I'm attending the tactical training. You?"

"That's funny, I'm guest lecturing for the tactical training. I'm out of Miami these days."

Elliot shook her head. Such a small world. "Really? I'm down in Key West."

"No shit? I went down there last month to consult with Commander Harriman."

Elliot had heard that one of the Key West patrols had brought back contraband, but that was all she knew. It was a need-to-know basis, and Elliot didn't need to—nor did she want to—know.

Grace narrowed her eyes. "How come your name didn't come up?"

"I like to keep my distance." After Seattle, Elliot had downplayed her law-enforcement background. She didn't want to get caught up in another Shaw incident.

"That's too bad. You're a natural."

"Just because I can doesn't mean I should. Besides, I like to drive the boat. Boarding is dangerous. You never know what you're walking into." This was an old argument, and she didn't know if she needed to hear it or if Grace did.

"True. Have you eaten? I'll buy you lunch, and we'll catch up."

"Careful, sir. You wouldn't want to be caught fraternizing." She was only half joking. She'd never seriously considered Grace dating material, but everyone had always assumed they were together. And those rumors got very ugly after Shaw's takedown. Yet another reason Elliot had kept her distance. But the rumors had started to die down in the past year, except for Weiss. And Elliot had missed Grace.

Grace slung an arm over her shoulder. "Then it's a good thing you don't report to me. Come on, I'm driving."

Elliot laughed. While the Coast Guard didn't forbid friendships among officers and enlisted, they did frown on those between superiors and subordinates. That artificial distance had actually made this friendship easier. There was never any "are you or aren't you" interested. Both Elliot and Grace had been at the same points in their careers in Seattle and had bonded over that connection. And then they'd put Shaw away together. Grace had moved up, and Elliot had moved on.

Grace took her to a barbecue joint where smoke curled up from the pits out back, and the smell made Elliot's mouth water. The sunlight reflected off a white concrete building that was plastered with signs for various drinks as well as a "no air-conditioning" one. After grabbing their platters, Grace picked a picnic table under an oak tree, and Elliot sat opposite her.

Within ten minutes, they'd filled in the blanks and Grace asked, "And how was Antarctica?"

"Long, cold, beautiful." And mostly drama-free, which had been the real reason she'd requested the assignment. She'd gotten tired of defending her actions and had wanted nothing more than to ship out to sea. By the time rumors started circulating about Seattle, she'd established enough of a reputation that her shipboard friends had ignored them.

Grace laughed. "Well put. How's work?"

Elliot shrugged. "Pretty standard for a tourist spot. Mostly recreational accidents and violations."

"No LE?"

"Oh, there's some of that, too. But nothing like Seattle."

The past sat between them for a minute. Grace broke the silence. "You did the right thing. You know that, right?"

"Yes, I do, but..." Elliot sighed and shook her head. She regretted bringing it up. She didn't want to talk about it. She'd spent the last few years putting it behind her. Being right hadn't made living with the consequences any easier.

"You could always come work with me." Grace smiled with a hopeful look, one that she'd repeated often enough.

But Elliot preferred the open water and short missions. Drawn-out investigations and divided loyalties chafed against her sense of honor and integrity. Not that the work Grace did was less than honorable—rooting out corruption and other illegal activities both within and outside the Coast Guard—but the duplicity required for that kind of work didn't sit well with Elliot. "I appreciate the offer."

"But you're going to say no. Again. I get it."

But there was more to her "no" this time. She liked Key West, and she liked what she had with Martine. She wanted to see where it was going. Moving away was not an option. She smiled and changed the subject.

CHAPTER TWENTY-ONE

Martine came downstairs to check the temp on Ernie, the potbellied copper still she'd chosen for her second distillation. Bert, the column still, had already distilled it once. The still was coming to balance, and she'd make her first cut soon. Under normal circumstances, she'd know exactly what she wanted from these cuts, but this batch was different. She'd been distracted from the start, doubling the mix in the fermenter the day after she'd slept with Elliot. She'd had to adjust the times and tinker with the stills, and she still didn't know what to expect. She'd been on edge all week because of it. She'd been so unbearable that Chloe had shifted her hours on either ends of the workday to avoid her. Ana Sofia had told her to stop being a pill.

She tried, but clearly, something was missing, and by the middle of the week, she knew it was Elliot. Even when they worked opposite schedules, Elliot was still around in the form of coffee in Martine's thermos or leftovers in her fridge. But this absence bothered her, and she wasn't sure why. They were still in this fragile place, and Martine hadn't heard a word from her. Not that she expected to, but it made her anxious.

"She's right in here," Chloe said behind her, and she turned.

Martine took her first deep breath in a week as Elliot sauntered in with a sheepish grin on her face. "You're back." Martine tucked her hands in her back pockets, oddly shy. She wanted to wrap her arms around Elliot and kiss her hello.

Elliot leaned in, the smell of sunscreen, salt, and coffee accompanying her. "I'm back. I was thinking of grabbing brunch at Blue Heaven. Wanna come?"

Barely a hint of sexual innuendo in that question, and Martine wanted to ditch work and drag her back to the house. Her cheeks got hot. "Uh."

Doing a quick check of the room, Elliot moved closer. "Miss me?"

Not until Elliot stood in front of her did she realize how much. "Yes."

Martine jumped away as the salesroom door banged open, and Ana Sofia popped her head in. "Oh, hey." She smiled at Elliot, then looked at Martine. "Can you work the floor for a bit? I got a call I need to take."

Martine shook her head, too flustered by everything around her to deal with customers. "I can't. I've got to make cuts. I think Chloe's in the barrel room. Want me to get her?"

"How close are you?" Martine's alarm went off, and Ana Sofia waved her hand. "I'll get her. Stay. Work your magic."

Pulling her attention back to work, Martine hustled to the still and checked the spirit safe. She opened the first bin, where a steady stream poured into it, and the smell of nail polish and vinegar wafted up. Not yet, but close.

Elliot followed, coming up behind her. "Cuts?"

She wanted to lean back and revel in Elliot's closeness, but work called. She quelled her carnal thoughts and brought her senses back in line. "Smell that?"

Elliot took a whiff and coughed. "Yeah, that's terrible."

Concerned, Martine touched her arm. "Careful. Those are heads. Methanol. It'll clean out your sinus."

Taking a step back, Elliot shook her head. "Isn't that toxic?"

Martine quipped, "Only if you drink it."

Elliot looked confused. "Isn't that the point?"

"Do you know how distillation works?" Warming to her subject, Martine linked their arms and gave her a quick overview of the fermentation process and distillation while keeping an eye on the heads.

Elliot listened and asked thoughtful questions. As Martine wrapped up, Elliot spread her arms. "Where did you learn all this?"

Martine usually got this question at some point of the tour, and her answers varied depending on the crowd. But Elliot's tour was personal, so she opened up. "Remember that woman I followed to Barbados? Well, I worked at her family's distillery for a few years. Her brother, Louis, had contacts all over the rum world, and he sent me to Jamaica, Martinique, and Guyana." She smiled as she shared her stories. She put so much of herself in her rum, and Elliot's interest touched her. While she talked, she kept an eye on the heads and occasionally smelled it.

When they got to the stills, Elliot smiled. "Love the names."

Martine preened under the compliment. "I came up with them."

"Do you always use both of them?"

"Usually. It depends on the flavor I'm looking for." She explained the role of copper plates, alcohol, and evaporation in creating flavors. She veered into more technical details before she caught Elliot's eyes glazing over. Reeling it back in, she walked back to Ernie.

The nail polish smell had diminished, signaling a change in the distillate. When dipping her finger in the alcohol coming straight out of the still, she caught only a slight whiff. Just enough to impart a citrus and cream taste if she cut over to hearts right away.

Holding up her hand, she said, "Let me do this first." She shut down the head lever and opened the heart valve. She shuffled past Elliot, brushing up against her and enjoying the heat of her body. She loved this part of the cut. If she got it right, it was amazing. If she got it wrong, well, a lot of time and effort went to waste. With Elliot beside her, the cut took on a different feel, more visceral and emotional than she'd ever experienced. *This could be the one.* And she had no idea if she meant Elliot or the cut.

Elliot spoke and burst her bubble. "What did you do there?"

Martine fell back to her earth and scolded herself for her

wandering thoughts. Distraction caused errors. She grabbed the distiller's log and made detailed notes about the cut before she came back to their conversation. Pointing at three blue valve handles, she tapped each one. "I switched the flow from tails to hearts. Now they're going to collect in the next bin. Heads. Hearts. Tails."

"What happens to it after this?"

All business now, Martine detailed the next steps, discussing the why and how behind the process and the way aging factored into how close a cut she made. "This one? I'm going for a tight cut because I'm not looking to age it."

"We'll be able to drink this today?" Elliot seemed surprised.

She shook her head. "No. I'll have to proof it with water. Then let it sit for a few months before we bottle it."

"Oh." Elliot's shoulders sagged.

Preoccupied with the cut and Elliot's presence in her space, Martine had forgotten the reason people visited her distillery. A bit nervous, she asked, "Did you want to try something else?"

"That you made? Yes." Elliot grinned, her delight obvious.

Martine's stomach fluttered. All of the rums were a reflection of hard work and emotion. What if Elliot hated it? She swallowed her nerves and said, "I've got a few more hours here. Let me finish up, and then I'll give you a tasting."

Elliot's bright smile and enthusiasm dispelled some of her hesitation. "Since you're stuck here, why don't I go run a few errands, get us something to eat, and we can do a tasting then?"

"That would be awesome."

Elliot took her order and left. Nervous and excited, Martine renewed her focus. Lots of people wanted to try her rum. And their opinions mattered in a cerebral and marketable way. Did they think it was good? Would they buy it? She could name off all the flavors and the way she wanted them to taste in someone's mouth, but that final bit where the rum met their tongue remained uniquely personal. She had no control after that, and she'd made her peace with it.

But Elliot bridged that gap between personal and professional. Having Elliot taste something she'd spent the last decade perfecting felt distinctly intimate. Fear shivered up her spine and settled in her gut. She poured her heart into her work, and letting Elliot taste it left her unguarded. What would she see? Martine hadn't even known she was this vulnerable. Maybe she should back off, but she knew it was already too late.

And what if Elliot saw something Martine wasn't ready to share? She couldn't be more exposed if she was lying naked on their kitchen table. Again. But physical intimacy and emotional intimacy had never been the same for Martine, and she couldn't pretend they were.

She almost missed the Queen's share with all her obsessing, and she finally put it to rest. It was just rum—important rum, but not enough for all this energy. She needed to get a grip, so she tamped down her fears and turned her attention back to the work. And if every now and then a stray thought popped up, she quickly corralled it. By the time Elliot texted to check in about food, she'd managed to shift those emotions into anticipation and excitement. If all went well, maybe she'd show Elliot the blend she'd been working on for the past few months. That would be special.

❖

Elliot came back in the early evening with takeout from a Caribbean restaurant on White Street, excited to taste Martine's rum. Martine greeted her at the door. "Let me give you the grand tour this time."

The building belonged to Ana Sofia's family. A converted cigar factory, the fourteen-foot ceilings allowed tobacco to dry in large stacks. The front half of the building housed the tasting room and the stills; the back half of the building housed the barrel rooms and the bottling line. A plate-glass window between the tasting room and the stills let the customers watch the rum being made while they drank it.

In the tasting room, Martine poured from four different bottles, only one of them was the clear white Elliot associated with rum.

"All of these are rum?"

Martine grinned. "Yes. Let me give you the rundown. We have

four main expressions. Cochin, aged three years. Bantam, aged one year. Crèvecoeur, aged five years. Sebright, unaged."

"What do the names mean?"

"They're chickens."

"What?"

"Breeds of chickens. Like the ones you see all over town."

"The same kinds?"

"No. They're mostly Cubalaya. And whatever breeds worked for cockfighting. They're all mixed up now."

Elliot smiled, tickled by the names and enjoying the one-on-one attention. "I see. Do you have a sheet of paper telling me what flavors to look for?"

Martine waved her off. "That's for helping people decide what they might like. Tasting's so subjective. One person's vanilla notes are someone else's caramel. You don't need that. Try them first. Then I'll tell you how they're made."

And she did. But Martine also revealed another side of herself that had Elliot hungering for more. Watching her distill that afternoon, Elliot had seen a detailed, clinical, and precise individual. But as Martine shared her rum, she shared her history, and another, more familiar side emerged—passionate, dedicated, and connected. She'd never think of rum the same way again, nor taste it without hearing Martine's voice.

Martine's roots went deep, and she celebrated them in her work. Elliot had no such history. Her entire life had been transitory. Her parents' families were distant relatives she'd grown up seeing once a year at Thanksgiving or Christmas. She'd never wanted something different. For the first time, she imagined a different future, a community around her. Not a work community like the Coast Guard but the one Martine had here in Key West.

"Am I boring you?"

Worried that she made the wrong impression, Elliot quickly reassured her. "No, not at all. I was just thinking…" That she wanted her life to feel like Martine described. That she loved the sense of belonging she heard coming from Martine's lips. How much she envied her.

Martine gave her a long look, as if she wasn't sure what to say. Then she abruptly leaned in and said, "Can I show you something?"

Already enthralled, this new intensity sucked Elliot in. She'd do almost anything Martine said right now. "Sure."

Martine held out a hand and brought her back to the barrel room. Not air-conditioned, the room retained the day's heat, and the humidity clung to Elliot's arms. Martine led her to a low table in the middle of the room. Several small jars with handwritten labels littered the space. It was the first unorganized part of the distillery she'd seen. Martine waved her arm over them. "These are called marques. I take various ones and blend them together to create something new." She grabbed a short jar and poured it into another jar. "I want you to try this."

Elliot took the jar and reeled as the high alcohol content burned her nasal passages. "Whoa."

"Shit. Sorry." Grabbing the jar back, Martine fished a water bottle from under the desk and diluted the mix.

This time, when Elliot put it up to her lips, the fumes didn't overpower her. She took a sip and suppressed the urge to spit it out.

Martine watched her intently, her eyes narrowed. "You hate it."

Forcing herself to swallow, she said, "It's a bit...raw."

Martine took the jar and sniffed. "Yeah. It's still a bit off."

"How can you tell?"

She gave her a slow, sexy smile. "Want me to show you?"

Not exactly sure if she meant rum or something else, Elliot nodded.

For the next few hours, Martine showed her how she blended her rum. They mixed and matched, pulled rum from casks. She taught Elliot how to taste for structure and texture. Was it open and supple? Or linear and firm? Was it silky and smooth or rough and gravelly? By the time the sun set, Elliot no longer cared about the terroir of the rum. With every lesson on taste, Martine touched her face, her arm, her shoulder. The intimacy of the work and the humidity of the room heightened Elliot's arousal. Every touch ignited tiny sparks from head to toe.

With a triumphant flourish, Martine put the bottle down. "There. That's it."

In that moment, when Martine was so in her element, Elliot could no longer hold back her desire. She gently spun Martine around and kissed her. Softly at first, barely there, enough for Martine to back out. But she pushed forward, pressed harder, reciprocated and demanded entry. Their tongues touched and stroked, charging and retreating. Elliot let go of her shirt and clutched her shoulders, wanting more, needing to get closer. Her world narrowed to this moment with Martine in her arms and was only broken when Martine's voice, low and breathless, set shivers up and down her spine. "Let's go home."

CHAPTER TWENTY-TWO

For Martine's birthday, Ana Sofia took her, Elliot, and Cass out on her boat. Elliot had been surprised by the boat part, but she'd packed her bags and joined Cass and Martine at the dock. Ana Sofia's boat was a seventy-six-foot yacht with three decks—a fly bridge, a main deck and a below deck that housed sleeping quarters for seven people. She moored it off an island, and they took the small dinghy back and forth to set up a bonfire.

Cass and Martine spread blankets around the bonfire as Ana Sofia set up the fanciest camping stove Elliot had ever seen. While the black beans and rice cooked, she laid out a blanket and cutting board with several cheeses, bread, and fruit. She opened jars of fig preserves, roasted tomatoes, olives, and hot peppers.

"Is there anything I can do to help?" Elliot asked. Everyone else worked with the practiced ease of having done something similar several times before. She felt a little left out until Martine touched her, sending sparks down her spine that comforted rather than excited.

"You're good. Have a seat." Martine cracked open a portable bar and dug out four glasses. She opened another bag and pulled a thermos from it. She stirred and tasted it before she poured its contents into the glasses, garnishing with orange peels. Handing them around, she waited until everyone had one and then said, "Cheers."

The gentle click of glass echoed across the dark water, and

the warm smiles from Ana Sofia and Cass made her feel included. "Cheers."

The cocktail hit the back of Elliot's throat with a pleasant sweetness and then a gentle burn down to her stomach. "Mmm. What's in this?"

Martine sat beside her and said, "El Presidente. Our own lightly aged rum, Pierre Ferrand dry curacao, Noilly Prat Extra Dry vermouth, and my homemade grenadine."

Elliot assumed that list of ingredients made sense to someone who knew about cocktails. Nothing told her why it tasted the way it did, but when she thought about asking for details, she found she didn't care. *Let the mystery stand.* "It tastes great."

Martine leaned back on her elbows. "It's one of my favorites."

They passed around the cheese platter and talked about work and life in the Keys.

Something Ana Sofia said triggered Elliot to ask, "You own this island?"

Ana Sofia shrugged. "Pilar does."

"Your mother?"

She pursed her lips. "Hmm."

Cass plucked an olive off the cheese platter and popped it in their mouth. "There's a history with this island. It used to have a lighthouse in the 1830s, but a hurricane washed it out to sea. Wreckers would moor here while waiting out storms. Then the sponge divers came and set up a seasonal camp. Just up the shore, you can still see the outlines of the buildings. During Prohibition, rum runners would meet Cuban boats out here before smuggling their rum into the US."

Martine smiled. "I sometimes wonder if our great-grandfather was out there waiting for them."

Ana Sofia fussed with the fire, creating a smaller side branch. "It could very well be. This island's been in my family since the turn of the century. My abuela says her father used his connections in Cuba to bring rum into the country. We might not have been the first Cejas-Roberts partnership."

Elliot loved the sense of place they all shared and envied their connection. She knew other Coasties who'd built lives for themselves off-base, setting up homes and putting down roots, sometimes leaving for assignments but always coming back home. Looking at Martine, she could see the allure of home, and an unexpected longing lodged in her throat.

Martine tilted her head and mouthed, "What?"

Caught in the moment, Elliot swallowed her feelings and smiled. "Nothing."

"Are we ready?" Cass asked Ana Sofia, who nodded. They brought a beach grill and set it down on the coals. Together, they grilled oysters and lobsters while telling jokes and more stories. Their shared connection pulled her in and held her. Not once did Elliot feel like an outsider.

After dinner, she stretched out, looking for somewhere to put her head. Martine tapped her thigh, and she automatically scooched over. She put her head in Martine's lap and stared into the night sky. Nothing beat stargazing out on the ocean. Even if she was on an island.

Martine glanced at her and then up. "It's beautiful, isn't it?"

She hummed her agreement, luxuriating in Martine's warmth and the drowsiness of a full belly. She breathed in and closed her eyes. The salt air, burning wood, and a faint bread and orange scent surrounded her.

Martine brushed her fingers through her hair. "Are you falling asleep on me?"

"Maybe." Opening her eyes, Elliot focused on her. She'd never felt so close to her. The fire lit up a tiny scar on her chin. Elliot reached up and touched it. "How'd that happen?"

Martine covered her hand and smiled, a distant look on her face as if the memory replayed in her mind. "Fishhook. When I was ten, I tripped. I needed stitches and everything."

Elliot winced. "Sounds painful."

"It was."

Something passed between them, a tenderness in Martine's touch that she couldn't name. Throughout the evening, Martine had touched all three of them, hanging off Cass at first, then lounging at Ana Sofia's feet, and now she lounged with Elliot. This kind of intimacy was new but totally welcome.

"I've been saving this for you. Happy birthday." Ana Sofia passed a bottle to her.

Martine leaned forward, and that citrusy smell grew stronger. "Oh, where you'd find it?"

"Jean-Claude owed me a favor."

"That must have been some favor."

Elliot turned on her side, and Martine held the bottle so she could read the label. The fire lit it from beyond, revealing a deep red-brown liquid. Appleton Estate, aged 50 years, Jamaica Independence Reserve, Jamaica Rum.

"This is the world's oldest barrel-aged rum." Martine cracked the seal and sniffed.

Elliot sat up, already missing Martine's closeness. Ana Sofia handed her a glass, and Martine poured two fingers' worth in her cup. Elliot waited until everyone had some and then took a tentative sip. For a second, she thought she was drinking bourbon, but then it changed, and she tasted a sweet and spicy blend of vanilla, cinnamon, and licorice. She swallowed, and the warmth traveled down her throat, leaving behind a taste that begged for more.

"Oh."

Martine moaned beside her. "Mmm-hmm."

Ana Sofia held her glass up and said, "Now, this is rum."

"They grow their own sugarcane." Martine shook her head, a wistful tone in her voice.

"Is that a good thing?" Elliot asked.

"Someday, I want to source all my molasses from the same farm. Maybe even dabble in cane juice fermentation. Make our own agricole."

While Elliot understood the words, the specific terms escaped her. Martine wanted to control the process, and as someone who loved fresh ingredients, that meant something. Their conversation turned into a comparison of other rums, and Elliot listened intently.

"I don't have a problem with adding sugar. People like what

they like. Sometimes, I want a sweet rum. But at least be honest and label your product."

"Isn't that illegal?" Elliot asked.

Ana Sofia laughed, and Martine bumped her shoulder. "You'd think. Rum is a pretty big unregulated category that's spread across several countries. With their own laws."

"I take it you don't add sugar to your rum," Elliot said.

"Only when we're making cocktails."

They talked late into the night discussing food and drink for most of it. As the night wore on, Elliot saw Martine's guard drop. At first, she thought it was the alcohol lowering her inhibitions, but it was deeper than that. Something about the way the three of them talked and laughed, a relaxed shorthand communication between them. This was Martine's home, these two people and their world. And for that evening, it included her.

Elliot passed on the third drink and stifled a yawn.

Martine whispered, "Did you want to head back?"

"To the boat?" She didn't think Ana Sofia was up to navigating in the dark. She could probably handle the dingy, but mixing water, liquor, and sleepiness was stupid.

Martine grinned and glanced at her two friends wrapped in a blanket and talking quietly among themselves. "Unless you want to camp out here. It might get cold."

"Then we'll cuddle, but I think we should sleep it off here." She wasn't letting any of them near the water in this state.

Martine stood. "Well, I'm going to pee. I'll be right back."

Taking that as a yes, Elliot grabbed another blanket and stoked the fire a bit. Neither Cass nor Ana Sofia looked their way when Martine returned and snuggled next to her. Elliot tucked them in, and they lay facing each other, so close she could smell the rum on Martine's breath. She wished they were alone so she could kiss her.

Across from them, Ana Sofia and Cass huddled together, whispering intently. Ana Sofia kept shaking her head at whatever Cass was saying.

"What's the deal with them?" Elliot whispered.

Martine glanced over. "They have this push-pull thing. Always have. Whenever one of them gets close, the other runs away."

"Why do they do it?"

Martine took a deep breath. "When I first met Ana Sofia, Cass had a huge crush on her. But Ana Sofia didn't notice them until college. They dated then. Cass even offered to move to New York when Ana Sofia went to law school. But Ana Sofia didn't want to hold Cass back, so she broke it off. Cass was devastated. When she came back for good, Cass had moved on."

"And now?" She stole another look, and they'd moved on to kissing. Elliot huddled closer to give them more privacy.

Martine rubbed her shoulder. "I think they still love each other. A lot. But Cass needs to move on, and they know it. And Ana Sofia is not ready to let go. What about you? Any first loves you couldn't let go?"

You came to mind, but that wasn't true. She didn't love Martine, at least not that way. And especially not back then. She hadn't even known who she was when they'd first met. "No."

"Me neither. Guess that makes us the last of the un-romantics."

"Guess so." Except everything about this night felt romantic. And if a tiny part of her heart hurt after Martine's comment, she didn't mind because she'd seen another side of Martine and wouldn't trade that for all the flowery words in the world.

Martine yawned and turned over. "Good night."

Elliot closed her eyes and breathed her in. "Good night."

❖

Martine got up in the middle of the night to pee again and added more wood to the fire before crawling back under the covers. Across the way, Ana Sofia lay sprawled across Cass's chest, totally asleep.

Martine snuggled into the smaller spoon slot, adjusting her ass to fit just so.

Elliot pulled her closer and whispered in her ear, her voice low, ragged, and full of sex. "I like that."

She wiggled a little more. "Like this?"

Elliot clutched her hips and rubbed against her ass. "Yes."

Her breath ghosted along Martine's skin, giving her goose bumps. Closing her eyes, she tilted her head and whispered, "That feels nice."

Elliot palmed her breasts, squeezing and circling her nipples. The gentle rubbing dulled her senses. Elliot had such wonderful hands, so supple and strong. The way she touched, so tender and firm.

Martine gasped as a sharp pinch brought her back into focus.

Elliot whispered in her ear. "Shh. Don't make any noise."

And then Elliot tangled their legs together, opening Martine up and pinning her in place. Martine offered no resistance. She let Elliot control the pace and the tempo as her entire world narrowed to the circle of Elliot's arms.

She bit her lip to keep from moaning as Elliot slid under her shirt, lingering on the curve of her hip and the swell of her stomach before moving lower. She shuddered as Elliot skimmed along her labia, parting her folds, and slipping through her wetness to circle her opening. She suppressed a gasp and trembled, undulating as Elliot touched her clit.

Elliot played with her, building up the intensity with each stroke before bringing her back down. Again and again, Elliot brought her to the edge only to ease away, but each escalation took less and less time to bring her to the brink again. When she finally came, she shuddered and bucked while Elliot cradled her in her arms.

Elliot soothed her with kisses at her temple and cheek and words she'd couldn't follow. But she didn't need to hear them. She knew the feeling that they shared was love, but she was too tired and too relaxed to freak out.

CHAPTER TWENTY-THREE

With no coffee, Martine's will to have breakfast on the beach evaporated. They packed and headed to the boat. Elliot and Cass crowded into the galley and made breakfast there. Ana Sofia made grapefruit-Campari drinks, Cass made toast and bacon, and Elliot poached eggs.

Elliot moved with ease among Martine's friends. Something had changed, and Martine couldn't stop thinking about it. They'd been doing their own push-pull dance for a while, and she'd been content to let it ride. After last night, she wasn't sure what she wanted.

"Do either of you need to get back? We're thinking of heading out to the Dry Tortugas. Do some snorkeling. Do you want to come?" Cass passed the bacon while Ana Sofia doled out the eggs.

Seven islands seventy miles to the west of Key West, the Dry Tortugas offered untouched coral reefs and various shipwrecks, along with gorgeous tropical islands. It had been years since she'd gone. Another romantic destination on their unexpectedly romantic getaway. She wasn't sure how she felt about it, but one look at Elliot's hopeful expression and her reluctance crumbled. "Sure."

After breakfast, Martine washed the dishes, and Elliot volunteered to help. But it quickly became obvious that Elliot had no desire to actually help. Each lingering touch sent electric shocks down Martine's spine. With Ana Sofia and Cass coming in and out of the room, her frustration and arousal grew. Exasperated, she finally spun around and pinned Elliot in the corner.

Elliot's eyes sparkled as if she'd been hoping for this move for some time.

Bracing her hands on either side of Elliot, Martine leaned in. "If you keep this up…"

Elliot met her halfway. All the pent-up energy from the morning erupted into a ferocious, open-mouthed kiss. Martine struggled to keep her balance while Elliot moved her tongue in the most delicious twists and turns.

Pulling back, Martine brushed kisses along her jawline. But Ana Sofia asked a question as she walked into the dining area, and Elliot pecked Martine on the cheek and spun away.

The entire day continued from there, with each of them teasing and testing until they jammed themselves into a tight corner and kissed hungrily. But they were never alone for long. And when they were underwater by themselves, they were both seasoned enough to stop the game for safety reasons.

They ate a late lunch from Ana Sofia's well-stocked fridge and pantry. She went topside to the helm while Cass went below to sleep. Alone for the first time in hours, and still buzzing from all that sexual energy, Martine leaned over Elliot's shoulder and kissed her neck. "I'm going to take a shower. Get some of the salt off."

Elliot hummed and tilted her head.

Martine took advantage of the move to kiss along the curve and up to her ear. "Join me?"

Elliot pulled her onto her lap and kissed her. She slipped her hands in Martine's shirt and held her close.

Martine twirled out of reach and extended a hand. Elliot had kept her aroused all day, and she needed to touch her. "Let's go."

❖

Elliot jumped awake when Ana Sofia's voice came through the speakers above their heads, the sound so close that Elliot thought she was in the room. "Hey, do you two want to join us for dinner at Santiago's Bodega? We dock in twenty minutes."

Martine rolled over and snuggled close, her damp curls brushing against Elliot's knee. Elliot shifted closer, her thigh coming to rest between Martine's legs. Martine hummed and kissed along her neck.

"Do you think she knows?" Even after spending an intimate weekend with Ana Sofia and Cass, Elliot didn't know them well enough to share her sex life. She hadn't sorted out her own feelings yet. She didn't need the added stress of Martine's business partner and close friend knowing all about them.

"No. She broadcasts that into all the rooms. Although she might have heard us." Martine winced.

Elliot glanced up. They'd been loud but not that loud. The boat moved at a pretty fast pace, and the wind alone drowned out all sound. "From two decks above? No."

Martine raised her head and said, "Well? Any dinner plans?"

"Not tonight." She leaned in and kissed along Martine's ribs.

"I need to take another shower. I smell like sex."

"You also taste like sex." And she liked that taste.

Martine inhaled sharply while Elliot continued kissing along her hip. She didn't want her to get up. If she got up, then this moment, this weekend, this closeness might end.

"El…"

The way Martine shortened her name turned her on even more. She shifted again and kissed along Martine's shoulder blades. Martine tilted her head and made no move to rise. Elliot slipped a hand between her legs, enjoying the sticky wetness while she kissed a line up her neck. "We have time, don't we?"

Martine turned in her arms and shoved her backward. "Yes. But it'll have to be fast."

Elliot smiled. "I can do fast."

But not fast enough. The boat slowed as Martine climaxed, and she nearly jumped out of bed.

"Hey, what about me?" Elliot laughed as Martine dashed out the door with no clothes on.

"Maybe later," Martine called and shut the bathroom door.

By the time Elliot dressed, Martine was already up on deck. Dinner gave them very little privacy. No touching under the table or stolen moments. But the food...well, the food made up for some of that.

Later, Ana Sofia dropped them off at their house and drove away as Elliot climbed the steps. Away from the house, everything had made sense. But now that the weekend was over...not so much. She paused at the threshold, and Martine bumped into her.

"Are you okay?"

Elliot stared at her hand on the knob, afraid to open the door and end the weekend.

"Did you forget your key?" Martine ran a hand down her spine.

"No." Elliot leaned into her touch, imagining where those hands had already been and where they might go. Their emotional intimacy had changed, deepened, and expanded. She didn't want to lose that. Would coming home change that or amplify it?

Martine reached around and opened the door. "Are you coming?"

Elliot closed the door behind her. What would she say anyway? She'd let her actions speak for her. And then, maybe, they wouldn't need to talk about it after all.

CHAPTER TWENTY-FOUR

Martine woke up slightly disoriented, unsure of the time and location. She squeezed the pillow in her arms and breathed Elliot's citrus-and-salt scent. Shouldn't she smell coffee somewhere? She'd lost track of the times she'd woken up in Elliot's bed with her gone, but the scent of coffee always permeated the house. Then she heard the shower going next door. Either she'd woken up earlier, or Elliot was running late. She'd bet money on the late part, considering what she'd come home to the day before:

"What is this?"

Elliot came over and patted the brand-new tabletop sitting in their kitchen. A slight hitch in her voice betrayed her nervousness. "Do you like it?"

Martine circled it, putting her palm down and testing its weight. Solid wood, not the polycarbonate of the previous table. She glanced over, somewhat surprised at the expectant look on Elliot's face. She wanted Martine to like it. Had she bought it for her? Elliot had spent a lot of money, and that made her uneasy. "I like the color."

"It's not too dark?"

"Not at all." The black matte finish accentuated the kitchen's tropical greens, blues, and whites.

"I almost called you." She shrugged.

Martine couldn't quite understand what Elliot wanted from her.

Something much deeper was at play, but she wasn't sure what, so she chose to ignore it. "It's your house, too."

She must have said the right thing because Elliot relaxed. She hoisted herself up and pulled Martine over. "We could test it out."

Martine toyed with the nape of Elliot's neck. "Seems sturdy enough. But I'd hate to have a repeat."

Elliot slipped her hands inside Martine's shirt, and she closed her eyes at the touch of skin on skin. Elliot leaned closer and said, "I'm not worried." Then she kissed her.

So much sex. And not just last night but for the past few weeks. Sore muscles that she didn't know existed kinds of sex. Not that she was complaining. But the on-demand sex was a perk Martine had never experienced. Closing her eyes, she buried her face in the pillow and basked in Elliot's smell.

"I'm not interrupting a moment, am I?"

Embarrassed at being caught, Martine tossed the pillow at her. Elliot deflected it but lost her grip on her towel. Those long legs, toned arms, and strong chest begged to be touched. Martine flipped the sheets off and crawled across the bed, snagged her hand, and tugged. "Come back to bed."

"You're killing me." Elliot groaned but let herself be pulled down on top.

"Am I? You don't feel very dead. You feel very much alive." She palmed Elliot's breasts and sucked a nipple into her mouth.

Elliot hissed but didn't pull away. "I'm late already."

Martine let go of her nipple with an audible pop and ran her hands up and down Elliot's back, brushing against the tiny pinpricks of wet skin. "How late?"

"Very." Elliot kissed Martine with a single-minded determination that left her breathless and wanting more so thoroughly, she didn't feel Elliot pull away until she was off the bed. So thoroughly, Martine didn't even protest while Elliot dressed.

But Martine couldn't let her leave without a final temptation. She flopped back on the bed with a melodramatic sigh. "Fine. Go. I'll just get myself off."

She almost jumped out of her skin when Elliot pounced back on the bed and pinned her arms above her head. "No. Wait for me."

Her tone and intensity made Martine even wetter, but she couldn't let it go. "Are you going to make me?"

"Are you asking me to?" Elliot quirked an eyebrow.

Well, fuck, there it was. They'd flirted on the edges of this power dynamic since the beginning. She didn't usually let other people take control. And she got the feeling Elliot didn't either, and yet they both kept asking each other to do it. "I'm not sure."

"Well, then, do what you will. But there will be consequences." Elliot smiled and stood, leaving Martine wanting to feel her weight again and reeling with the possibilities. Elliot fixed her with a direct look. "That is, if you want there to be."

Martine didn't look away as she said, "Let me think about it."

Elliot grinned, and the whole mood shifted. "I'll make you coffee before I go." She finished getting dressed and called over her shoulder on the way out, "No breakfast, though. Someone distracted me."

Martine's stomach rumbled, and she mourned the loss of both food and sex as she lounged in bed and wondered if she'd masturbate. Just the way Elliot had said consequences thrilled her. Did Elliot want to spank her? Her heart fluttered. Did she want to be spanked? She clenched her legs. She'd dabbled in light bondage before but in very controlled circumstances. Even when she'd been tied up, she'd run the show. She already knew that Elliot would be different. And she needed to know her own boundaries before she could explore them with Elliot. If they did this, they'd need to talk.

But first, coffee.

Elliot managed to get to work just under the wire. Martine had emerged from her bedroom, tousled and drowsy, as she had rushed out the door. Good thing she'd come out later because after a few more minutes, Elliot wouldn't have cared how late she was.

From the moment she'd walked in and seen Martine holding that dildo, she'd wanted to use it on her. And then she'd thought it'd be over, sexual tension dispelled in a night of tremendous fucking. But not so much. Then after Martine's birthday trip, the sex had changed, becoming more intense. Elliot couldn't keep her hands to herself, and judging from Martine's willingness, the feeling was mutual. They'd had sex in almost every place in the house, including the pool. They'd sometimes have bouts of domesticity followed by sex. That was how she'd ended up going down on Martine at the edge of the pool when she'd gone out to skim the leaves. Or the time she'd been doing laundry and Martine had backed her onto the dryer and fucked her until she'd banged her head on the vent. Her desire only increased with knowing what she was getting instead of imagining what she was missing.

Although this morning, the reverse had been true. Imagining Martine masturbating without her turned her on. A sudden feeling of "mine" hit her, and she wanted to possess her. Something had passed between them, another step in their relationship that Elliot had put out there sooner than she'd meant to. But now that it was out there, she was ready for what came next.

She adjusted her uniform a final time and left the locker room. She spent the next hour getting the boat ready for their field trip. They had two hours before they were due to meet the Truman Summer Camp at the Key West Historic Harbor. She wanted to make sure the boat was pristine and also safe for the kids to wander around in.

She went over her checklist while the crew finished scrubbing the deck. She wandered in and out of the cockpit several times, overhearing snatches of conversation about bars and baseball. Done topside, she went below. Rounding the corner, she heard Weiss say, "...transferring if she gets promoted."

Elliot came up behind her and said, "You should get that paperwork in order." She met Riviera's eyes over Weiss's shoulder and winked before they stepped aside to make way. "Riviera, if you're done in the galley, I could use some help in the engine room."

Riviera gave the same version of "Don't listen to her" that

Elliot had been getting each time Weiss had publicly dragged her. Sooner or later, Elliot would have to deal with her or face serious morale problems with her crew. She'd asked around and had learned that Weiss had served under Shaw during her first posting. She knew from experience that Shaw cultivated loyalty, and Weiss had been mentored by him. If Weiss didn't stop on her own, Elliot would have to call her on the carpet, and she knew from experience that it could go either way.

They were under way within an hour. Elliot took them out into the bay for a bit before turning around and heading back to shore east-northeast. She came in alongside the dock, waving at the group of elementary kids. Several hands waved back, and more than a few were jumping in place. With a wave of his own, Riviera hopped over to secure the lines while Elliot powered down.

Weiss met her on deck and smiled. "I love this part."

Surprised at the unexpected thaw in their relationship, Elliot grinned. "Me too." Maybe she could change Weiss's opinion of her. Staying angry took a lot of work. All Elliot had to do was nudge her in another direction. Nodding toward the kids, she said, "Wanna do the honors?"

"You want me to do the tour?" Weiss gave her a skeptical look.

"Why should I get all the fun jobs? If you're not interested…" She dangled it out there, ready to pull it back.

Weiss narrowed her eyes, and Elliot could feel her wheels turning before she nodded. "Okay. Let's do this."

Elliot followed her into the fray but let her take the lead. Most of the equipment was stowed away, but managing twenty or so seven-year-olds on a Coast Guard boat required constant supervision. About a quarter of the way into the tour, one of the adult chaperones sidled up to Elliot and said, "You're a natural with them."

"It's not so different than dealing with adults. Clear boundaries and set expectations." Elliot quickly glanced at the speaker and paused. "Brynn?"

Brynn grinned. "I was wondering if you were ignoring me."

"After you ghosted me." She grinned, both acknowledging

their past and teasing. She didn't hold it against Brynn, especially now that things with Martine had taken off in a new direction.

Brynn had the decency to look a bit embarrassed. "Yeah. Something like that."

Elliot shook her head. She'd quickly scanned the adults but hadn't recognized her. She sometimes glossed over details when looking for specifics. "No. Just keeping them safe. I didn't know you were a teacher."

"Teacher's aide. Bartending's a side gig."

Elliot spotted one of the young girls reaching toward a knob. "Gotta go."

They chatted here and there while Elliot remained focused on Weiss's talk and the kids. Brynn's easy presence reminded her of Martine. Was it genetic, or did they have similar styles? In bed, they were completely different. Martine liked to dominate, and Brynn liked to submit.

But sex with Brynn, while intense, had been…boring. Elliot had fallen into a familiar pattern where she took charge and made all the moves. And she never would have noticed that difference if she hadn't started sleeping with Martine. Martine shared power. She gave as good as she received. Elliot had never trusted anyone to do that for her, and it probably had to do with that kernel of trust planted when they were kids. The way they saw each other then, without the armor of adulthood. This fundamental connection that linked them as friends made sex so…addictive. Yeah, that was the word for what was happening between them.

But the physical intimacy wasn't the only draw. She liked the life they'd started building together. And even if the sex faded away, she planned to do everything in her power to keep that life protected.

The tour ended, the children clapped, and Elliot helped them file off the boat. As they gathered, Brynn leaned in and said, "We should do coffee sometime."

And by coffee, did she mean sex? Probably. Elliot wasn't about to take her up on that offer, but Brynn was Martine's cousin, so she couldn't just brush her off. "Sure."

Brynn trailed her fingers along Elliot's forearm. "You have my number. I promise, I won't ignore you."

Elliot didn't have the heart to say she'd be doing the ghosting this time.

CHAPTER TWENTY-FIVE

Martine worked a half day, wanting to get home before Elliot. She'd make up that time on another day. Taking a quick shower, she dried off and crawled back into bed. A quick text told her she had about twenty minutes to get ready. It didn't take that long. She'd been horny and wet all day thinking about the way she wanted to entice Elliot tonight. Would Elliot step into the room and watch her get off? Would she tell her what to do but deny her a touch? Would she use force? Tie her up and tease her? She heard the door open and came while imagining Elliot's face as she walked in.

Her hand still between her legs, Martine listened as Elliot closed the door and headed into her bathroom. Careful to avoid her sensitive clit, Martine slowly circled her opening as the shower came on. She closed her eyes as she pictured Elliot under the spray, soaping her body. She rubbed along her labia, swirling and massaging her folds, becoming more and more aroused.

"Didn't I tell you there would be consequences?"

Martine's eyes snapped open. Shit, when did the shower stop?

Elliot stood at the edge of the room, her gaze trained on Martine's hand still moving under the covers.

"Yes." Her need had become unbearable.

"Is that something you want?" She spoke, a low and almost choked quality. Martine could see her desire written in the set of her jaw and the way she held her body rigid.

She stilled her hand trapped in her warm wetness. "Yes."

"Well, don't mind me." Elliot leaned against the doorjamb and crossed her arms. "Continue."

Acutely aware of Elliot watching, Martine eased back into the wetness surrounding her opening.

"Wait." Elliot flew across the room and pulled the covers down to Martine's ankles. "That's better. Now, open your legs. Yes."

Martine held her gaze for a moment before Elliot's focus shifted between her legs. She relished Elliot's reaction, so much better than her earlier fantasy. Her fists opened and closed as she stood at the end of the bed and watched. Martine wanted to break that calm, that distance, and force Elliot to do what she said she'd do.

Elliot's jaw clenched, and her nostrils flared as Martine spread herself wider for inspection. Her breath came in shorter and shorter pants, and still, Elliot stood there. "I thought you said there'd be consequences."

For a brief moment, Elliot's confidence flickered. If Martine hadn't been staring so intently, she would have missed it. This was new territory. And then it was over. Elliot squared her shoulders, an aura of command dropping down. "Get off the bed."

Time to test the boundaries of this arrangement. "And if I don't…"

Elliot paused, the command persona slipping as she offered Martine one more out. "We don't have to do this."

Martine needed to own this moment, and so she stood. "Oh, I want this."

Elliot grinned. "Good." She circled Martine, trailing a hand along her bare skin, each touch a pinprick of desire. Her breath tickled Martine's neck as she leaned into her from behind. "Tell me, what do you think should be a consequence for your coming without me?"

Martine turned in her arms and said, "I think you should spank me."

Elliot whooshed out a breath. "Oh, okay."

"Too much?" Martine adjusted Elliot's lapels and ran her hands down her shirt. She tucked her hands into the belt and tugged her closer.

Elliot shook her head, and again, Martine wondered how much experience Elliot had with this kind of power play. "No, not at all. How rough do you want me to be?"

"I'll say 'sugarcane' if I need you to stop."

Elliot quirked an eyebrow at her word choice.

She rolled her eyes. Was Elliot seriously hassling her about her safe word? "I make rum."

Elliot relented and smiled. "I get it."

Then Elliot stepped away, leaving Martine grasping at nothing, standing alone and naked in the room. Elliot's hot stare stripped away her doubts. She embraced her vulnerability and straightened her back, prepared to accept what Elliot had to offer.

When Elliot spoke, her voice crackled with authority. "Bend over the bed."

Martine leaned over, her stomach resting against the edge, her ass on display. Elliot ran a hand, warm and rough, along her cheeks. She clenched and unclenched her ass, anticipating the blow that never came. Instead, Elliot gripped her cheeks and pried her open.

She squirmed, the urge to stand up and take control surged through her. This was too much, too soon for that kind of trust. Oh... she moaned as Elliot licked a path from her perineum to her clit. She pushed back into Elliot's mouth, but she moved away, kissing first one, then the other cheek before murmuring, "You taste so good. All this for me?"

Martine nodded, unable to speak.

Elliot slapped her ass, a light touch meant to get her attention but leaving her wanting so much more. "I asked you a question."

"Yes." Her voice sounded too breathy and almost squeaked.

"Better."

Martine closed her eyes, imagining Elliot on her knees behind her as she lapped the length of her, slow and firm circles, building her arousal with teasing touches of her clit. Martine moved against the bed, curling toward it to get more friction where she needed it most. Each lick adding to her growing wetness until she finally begged, "More, please."

"Not yet." Pulling away, Elliot spread her wider, her thumbs rubbing in the crease and along her anus. Martine got wetter at the delicious pressure of being held. She twitched at the touch and arched toward her, begging with her body as well as her words, but Elliot held her in place, tightening her grip. "Such a lovely ass. It's almost a shame to hit it."

Aroused and frustrated at how close she was, Martine turned over and said, "Fucking do it already." She immediately regretted her outburst. Judging from Elliot's stunned expression, she'd thrown them both out of the moment. "I didn't mean…"

But then Elliot recovered. Her eyes narrowed, and a slow hungry smile preceded her quick movement. Before Martine could react, Elliot sat next to her, hooked a hand around her waist, and hauled her over her lap. She flopped across Elliot's legs and scrambled to adjust, but not before Elliot smacked her.

The sharp sting shot up from her ass and jolted her upright. "Oh!"

"I'm not done with you yet." Elliot nudged her back down.

She squirmed against the fabric of Elliot's shorts, trying to find a less awkward position.

Elliot stopped touching her. "I don't hear 'sugarcane.'"

She stilled. She didn't want her to stop. The pain had been brief, but the thrill of being held down was exquisite. Taking a deep breath, she relaxed. "I'm ready." She clenched her ass just before the blow hit, a loud crack echoing around the room. She jolted, her clit brushing against the fabric, and a burst of pleasure accompanied the pain. The mix of pleasure to the pain tipped the balance, and Martine looked back at her. "I need you to touch me."

Elliot smiled and slipped a hand under her. "Like this?"

She hissed as Elliot touched her, tangling in her folds but not moving. A maddening, almost touch. "Yes."

Her hand came down again, a little less painful. But Martine didn't have time to focus as Elliot stroked her.

Elliot pushed her toward the edge, rubbing her clit until Martine almost forgot what was coming and then smacking her back into her body. Her heart raced, her breath caught. She lost track of the individual slaps, the painful stings becoming hot throbbing. She wanted—no, needed—to come, but Elliot held her at bay. She could stop this, demand Elliot finish her off. All she had to do was say it.

She glanced back, seeing the sweat on Elliot's face, her furrowed brow, and the firm set of her jaw. Such intense concentration devoted to her pleasure. A warm feeling bubbled inside her. Her defiance melted, and a part of her she hadn't known existed emerged. She swallowed hard and asked, "Can I come?"

Elliot paused, and once again, Martine worried that she'd killed the mood. The whole idea of submitting to someone had been a huge mistake. Embarrassed by her vulnerability and humiliated by her question, she started to move away. But Elliot held her fast.

"Did I tell you to move?" Sandwiched between her hands, Martine clutched the sheets as another blow hit. "Answer me."

"No." Her voice came out strangled and desperate.

"Of course you can come." She kissed her shoulder blade and whispered, "When we're done."

Martine shuddered in relief and anticipation. Closing her eyes, she flexed her ass and raised her hips to meet the next blow. This time, there was no gentleness but a furious rubbing that sent vibrations throughout her body as Elliot slapped her ass. The endorphins kicked in, and the pain transformed into something brilliant and profound. "Oh, Elliot…"

Her vision blurred, and she tensed, her legs splayed and her back bowed as she came without permission. The last smack rang out in the room. She lay limp across Elliot's lap, wondering if they were done or if Elliot still had plans.

Elliot helped her roll over and gently inched her up the bed. The cool fabric did nothing to stop the burning of her ass. Sitting was going to be a problem. Elliot kept pushing her until she could lie down on top of her. She gasped as the weight of her ignited more sensations.

"We're still not done." Elliot thrust inside her. Each move rubbed her raw ass against the fabric and sparked the pain-pleasure connection until she was teetering on the edge again.

This time Martine warned her. "I'm close."

Elliot stared with a satisfied and feral smile as she kept up the pace. "Now you can come."

Another thrust and Martine's orgasm barreled through her, spreading outward, leaving her hands tingling and her chest flushed. Her whole world suspended on the border of not enough and too much, and then she crashed.

She collapsed and exhaled, all the tension bled out. "Well, that was…"

She struggled for words against the noisy backdrop of her conflicted emotions. Amazing, yes. The sliver between pleasure and pain was so unexpected. And scary, not in a physical sense but an emotional one. She liked it more than she'd anticipated, and that alone made her feel vulnerable.

"Well?" Elliot poked her in the ribs, playful and a little unsure.

Elliot's uncertainty pulled her back. She wasn't the only one who'd moved out of their comfort zone. She propped her head on her hand and grinned. "That was…something."

"Good something or bad something?" Elliot rolled on her side and mirrored her.

Martine pushed her over and climbed on top, ignoring the prick of pain as she stretched her sore ass. She held Elliot's wrists to the bed and leaned down. "More like something you're going to try next time."

Elliot's lips twitched. "Really, like what?"

She breathed the words against her lips. "So, so many things."

CHAPTER TWENTY-SIX

Too tired to make dinner, Elliot sprawled on the couch and flipped on the TV. She'd been working nonstop since the spiny lobster sport season. She groaned as she watched the coverage of Hurricane Dawn as the storm rolled into the Gulf Coast.

"That bad?" Martine joined her on the couch. Elliot tucked her feet up to give her room. Martine set them on her lap. She loved how physically relaxed they were together. Their future lived in these small gestures, but she didn't know how to get there. For now, she lived in the moment.

Elliot waved at the screen. "I'm probably going to be called up for that."

"Called up?" Martine dug her thumbs into the bottom of Elliot's foot and worked her way up to the balls of the feet.

Something deep inside Elliot uncoiled, and she sighed. "That feels nice." Tilting her head back, she closed her eyes and drifted.

Martine tapped her foot.

Oh, right she'd asked a question. "SAR. Search and rescue. All hands on deck sort of thing."

"Does that happen often?"

She shrugged, eyes still closed. "Depends on the location, size, storm surge." She struggled to concentrate as Martine continued to massage her foot. "Dawn's coming in on a high tide, so there'll be flooding. Oh…right there. She's moving fast. I might have to leave quickly."

"But not tonight?" Something in Martine's voice sounded odd, but the foot rub proved too distracting.

"No, not tonight. Maybe tomorrow. Or the next..." She let go of the conversation and floated off. How did her feet hold so much tension? Bit by bit, her stress decreased as Martine moved from one foot to the other. Her thoughts mixed and mashed together, a jumble of emotions and events that finally jelled in a moment of clarity. What was she saying? Tonight. Something about tonight.

The touch changed, less soothing and more sensual. Different nerves came alive as Martine moved from her feet and started pulling against the muscle in her calves, each finger curling around her leg and dragging down to her ankle. She started a slow rhythm up and down with each pass, settling a different sort of tension, each time getting higher and higher until her fingers brushed along the inseam of Elliot's crotch.

She gasped and opened her eyes.

Martine smiled, a slight twinkle that said she knew exactly what she was doing. She tugged Elliot closer. They hadn't touched like this since that night. Elliot hadn't given it much thought. Sometimes, work interfered with their sex-on-demand deal. But this time, something had changed. Some boundary had been crossed.

Elliot sat up and stopped her. "We need to talk."

Martine stilled and held up her hands. "I'm sorry. I didn't ask."

Did she really not know? "The spanking. We never really talked about it."

"I thought we did." Martine plucked something off the couch and wiped her hands together.

"Well, briefly." Two minutes of pillow talk didn't count. "Have you ever done that before?"

Martine smiled, a slight wistfulness to it. "Once or twice. You?"

Elliot shook her head. She'd tied women up before, given them a light tap on the ass, but never anything like that night. It had caught her off guard, and she wondered if Martine expected more where that came from. She kind of liked it but wasn't sure she'd done it right. She wanted another chance to do better.

"I figured."

Mortified, Elliot said, "Could you tell?"

Martine reached for her and smiled. "Only because I was looking."

Staring at their hands, Elliot asked, "Do you want to do that again?"

"No."

Elliot's heart sank. She'd totally fucked it up.

Martine tilted Elliot's head toward her. "Listen to me. You were amazing. That was amazing. It's just not for me."

Elliot searched her face for some clue about where this conversation was going because it definitely had a direction. Maybe Martine wanted her to do something else. She'd try anything once. "Is there something else you'd want?"

Martine leaned in and whispered, "Do you trust me?"

Elliot swallowed around a suddenly dry throat. Fear coiled around desire. What was Martine asking? Did she want to spank Elliot, too? Or something else? "To do what?"

Martine's phone dinged, but she ignored it. "Do you trust me?"

Elliot's stomach fluttered, and the slow build arousal from the massage shot up by several degrees. Intellectually, she had doubts, but physically, she had her answer. She nodded, sure of that if nothing else.

"I need to hear you say it." Martine caressed her face, a gentle counterpoint to her intense stare. Her phone dinged again.

Elliot shifted, acutely aware of how wet she was. "I trust you."

Then her phone rang. "For fuck's sake." She fished it out of her pocket and slapped at it. "What...No, I'm busy." She leaned in and nipped just under Elliot's ear.

Elliot gasped and grabbed her arm, pulling her into a kiss. She didn't care who was on the line.

Martine wrenched away. "Oh, shit, I forgot...No, I'm coming." She sighed and put the phone against her head. "Do you like spiny lobster?"

After the past two days, the last thing Elliot wanted to see was another spiny lobster. But there was no way she was leaving Martine's side. "Sure."

"Come on. I'm late." She hauled her up and took her mouth in a kiss that said "to be continued."

❖

Martine cursed Cass's bad timing as they got in the car and left the house. The annual Roberts spiny lobster bake also doubled as a birthday celebration for Aunt Elise, her father's sister and the de facto leader of the family. She really couldn't miss it for sex with her willing, and now possibly very compliant, roommate.

Their last kiss still burning through her, Martine waited until the first traffic light to put a hand on Elliot's knee.

Elliot looked over and smiled with a slightly raised eyebrow.

Time to see how far Elliot would go. "Unbuckle your belt and loosen your shorts."

Elliot took a deep breath, and Martine wondered if she'd pushed too far too soon. Then Elliot's hands went to her belt. As the light turned green, Martine tore her eyes away, but the clang of buckles and the metallic rip of a zipper being pulled down told her Elliot had done it.

Martine kept her eyes on the road, the way to Elise's house instinct by now, while she reached across the seat and slipped a hand inside Elliot's shorts. Elliot moaned and pushed against her, the fabric between them warm and wet.

Elliot covered her hand with her own and started to move them together.

Distracted by her touch, Martine almost missed the turn. She'd need to pull over if Elliot wanted to play. But she had a better idea. "Let me do the work."

Elliot pulled back, holding up her hands while Martine slid her fingers into her boxers and grazed against her wetness. She stroked the length of her, searching for a way inside, but the angle was all wrong.

Martine pulled up to another light and looked over. Elliot sat ramrod straight, her hands gripping the door handle. "Slouch a little. Spread your legs. That's it." She moved lower and slipped inside.

Elliot threw her head against the headrest. "Oh yes."

Martine clenched her legs together as her words washed over her. "Do you want more?"

Elliot nodded vigorously.

She grinned. "I can't hear you."

"More." She rolled her head on the headrest, eyes matching the plea in her words. "Please."

Martine plunged two fingers inside, and Elliot arched off the seat. *Beep, beep.* Startled, Martine whipped her head around. What, oh, the light was green. "Shit." She withdrew her hand over Elliot's protests and drove on. "Sorry. We're almost there."

"Me too."

Martine chuckled at the grumbled comment. She touched Elliot's chin. "Good things come to those who wait."

Still grumbling, Elliot rolled her eyes and zipped back up.

As soon as she opened the gate to her aunt's backyard, Martine lost Elliot in the sea of extended family. Right away, Aunt Elise swept her up for a round of introductions. Elliot shot her a lingering look, part longing and part "help me."

She shrugged and mouthed the word "Sorry." But she wasn't really. She liked teasing Elliot way too much. She'd never had this much fun in a sexual relationship before. In the past, if she'd wanted something different, she'd switched partners. With Elliot, she didn't have to.

But her ebullient mood soured as soon as she saw her cousin Brynn talking with Elliot. She didn't know why it irked her so much. They didn't have any hold on each other. But when Brynn clutched Elliot's arm and giggled, Martine made her move.

And nearly bowled Cass over. "Whoa."

Cass handed her a Coke and said, "I was just coming to see you. What's got you so pissed off?"

"Who says I'm pissed off?" Martine snatched the can and popped the lid. Its contents spilled out over her hand. She cursed and shook her hand to dry it.

Cass stared at her with their "seriously, you're going there?" look.

She sighed and sipped her Coke. Brynn threw an arm over Elliot's shoulder, and they laughed as a bunch of kids circled them, chasing each other with water guns. She frowned at the delighted squeals and screaming laughter. "I don't know. I'm just annoyed."

"Yeah, must be so annoying to have someone who fits in so well with the fam."

"Right." Grateful to have Cass in her corner, Martine tore her attention away from Elliot and Brynn.

Cass wore the same no-bullshit expression from earlier.

"Oh." Martine had missed the sarcasm on that one.

"Are you going to tell me what's going on for real? What did Brynn do this time?"

"Slept with Elliot."

Cass's mouth hung open. "Recently?"

"No."

"Then what's the deal? Are you and Elliot exclusive?"

"No. Maybe. I don't know." Should they be exclusive? Brynn leaned in and whispered in Elliot's ear. Elliot laughed, and Martine's blood boiled. "That's not the point. I mean, look at her. She's practically throwing herself at Elliot."

Cass bust out laughing. "Oh, you are jealous."

"Of Brynn? *Pfft.* No." Okay, maybe. But that was only because she'd had her hand down Elliot's pants about an hour ago. She didn't like to share. And that was all it was.

Just before dinner was served, Brynn plopped in the chair next to her. "So what's the deal with your roommate? She keeps ducking my texts."

A red-hot rage surged inside Martine that she quickly and quietly suppressed. "Oh, really? I thought you two had called it quits."

"We did. Well, I totally ghosted her. But then I ran into her during a field trip. And she's just so yummy."

Yummy? Not the word Martine would use. Although she did like the taste of her. "Oh, I hadn't noticed."

"Is she seeing someone?"

Not you. She should have said, "Ask Elliot," but what came out instead was, "Yes."

A dark satisfaction bloomed in her heart when Brynn's face fell. "Is it serious?"

Martine couldn't help herself. "Why? It's not like you're into long-term."

Brynn stared, her eyes narrowed.

"Sorry. That was rude."

Brynn nodded. "Yes, it was. What's got in your craw?"

"Nothing." She folded her arms, wishing any other member of her family would come over and break up this conversation. Where was Elliot anyway? She spotted her playing cornhole by Cass.

But Brynn would not let it go. "If she's off-limits, just tell me, okay?"

Through the years, they'd occasionally dated the same person—not at the same time—but none had generated this level of animosity. Elliot caught her looking and waved. "That's not my decision."

"No, it's not. But you can say if you'd rather I back off. I like her, but I think you like her more."

Annoyed at having to say anything at all—Brynn should have known better—Martine said, "Maybe you should." With nothing more to say, she excused herself and joined Elliot across the way. "How's it going?"

"Your family's lovely." Elliot grinned and then made a face. Leaning in, she said, "But they think we're dating. I didn't say anything."

Martine shook her head. "They always think I'm dating anyone I bring."

"You bring other women?"

"All the time." But only friends, never anyone she was sleeping with. She'd already had enough uncomfortable conversations at this party, so she didn't bother elaborating.

Elliot laughed. "Huh, that's not what your cousin told me."

"Which one?" Because if it was Cass, she'd have their head.

"Short, very in your face. Dark curls."

"Gabrielle." She shouldn't be surprised. There wasn't a pot she didn't like stirring.

"That's her."

"Well, she's not the most reliable narrator."

"What about Cass?"

Martine's stomach dropped. If Cass said anything…

"Cass told me Bantam had been nominated for an award."

The shift in gears set Martine back for a minute. "Oh. Yeah. That."

"It sounds like a big deal."

"Kind of." Once again, she was up for another award, but she didn't want to get her hopes up. She'd lost last year, and she didn't think this year would be any different. Awards tended to favor bigger distilleries with larger inventory and vast distribution chains.

"You don't sound excited."

"There's a lot of variables involved."

"Still, we should celebrate."

She shrugged. "Sure." Something about Elliot's enthusiastic support made her wary. Her successes were her own; she didn't feel comfortable sharing them with anyone else. Maybe if it was a private celebration. The naked kind.

One of her uncles bellowed across the yard, "Come and get it!"

Martine hooked her arm through Elliot's elbow. "I hope you're hungry." Because she'd need an appetite for what she had planned when they got home. But they were halfway through the food line when Elliot's phone emitted a long and low foghorn sound.

"Is that your ringtone?" Martine had heard her phone ding and ring before but never with that sound. How cute.

Elliot shrugged sheepishly. "It's for work. I needed something different. I've got to take this." She stepped out of line and moved away.

A growing unease churned Martine's stomach as Elliot walked off. She'd been slightly worried about Elliot going to work in a hurricane. She finished filling her plate, and Elise called her over. When she sat, Elise nudged her. "Something wrong?"

She ripped off a piece of cornbread. "I think she's being called in."

"For that hurricane in the Panhandle?"

She nodded, picking at her plate.

Elise squeezed her hand. "She'll be fine."

She looked up. "I'm not worried." Was she? She had a vague idea what Elliot did, and working in high seas was exactly what Elliot was trained to do. But the ocean had taken from Martine before. She didn't trust it not to hurt her again.

"Uh-huh." Maybe she was worried. Elise often sussed out her emotional state before she did. Elise took a long sip of her iced tea. "She reminds me of that woman you used to hang out with in college. Tonya. No, that's not right."

Martine tilted her head, surprised. "Toni?"

"The rich one. Yes."

She chuckled. "There've been a few rich ones."

Elise narrowed her eyes and shook a fork at her. "You know what I mean."

Elliot and Toni had nothing in common. Well, maybe the fact that they'd started as friends before they'd slept together, but Toni had left her for another woman in her upper-class social circle. And Elliot, well, they weren't dating, so she couldn't leave her. Martine watched out of the corner of her eye as Elliot hung up the phone and came back.

"Everything okay?" Martine asked.

"I'm being called in." She set her beer on the table.

Martine hid her disappointment and stood. "Oh, okay."

"Leaving so soon?" Elise asked. "Let me fix you a plate."

"I'm sorry. Duty calls."

"Not on an empty stomach."

"That's not necessary," Elliot said to Elise's back.

Martine touched Elliot's forearm. "Don't bother. She's not going to listen anyway."

"I'm sorry I'm leaving." She leaned closer. "I really wanted to finish what we started earlier."

Martine turned and kissed her cheek; worry had replaced desire. But she wanted to send her off with positive vibes. "It'll keep."

Elise returned with a big plastic container full of food. "I'll send Martine home with some cake."

"I probably won't be back in time to eat it," Elliot said.

"Oh, it'll freeze."

Elliot hefted the container. "Thank you for having me."

Elise wrapped her up in a big hug. "You're welcome anytime, honey."

"Thank you." Elliot's grin nearly split her face.

"I'll take you home," Martine said as she headed toward the gate.

Elliot stopped her. "Stay. I've got an Uber coming."

Confused, Martine said, "Oh. Then I'll wait with you."

They sat out front while Elliot nibbled on her food. "This is good. You should have brought your plate."

She was too worried to eat. Her earlier possessiveness had been replaced by concern. "Do you know how long you'll be gone?"

"No." Elliot swallowed and put her food to the side. "Do you want me to call you?"

"You don't have to."

"That's not what I asked."

Feeling as if something had shifted, she said, "Yes."

A car pulled up, and Elliot gathered her things. She reached out for a hug. "Sometimes, cell service is spotty, but I'll find a way."

Martine tightened her arms and said, "Be careful. I've got plans for you."

Elliot kissed her, a light and tender touch that scared her with its hint of finality. What if Elliot never came back? She shoved that thought aside and squashed her fears. Elliot knew what she was doing. This wasn't her first time, and she'd trained for these kinds of missions. Martine would see her again; she was sure of it.

She stepped back and forced a smile. "Good luck." When had their relationship gotten so serious? She should pull back, but it was too late. She already cared too much to let go.

CHAPTER TWENTY-SEVEN

Elliot dropped her go bag on the floor of her bedroom and stumbled into the shower. She let the water sluice off her and closed her eyes. Right away, she was back in the boat, cruising down flooded streets and looking through the debris for survivors. She didn't even know the number of people she'd rescued, and after a while, their faces blurred together. A composite of women, men, and children. No one looked alike, and yet they all blended together. Older Coasties talked about Hurricane Harvey in the same breath as Dawn. She'd been in Seattle at the time, and although she knew other Coasties had been called down, she hadn't. So she had no frame of reference for the operation she'd just experienced.

Although efforts were shifting from rescue to recovery, boats were still out there when she'd been called back to Key West. She'd called Martine twice. Once to let her know she'd gotten there and the second time just to hear her voice. She'd found a quiet bench at the edge of the barracks, a series of squat green tents that reminded her of every war movie she'd ever seen:

Martine answered after the third ring, and Elliot checked her watch. Time had lost its meaning. She ate when she was hungry, slept when she could. The sun was up so it couldn't be too early. Still. "Did I wake you?"

She heard some rustling. "No, I was trying to make coffee. Emphasis on trying."

Elliot smiled, imagining Martine standing in their kitchen, holding the beans in one hand and the measuring spoons in another. "Do you want help?"

Martine sighed. "Totally."

Elliot walked her through the process, and when they got it brewing, she said, "Next time, I'll leave you directions."

"That would be awesome."

She stared ahead, not really wanting to talk but not wanting to hang up either. Just hearing Martine breathe helped.

"How's it going? It looks terrible."

Elliot rubbed her hand through her hair and sighed. "It's bad. Whole neighborhoods underwater. People have lost everything." The enormity of their loss pushed against her, and she choked up. Maybe calling Martine had been a bad idea. She needed to keep an emotional distance to do this work. Talking to Martine opened an unexpected door. She took a shaky breath and brought it back under control.

But Martine seemed to hear it. "Are you okay?"

She could cry later. "I will be."

"When are you coming home?" Home. No longer a place but a person. She belonged somewhere with someone. Did Martine think of her as home? She hoped so.

"I don't know. There's still so much to do." So many people stuck in their homes with no way out.

"Well, I'll be here when you get back. Call me if you need me."

"You too," she said automatically, even though she didn't know if she could pick up.

She opened her eyes and turned off the taps. She toweled off and wiped the steam off the mirror. She looked as tired as she felt. After she brushed her teeth, she walked into her bedroom and paused. She should just sleep in her own bed, but the pull toward Martine proved more enticing. And that pull was only getting stronger. In the quiet moments, when the exhaustion hadn't taken her, she'd fantasized about their last day together and had wondered what Martine wanted from her that needed trust. What part of her had she not already given freely? What boundaries did Martine want to expand? Would she strap her down and flog her? Fuck her to the brink and then deny her?

She got as far as the open door to Martine's room before she stopped again. She didn't want to wake her or scare her.

"Stop lurking out there and come to bed." In the dim light, Martine threw back the covers and haphazardly patted the bed. She didn't have to ask twice. As soon as Elliot lay down, Martine snuggled up. "You're warm." She chuckled. "And naked."

Elliot drew her close, tangling their legs and burying her face in her hair. She breathed her in. She'd missed that smell. "I took a shower."

"I heard." Martine ran a hand through Elliot's hair. "I wasn't sure if you wanted space."

"Not tonight." She relaxed for the first time in days and sighed.

Martine kissed her neck, her throat, along her collarbone, featherlight touches that comforted without arousing. "Tell me what you need. Talk, fuck, sleep?"

Elliot hummed. "That feels nice." She closed her eyes, a warm, drowsy feeling spreading outward.

Martine continued touching her and whispered in her ear, "Go to sleep. I've got you tonight."

She drifted off, searching for the exact moment when they'd changed from friends with benefits into something more, but not one single moment stood out. Just a series of moments building to the inescapable truth that Martine meant more to Elliot than anyone else.

Martine exited her favorite coffee shop carrying two cups of café con leche and a white bag filled with an array of sweet and savory pastries. She whistled on her walk home, happy to have Elliot back safe and sound.

Elliot was still in bed when she walked in. She tiptoed into the room and set the coffee on the nightstand.

"I'm awake." Elliot rolled over and sniffed. "Is that coffee?"

She smiled. "Yep."

Elliot sat up. "Did you make it?"

She handed her a cup. "Nope."

"Café con leche?" Elliot hefted the cup and took a sip. Tapping the bag, she said, "What else did you bring?"

Martine sat beside her and opened it up.

"Oh. Yummy." Elliot pulled a muffin out and took a big bite. Crumbs sprayed everywhere. Martine laughed as Elliot apologized and started brushing them off, only to create a larger mess.

"What's on the agenda today?" Martine hadn't expected her home so soon. For a few days after she'd left, Martine had puttered around the house doing laundry, vacuuming, and dusting. When Elliot had finally called, Martine had admitted to herself that she was lonely. A lonely that had nothing to do with being alone but more with longing. She'd grown accustomed to Elliot's presence in the house, even when she wasn't there.

Elliot leaned back. "Sleep. Food." She grinned. "Sex."

"I think I can accommodate all three. Where do you want to start?"

"You've already taken care of the first two." She set aside her coffee and threw back the covers.

Martine slid off the bed, pulled her T-shirt over her head, and tossed it across the room. Her sports bra followed. Elliot's smile grew as she lost each layer of clothing, and she took her own time staring at Elliot's broad shoulders, small breasts, and muscular thighs, her skin fading from her dark hands to her light, lean torso, a sailor's tan.

Starting at Elliot's feet, Martine kissed and nipped along her calves and toward her thighs. Elliot caressed her head, her neck, her hair, constantly keeping them connected by touch. As she skimmed over Elliot's center and inhaled, Elliot clutched her head.

"Not yet," Martine murmured and continued upward, brushing open-mouth kisses along the curve of Elliot's hip and the underside of her breast. She licked along her areola and gently sucked a hard nipple into her mouth.

Elliot groaned and arched when Martine scraped the nipple with her teeth, giving it a tiny bite as she pulled back. Elliot clutched Martine's head and hissed. "Don't stop."

Pleased with her reaction, Martine moved on to the other nipple. Elliot tightened her grip, and Martine answered that by increasing her suction. Elliot writhed, her moans growing louder until she wrenched away and rolled on her side. "Stop, you're going to make me come."

Sliding down to face her, Martine wet a finger and traced a circle around the nipple's base. "And that would be bad, why?"

"Mmm, good point."

Martine kissed her, deliberately teasing with her tongue and teeth while she moved her hand lower. She inched closer, and their kiss collapsed when Elliot threw a leg over Martine's waist, allowing Martine easy access to her folds. The wet sounds turned her on even more before she dipped inside. Elliot gasped and clenched around her. The tightness drew Martine in and held her in place before she pulled out and pushed back in. Elliot dug her heel into Martine's ass, bringing her closer. Using three fingers, she thrust again and again until Elliot's grunts became pants. Martine watched her face contort and twist, revealing and reflecting the raw desire they shared. Finally, Elliot went still, her eyes focused on Martine with such openness, she almost flinched. Then Elliot came with a loud "Fuck!" and collapsed on her back.

Martine pulled out.

"That was…"

"Yeah." Still riding the high of fucking her, Martine stared at Elliot's flushed face and heaving chest. That wanton look with the barriers down cried out for more. Seeing this side of Elliot, unguarded and open, sparked a deeper urge to dominate and explore, something that had been tickling the back of her mind since the first time she'd taken control. Something that had grown after she'd let Elliot spank her. Something she'd skirted the edges of with other women, but she hadn't wanted to take the time and trust to go further with them.

She leaned across Elliot, enjoying the lazy touches as she pulled a black box from her side drawer. "I have a present for you."

CHAPTER TWENTY-EIGHT

Elliot held the black box, surprised that Martine had bought her something. Curious, she opened it. Sitting on a tiny black cushion was a stainless-steel anal plug. She picked it up and looked closer. Teardrop-shaped and hefty enough to feel it but not so large as to be overwhelming, with a loop on the end. Tucked underneath it was a packet of lube.

"Do you like it?"

Elliot smiled and held it in her palm, enjoying the feel of it. She didn't own any anal toys. Once or twice, a woman had asked her to use them, but no one had used one on her. She'd never trusted anyone that much. "I've never used one before."

"Will you wear it?" Martine asked, all hunched excitement, with an expectant smile on her lips. "For me?"

Elliot had spent hours imagining the ways Martine would want *her* to take control. But having someone else make the decisions and letting them do it was much harder than Elliot had thought. Was this what Martine wanted her trust for? Elliot hesitated, nervous but excited.

Martine set the plug aside. "If you don't like this, we don't have to do it."

"Have you done this before?" Needing reassurance, Elliot moved closer.

Martine rubbed her neck, something Elliot knew she only did when she was nervous. And that made her feel better. Like she wasn't the only one vulnerable here. "No. I've wanted to, but I never had anyone I wanted to share that with. You know?"

"I know." Touched that Martine trusted her with that revelation, Elliot made her decision. She leaned in and kissed her, a simple brushing of the lips that she let linger. She picked up the plug and put it in Martine's hand. "I trust you."

Smiling, Martine kissed her again, a quick peck and a slight nip that Elliot chased as she pulled away. "Good. Here."

Elliot leaned back as Martine gently tucked a pillow under her lower back. Her stomach fluttered, and her heart raced as Martine slowly spread her open.

Martine settled between her legs, and she leaned forward to watch. With a smile, Martine pressed a palm against her stomach. "Lie back."

She did and sighed as Martine peppered kisses along her inner thighs. Everywhere Martine touched tingled, a live wire of sensation. She moaned when Martine moved lower, licking her labia and teasing the edges of her clit. She gasped as Martine ran her tongue lightly along her perineum, up and around her anus. Arching her hips toward the slight pressure against her closed pucker.

Martine murmured, "You like that, don't you?"

Elliot nodded, unable to form words.

Martine continued licking her ass, moving her tongue back and forth, stopping to press against her anus. Elliot moved with each lick, getting hotter and wetter and needing more. She reached down and dipped into her wetness, brushing Martine's forehead.

Martine adjusted her angle, smiling between her legs. "Are you ready for more?"

Was she? She had control here. She could say stop, and it would be done. She didn't need to be in total control, though. Martine would take care of her. Something inside her released, and she exhaled. "Yes.

Martine put the plug next to her and ripped open the lube. She poured it over the tips of her fingers while Elliot touched the cool silver metal.

"Don't worry. It'll warm up inside you." She smiled and kissed her, a possessive kiss that reassured as well as aroused. A kiss that distracted as well as demanded.

Elliot caught her breath as Martine rubbed against her anus, the sticky substance adding to the slipperiness.

Martine paused. "Are you okay? There's sugarcane if you need it."

Elliot relaxed, her legs opening more, and smiled. "I know. I trust you." But she could have said "I love you" and meant the same thing.

Reaching down, Martine slipped a finger inside her. "You look so hot right now."

The words washed through Elliot, leaving her more aroused than before. She clenched her ass around the finger and moaned.

Martine slipped out again and rubbed, a circular motion that soothed and excited. "Your ass is practically begging for it."

Would Martine make her beg? Elliot probably would. But Martine reached across her and palmed the plug. "Oh, it's a bit chilly." She pulled her other hand away, and Elliot groaned her disappointment.

"Patience." With a wink, Martine rubbed the plug between her hands and poured more lube on it. "Ready?"

Elliot nodded and closed her eyes as the hard metal pressed against her. Martine leaned over her and whispered in her ear. "Take a deep breath."

Elliot shuddered as Martine brushed a kiss behind her ear, the gentle command giving her permission to enjoy it. She inhaled, and that firm pressure disappeared, replaced by a feeling of fullness and the weight of the plug inside her.

Martine grinned, an almost feral look on her face. A delicious chill crawled up Elliot's spine, adding to the feeling of the plug snug inside her. "Someday, I'd like to fuck you like this. Would you let me do that?"

Elliot groaned and nodded, her voice lost to the exquisite intensity.

Martine leaned in and tapped the plug inside her. "I can't hear you."

Elliot gasped and closed her eyes while she fought through the dryness in her mouth. Martine's insistent demands resonated with her base emotions, and she answered without hesitation. "Yes. Yes. Please."

Martine gently pulled her up, and the plug in her ass was noticeable but not uncomfortable. "How's that feel?"

Elliot wrapped her legs around her as they stared at each other. So many feelings jostled for space inside her. *Don't stop, please fuck me, I love you.* But all she could say was, "Different, good."

"That's just the first step." Elliot barely had time to savor the anticipation before Martine kissed her, open-mouthed, fierce, and needy. In between kisses, Martine leaned back and tugged on her hand. "Come here."

Elliot crawled up, the plug moving wonderfully inside her, and paused at her waist.

Martine shook her head. "Keep going."

Elliot inched up under Martine's guidance until her knees were on either side of Martine's head. A slight vulnerability at being so open over Martine washed through her, all the more astonishing considering what they'd just done. "This?"

Looking up from between her legs, Martine grinned. "This."

Elliot shivered under her gaze and sat on her chest. The plug shifted, and she gasped.

"Feel that?"

She nodded.

Martine grasped Elliot's hips and buried her face between her legs.

Closing her eyes, Elliot leaned forward and braced her hands against the headboard as Martine tasted her. A bold lick across her entire labia and a slight tug on the plug made her breath catch. Then Martine went for more focused strikes, diving into her with abandon. Gripping her ass, Martine played with the plug, pulling it in and out and twisting it, the angle deeper and more direct.

Elliot moved with her tongue, riding Martine's face, bucking her hips. And where one sensation left off, another picked up, the plug a counterbalance to Martine's relentless licking. Elliot had never been so thoroughly possessed, all her senses reeling. A heady combination of trust and lust that she'd never had with anyone else.

Her heart raced, and her breath came much quicker as Martine moved faster with a slight tug—a bite and then a suck—long and then short, alternating with quicker licks. Martine brought her to the edge only to pull her back down. Her release took longer to build, but when she finally came, her orgasm tore through her at full strength, the insistent pressure in her ass a delicious addition to all the other sensations, and she lost her grip on the headboard.

Martine caught her as she crumpled and adjusted their positions so they were both lying down. "Do you mind?" Martine tapped on the plug, and Elliot just nodded.

A gentle pull, a tight press, and it was gone. Elliot sighed, a little disappointed. She knew they'd use it again.

"You like that?"

"Mm-hmm...yes." She lay quietly, her head resting on Martine's chest, listening to her heartbeat slow and her breathing get deeper. Something had been clawing at the back of her thoughts since her first visit to the distillery, but it had been growing long before that. Even before they'd started having sex. A truth that Elliot had danced around that now stared her in the face. She'd opened her life to Martine, and they'd done things that she would have never done with anyone else. Not just sex but little things. Furniture, grocery shopping, all the mundane tasks of a relationship. Elliot trusted her, yes, but more importantly, she loved her. And not as a friend, although she was, but as the whole package: friend, lover, partner.

"Are you staring at me?" Martine murmured sleepily.

"Yes." And now that she knew, Elliot wanted to tell her, too.

"What do you see?"

"I love you."

Martine laughed. "Of course you do. I just gave you the best fuck of your life."

"No, it's more than that." She leaned in and kissed her, tender and heartfelt and awestruck.

Martine pulled back, a slightly confused look on her face. "Shh…you're fuck drunk. Take a nap. Let's talk later."

Elliot would feel the same way later, but she was willing to give Martine some time to think about it. She was worth the wait. "Okay."

Elliot closed her eyes, but she did not sleep, too excited for what came next.

❖

Martine crept out of bed a little before noon. She dressed quickly, hoping to be out the door before Elliot woke up. After Elliot's confession, she needed time to think.

Elliot stretched and yawned. Too late. "What are you doing?"

Martine paused. What was she doing? If this was any other woman's bed, she'd be halfway home by now. But she was already home, and this wasn't some woman.

Elliot tucked her hands behind her head. "Is this about what I said?"

How could she look so casual? And why was Martine so freaked out? Elliot wouldn't be the first person to tell Martine she'd loved her during sex, but the possibility hit too close to home. *It's more than that.* But what did *that* mean? "What? No. I just remembered, I have work to do. I should go in." She couldn't even come up with a good lie.

Elliot didn't say anything, but she looked skeptical. "You don't have to say it back, you know."

"I know." But she felt like she should. And that bothered her more than saying it. She'd never felt this pressure to return someone's feelings. She'd always compartmentalized sex, but she was friends with Elliot as well, and she cared about her feelings.

Elliot sat up and tossed the covers aside. "Will you be home for dinner? I could make something."

"Ah, yeah, about that. There's not a lot of groceries." She lingered by the door. Now that she'd been caught sneaking out, her urgency had left.

"Why am I not surprised?" Elliot looked around the floor and on the bed, obviously perplexed.

"You came to me naked, remember?"

Elliot straightened, and a slow smile spread across her face, playful and filthy. She sauntered over and cornered Martine by the door. "Oh, I remember."

Martine swallowed hard, all of a sudden out of her depth. What was wrong with her? She'd totally fucked Elliot's brains out a few hours ago, and now she couldn't even look her in the eye. She needed to get a grip.

She ducked under Elliot's arm and darted down the hall. "I'll catch you later." But as she left her alone, she wondered if she was making a mistake.

❖

Martine avoided Elliot for the next two days, sleeping on the couch in her office. She knew she'd have to face her eventually, and the longer she stayed away, the worse she felt about her leaving. Ana Sofia found her on the second morning.

"Did you sleep here?" She strolled in and kicked Martine's shoes out of the way.

Martine covered a yawn and scratched her neck. "Maybe."

Ana Sofia leaned against her desk. "What's going on?"

"Nothing."

Tapping her leg with her shoe, Ana Sofia leaned forward. "Then why aren't you sleeping in a bed at the house you're renting from my mother?"

"Well, it's Elliot. No, it's me. It's complicated." Complicated didn't begin to explain it. She'd fucked a really close friend who'd told her she loved her, and she'd run away. Okay, so not so complicated, but she felt like shit. She didn't treat friends this way. Well, not good friends. And not friends like Elliot. Shit.

Ana Sofia's face changed. "Oh my God, you've been sleeping with her!"

Martine pulled back, stunned by her vehemence. "Yes?"

Ana Sofia smacked her on the shoulder.

"Ow." She rubbed her shoulder. Ana Sofia had never smacked her before.

"What the fuck's wrong with you?"

"What's wrong with me? What's wrong with you? She's my friend. We can do what we want."

"'Friends with benefits'?" Ana Sofia used air quotes. "Since when has that ever worked?"

"Well, it was working just fine until…" She couldn't even say the word. Those three words had changed everything. But what did she think would happen? She'd fuck Elliot for a few months, and then Elliot would go away?

"Until?" Ana Sofia crossed her arms.

"Until nothing. Who are you to judge? What do you call that thing with Cass?" Ana Sofia's on-again, off-again relationship with Cass was a sore point, and she regretted bringing it up when Ana Sofia's face crumpled.

"Over." She sobbed.

Shock knocked the wind out of Martine's sails, and she held Ana Sofia while she cried. "I'm so sorry."

She'd never seen her this broken up over Cass. Angry, yes. Defiant, definitely. In tears, no. She could count on one hand the number of times Ana Sofia had cried over anything. Martine's angst over Elliot faded away while she brought Ana Sofia over to the couch and waited for her to let it out.

The sobs subsided, and Ana Sofia sniffed before pushing off Martine and sitting up. Martine handed her a tissue box. Ana Sofia thanked her and wiped her nose. She dabbed at the corners of her eyes and sighed. "I must look terrible."

"You look gorgeous. As usual."

"Liar." She squeezed her hand. "But thank you."

Martine hated to see her so deflated. "You've broken up before. Maybe this is just one of those times?"

Ana Sofia wiped at her tears and shook her head. "Not like this. It's really over." She hiccupped on another sob. "I don't even think we're friends anymore." And a fresh wave of sobbing began.

Martine's stomach dropped, and she swallowed back the fear that she'd made the same mistake with Elliot. She'd have to figure out a way to deal with Elliot's feelings so she wouldn't lose their friendship. And if she had feelings for Elliot, well, she'd keep them to herself. She loved her too much as a friend to mess this up.

CHAPTER TWENTY-NINE

When Martine didn't come home for two days, Elliot worried that she'd ruined their friendship. She'd spoken without thinking, and Martine had run away. She wouldn't take it back, but she wished that her timing had been better. Less spontaneous and more thought-out. Maybe a conversation first.

By the third night, Elliot had gone from concerned and anxious to angry and disappointed. She didn't even have the decency to show up and speak?

Grace called while she was still fuming. "I'm heading your way next week. Lunch?"

"Sure." Maybe she should call her. No, she wasn't going to chase her.

"Well, don't get too excited. What's wrong?"

Grace's skills as an astute investigator also made her an annoying friend. Elliot sighed and tuned in to the conversation. How much did she share? What was there really to tell? "I might have fucked up my living arrangement."

"Go on."

"It's complicated."

Grace countered, "I had one of those."

"Did you?" Grateful for the distraction, she grabbed on.

"Not a living arrangement complication, but she was an ambassador's daughter, and she broke my heart. Is this about your childhood friend?"

"Yes. Martine." She took a deep breath and filled Grace in. Their friendship connection, the sex without all the details, her feelings, the I-love-you.

"Oh, that sucks. What did she say?"

"She left."

Grace exhaled. "Not then. Right after you said it."

"Nothing. Well, she told me I was fuck drunk. But we haven't talked since."

"And what? Your phone's broken?"

Elliot bristled. "No."

"So at the first real point of conflict, you pull up stakes and run?"

"I did not run. She did."

"You still have access to all the modern communication devices. Call her." She had a point.

Although Elliot loved having sex with Martine, there'd been no one like her in Elliot's life, and she didn't want to lose their friendship. Maybe she wasn't mad at Martine so much as she was pissed at herself. She'd lost track of what she'd wanted in their relationship. Distracted by her libido, she'd almost ruined all of it.

"I'm just saying. Better to clear the air now than later. And if that doesn't work, well, I've got an opening up here with your name on it."

Elliot brushed it off as usual, and Grace didn't press. After they hung up, she scrolled through her contacts and clicked on Martine.

The phone rang several times and then went to voice mail. She considered hanging up, but then Martine would know she'd called without leaving a message. Time to own up to her adult decisions. "Hey, it's me. I'm calling to check in."

The door opened, and her heart soared. Her emotions settled for the first time in days. Ridiculous how much relief poured through her at her voice.

"Did you just try to call me?" Martine strolled into the kitchen, her voice a welcome return to normal.

Elliot shrugged and went for nonchalant teasing. "You're lucky I called you instead of the cops."

Martine stilled as the barb landed. Then she smiled and dropped next to her. "Yeah. You're right. But I'm back."

Elliot shifted and stared. "Are we going to talk about it?

Martine tilted her head back and exhaled. "Do we have to?"

Elliot folded her arms. "I told you that I love you, and you ran away for three days. Yes, we have to talk about it."

Martine sighed and rested her head on Elliot's shoulder. "I sort of freaked out."

Her willingness to touch gave Elliot hope, and she slung her arm behind her back. "Yeah, you did. But it's okay."

Martine twisted and looked up at her. "Really?"

She'd missed the feel of her after only three days, more if she counted the time she'd been on mission. And that alone made her decision easier. She'd rather have these small moments together than to lose it all, so she lied. "Really. I wasn't thinking when I spoke."

"But you meant it?" Was that hope or fear in her voice?

Elliot couldn't tell, and the last time she'd told the truth hadn't gone so well, so she went for a half truth. "In the moment, yes."

"And now?" Martine started rubbing small circles on her stomach.

Elliot gently pulled her hand away and held it. "I need a little more time before we can...go back."

Martine squeezed her hand and nodded. "I get it. For what it's worth, I'm sorry."

Sorry for what? Running out? Not loving her back? And as much as it hurt to sit there and pretend it didn't matter, Elliot stayed.

CHAPTER THIRTY

Handing Elliot a drink, Ana Sofia plopped beside her and nearly tipped into the couch. She yelped, and Elliot fished her out. "What the fuck kind of furniture is this?"

"The sentient kind."

She stared. "You are a find, aren't you?"

"You'd think." Elliot looked at where Martine chatted with some redhead and laughed a little too loudly. After Elliot had backpedaled from her feelings, everything between them had changed, and not for the better. How Martine could just pretend nothing had happened infuriated and troubled her. There was this brittleness to their interactions when they were alone, and Elliot couldn't shake the feeling that she'd broken something precious.

She sipped her cocktail, a mix of sweet and sour that overlay a distinctly bold alcohol. She pulled it away and stared at it. "What is this?"

"A daiquiri. A real one. Not that frozen shit."

She took another sip, and it went down as smoothly as the first. "These are dangerous."

Ana Sofia grinned. "Oh, there's more where that came from."

"Are you trying to get me drunk?" Too late, judging from the ease with which she teased her.

Ana Sofia splayed her hand against her chest. "I would never."

For a second, Elliot worried that this was a prelude to a sexual advance. She'd already bitten off more than she could chew with Martine. Ana Sofia played in an entirely different league.

Ana Sofia stood and held out a hand. "I think there's something else you'd enjoy."

Elliot didn't move.

Ana Sofia wiggled her fingers. "Come on. I don't bite."

Elliot wasn't so sure, but she stood anyway. On their way outside, Ana Sofia swiped a box from the table. They sat near the pool, and Ana Sofia leaned over and popped the lid. Inside were several cigars.

Elliot shook her head. "I don't smoke."

"Neither do I, but these go really well with that." She nodded toward the daiquiri.

Elliot listened closely while Ana Sofia showed her the proper way to trim, light, and smoke a cigar.

Then, Ana Sofia said, "But do it however you want. Part of the beauty of tradition is knowing when to flaunt it." She blew out a puff of smoke and grinned.

Elliot sucked in her own smoke and started coughing.

Ana Sofia laughed. "Give it another try." Elliot finally got the hang of it, and Ana Sofia shook her own glass, an amber liquid swirling inside it. "Now sip."

She did, and the rich smokiness created another dimension to the daiquiri. "Wow. How'd you know?"

"Cigars and rum are processed in the same areas of the world. Like certain cheeses go with certain fruits. Regional affinity."

Elliot took another drag and slowly released it. Not something she'd do all the time but surprisingly satisfying.

"I see she's introduced you to her bad habit." Martine plucked the cigar from her hand and took her own puff before nodding toward Ana Sofia's glass. "Where's the rest of that?"

"In the kitchen."

Martine handed the cigar back to Elliot, leaving her with a slow, lingering look. "Be right back."

Elliot's heart clenched as she watched Martine walk away.

Despite the change in their relationship, sexual tension still simmered just below the surface. Worse than before because Elliot knew what she was missing. She didn't know how much longer she could hold out or if she even wanted to.

Ana Sofia touched her hand. "You should tell her how you really feel."

Elliot choked on the smoke coming in. Any chance she had to blow off that comment died with her coughing fit. When she finally spoke, she heard the bitterness in her voice. "I already did. She freaked out."

"I know. She told me."

"Then why would you want me to say anything?" Elliot could feel herself closing off pieces of herself.

Ana Sofia took another pull on the cigar and blew perfect rings into the air. "I've never seen her like this."

Warmth crept up Elliot's neck that had nothing to do with the alcohol, and she covered her embarrassment by drinking. Yet another surprising secondary taste emerged, even better than the first. More mellow and almost like caramel. "Like what?"

"So centered."

Elliot laughed. Centered was not the first word she'd use to describe Martine.

Ana Sofia smiled and took another drag. "Don't see it, do you?"

"No, not at all."

"What do you see?"

Elliot looked around and found Martine with that damn redhead again. "Passionate, strong, competent...impulsive, guarded, and loyal."

"Then you do see her as she is." Ana Sofia stared across the room. "The things she feels passionate about, she stays with to the end. Rum, Cass, me, family. But she's always afraid that one day, we'll all disappear, so she keeps us at a distance."

"Why?"

"Well, you know. People leave her, so she lets go first."

But Elliot didn't know. Who'd left Martine? Did Elliot even know her at all?

"I'm always surprised she stayed in Key West. When I met her in high school, I thought she'd go to college, then move away, flitting from place to place."

Still trying to figure it all out, Elliot asked, "What do you think made her stay?"

"The distillery. I think it gave her stability that she could control."

Stability? Martine was the most stable person Elliot knew. She had a family and a community that cared about her. Her mind reeled.

Ana Sofia snuffed out her cigar and started to stand. "I'm sorry, I'm a little drunk. I shouldn't be sharing all this."

Elliot reached out. "No. Stay."

Covering her hand with her own, Ana Sofia sat back down.

Martine watched as Elliot flirted and joked with Ana Sofia all evening. Her anger grew with every casual touch between them.

Cass sidled up to her and followed her glare. "What do you think that's about?"

"I don't know. But I'm going to find out." She'd already gone over once, and she planned to do it again.

Cass held her back. "Don't."

"This is your going-away party." How could Cass be so calm?

"Yes, it is. So don't cause a scene."

"Aren't you the tiniest bit interested in what's going on?"

Cass smiled and shook their head. "No. They're just talking. Probably about us."

Martine paused. Why would Elliot talk to Ana Sofia about her? Things between them had been off since the I-love-you incident. She missed that closeness and struggled to find ways to get it back. She could feel Elliot leaving, and it scared her. "You're really leaving?"

Cass folded their arms. "I'm really leaving."

"You're going to miss Fantasy Fest." The Halloween extravaganza was Key West's answer to Mardi Gras, and it happened in another week.

"I know."

Martine's attention wandered back to Elliot and Ana Sofia. "You really don't care?"

Cass shook their head. "No. I've caused her enough grief. It's time to let go."

Martine's throat tightened, and she looked away. Cass and Ana Sofia had been her rocks. Even when they weren't together, they had been there for her.

Cass hugged her tight. "You're going to be okay. You're not alone."

Martine grabbed hold. "I know, but no one knows me like you do."

Cass held her a little longer, then pulled back. "What about Elliot?"

"It's different. You're family."

"Elliot could be family."

Martine shrugged. Not because she hadn't thought of that but because she didn't want to. She'd been avoiding Elliot's emotional pull but with less and less success. Without the sex to hide behind, their relationship had become strained under the weight of all the things they didn't say to each other. Eventually, it was going to break.

Several hours later, after she walked the last guest out, Martine came back to the kitchen to find Elliot cleaning up. "You and Ana Sofia looked pretty cozy tonight." She wandered the living room, picking up glasses and plates.

Elliot raised an eyebrow while she finished loading the dishwasher. "You think?"

She scoffed. "Yes."

"Are you jealous?" Elliot didn't bother to look up.

She shrugged. How could Elliot be so nonchalant? Did she think Martine didn't notice her ducking out of sex for the past two weeks? "Maybe."

Elliot shut the door and faced her. "No."

Confused, Martine asked, "No?"

"You don't get to do the jealous girlfriend."

"What?" She came back to the kitchen and put her stuff on the counter.

Elliot moved into her space. Her eyes glinted. Martine had seen her like this once before, when she'd come home from work angry.

Martine lifted her head and matched her intensity. "Are we going to fuck or fight?"

"Both." Elliot swept both hands across the table, and everything crashed to the ground.

Martine sidestepped a bowl and grabbed Elliot's collar. She kissed her roughly, tongue and teeth, pouring all her pent-up frustration and fear from the past few weeks into it.

Elliot matched her, pressing her up against the table before she spun her around and bent her over it. Martine caught herself with her hands, her blood pounding in her ears, and her breath coming in short gasps.

Elliot yanked her shorts down. Her belt dropped them to the floor. Her underwear was peeled off, and Elliot's knuckles brushed down her legs. She tried to turn, but Elliot held her down. "Did I say you could move?" Her tone was quiet but no longer angry, echoing that moment when Martine had lain across her lap, so open and aroused, begging to come. A moment she'd relived again and again with different outcomes. Where Martine had told her the truth. That she'd loved the way Elliot dominated her, but it had scared the shit out of her. To be seen so clearly left her vulnerable and defenseless.

Elliot brushed a kiss along her shoulder, that touch grounding her. Then Elliot stretched along her back, whispering in her ear, "Sugarcane?"

Her breath sent shivers down Martine's spine. Sugarcane? Oh. Safe word. Would she need a safe word? "No. I mean yes, that word. But not yet."

She barely finished her sentence before Elliot was inside her, twisting and turning with each thrust. Martine skittered along the table, reaching out to grip the far edge.

Elliot pulled back and growled. "Sit up." Martine scrambled around and wrapped her legs around Elliot's hips, pulling her closer. "I want you to know it's me fucking you. No one else."

Those words said with such fierceness pierced her heart. As if she'd let anyone else do this to her. No one saw this side of her. Not even Ana Sofia. She dug her heels into Elliot's ass and arched into her. "No one else." Then she lunged and kissed her, hard and fierce, with all the emotion coursing through her.

Elliot met her all the way, demanding and insistent with every push and pull, in and out as they kissed. Martine tore away from her mouth and lost all focus as Elliot fucked her harder. She met Elliot's stare, the crackling intensity that matched their physical connection. Emotions flashed across her face that Martine couldn't read. She wanted to know what Elliot was thinking, what she was feeling, but before she could ask, Elliot blinked, and when she looked again, whatever had driven Elliot before had fled, taking with it the intense emotional connection she'd felt between them. Only the physical remained, and when she came a few minutes later, she felt only relief, not release.

Elliot pushed away. Martine reached for her, but it was too late.

Elliot leaned against the sink, her fist against her mouth, shaking her head.

"Elliot?"

"I'm sorry. I can't." She moved away, heading toward the hall.

Panic seized Martine. Elliot was leaving? Not after this.

"Wait!" She chased her, her feet crunching on spilled chips.

"I need some air." Elliot kept going until she was out the door.

CHAPTER THIRTY-ONE

Elliot walked along Duval Street, dodging the late-night tourists and trying to figure out her next steps.

She'd let weeks of sexual tension boil over into a quick fuck on the table. And for one glorious moment, she'd felt that connection to Martine she'd missed since she'd said she loved her. But sex no longer filled the emotional gap in their relationship, and she couldn't pretend it did. If Martine had been anyone else, she might have continued, taking the pleasure without the commitment. She had so few people in her life, and Martine had tied together her past and present in ways that made her complete. She hadn't known what she'd been missing until Martine had shown up.

While Elliot was sure Martine felt something more for her than friendship, continuing without addressing their underlying feelings would eventually kill any relationship at all. Listening to Ana Sofia last night had convinced her that Martine wasn't going to change. At her core, Martine believed people would leave her. She wouldn't be wrong. Elliot's job required travel. She left all the time. Could their relationship weather those changes? Should she cut the cords now and avoid the messy breakup later? Who was she kidding? It was already messy. But at least her heart would only be slightly broken instead of completely devastated. She'd be doing Martine a favor letting her loose before either of them had a chance to get in any deeper.

And what about their house? She loved the life that they'd built together. That house had become a home in less than a year. The closest Elliot had ever come to feeling settled. As a child, Key West had been the place she'd fit in, and as an adult, that still held true. She belonged here, but whether that was with Martine, she didn't know.

She came back to a dark house. Hoping to avoid Martine, she slipped inside and ducked into her bedroom. She slept lightly, waking up just after dawn.

While she made coffee, she texted Grace and got an immediate call back. "Are you serious?"

Was she? She needed space, and she couldn't get that in Key West. She topped off her coffee and went out back by the pool. "I think so. I need more details."

"Is this about your living situation?"

"I need something...different."

Grace made a sympathetic noise. "I'm sorry. Is it *done* done?"

She exhaled. "I don't know, but I need time to figure that out."

"As much as I'd love to give you a quick out, I need to remind you that you've been ducking this job every time I've offered."

"I know, but maybe it's time to accept the inevitable." The Coast Guard was her life. She didn't need a home.

She waited while Grace typed something. "Why don't you come up for this operation? I'll clear it with your CO. Sort of a trial run for both of us. Then we'll go from there." Elliot went back inside to find Martine waiting at the kitchen table, her thermos sitting next to her. Elliot didn't remember making her thermos; it had become automatic.

"I didn't hear you come in last night."

Elliot closed the door behind her. "It was late."

"Can we talk?"

Elliot owed her that much. Sitting across from her, she grabbed her own coffee. "Sure."

"This is not working."

Last night had proved that. She shook her head. "No."

"I don't know how to fix this." Martine looked at her as if she had the answers.

"I'm not sure we can." Whatever they had before was done. It had finished the day she'd admitted her feelings and changed from friendship into love.

Tears shone in Martine's eyes. "This was never supposed to ruin our friendship."

"I don't think it has." Even if Martine could somehow see her way to loving Elliot back, Elliot needed time to sort out her own feelings.

"But you just said it couldn't be fixed."

"I don't think we can go back to before. I think we need some space to work out the new us."

"Friend us?" Was she looking for something more?

Elliot had already put herself out there more than once and had been disappointed. If Martine wanted something different, it would have to come from her. Elliot didn't have the stamina to do it again so soon. She nodded. "Friends, yes."

Martine exhaled. "What does space mean?"

"I'm taking a temporary assignment in Miami."

Shock registered on Martine's face. "Oh. Okay. When?"

"Next week."

"Is it a promotion?"

"Yes. Kind of. It's not the direction I want to go, but it's what I've got."

Martine tilted her head. "Don't do this on my account. Can't you say no?"

She wiggled her hand. "I kind of have. I'm too skilled to stay at the rank I am for much longer. But I ducked out of it the past few years by switching assignments."

"And if it works out?"

Elliot didn't really want it to work out. She wanted to stay here. "I don't know."

Martine could end all this by giving her a sign that she wanted Elliot as something more, but she just sat there asking questions and giving nothing in return.

Elliot stood. "I need to take a shower and head into work. Let's try to make it work for another week, okay?"

Martine's nod and blank expression was all the confirmation she needed that she was doing the right thing.

❖

Martine worked extra hours the week before Elliot was due to leave. Fantasy Fest created extra traffic at the distillery, so she had an easy excuse. But each morning that she came out to hot coffee, her heart cracked a little more. She didn't know what to do. She cared about Elliot, but saying that she loved her? She didn't know how to make those words come out of her mouth. And what was love, anyway? She'd made Elliot a priority in her life. She'd slept with her exclusively. Shouldn't that count for something? What more did Elliot want?

Fantasy Fest passed in a blur. Without Cass, the parties lacked appeal. Martine had been looking forward to bringing Elliot, but now she could barely drag herself to anything. More than once, she turned to make some observation and then remembered she'd come alone. Once, she even brought Ana Sofia, who turned out to be worse company than she was. At least with Elliot, Martine didn't have years of memories to drag her down. Ana Sofia had no such luck.

At the Blue Pelican, Martine nearly tripped over a woman on her way out.

"Briar Rose." That Mississippi drawl brought back memories of being pulled over by a hot sheriff in the middle of nowhere.

Martine took in her crisp shirt, broad shoulders, and mirrored sunglasses tucked in her pocket. "Sheriff...I don't think I ever got your name."

"Dianne. It was on the ticket."

"Really? I must have missed that." She'd driven up to the Glades County courthouse a few weeks after Elliot had moved in. She'd been slightly disappointed that Dianne hadn't been there and then had forgotten all about her. "What brings you to Key West?"

She waved around. "I got a few days off and thought I'd come and see all this for myself."

Instant tour guide kicked in, and Martine said, "Well, it's definitely one of our signature events."

"Can I buy you a drink?"

Martine hesitated and glanced around. She'd been on her way out the door.

Dianne caught her looking. "I'm sorry. You're not alone."

Understatement of the year and yet completely wrong. "No, I'm...I'm...sure."

"You don't sound so sure." Dianne gave her a half-smile.

Martine ordered an El Presidente, and Dianne ordered a daiquiri. Martine regretted it when it came, both for the poor quality—she should have known better—and the memories of the one she'd shared with Elliot on the beach.

"This is good." Dianne hefted her red Solo cup. While not the same level of daiquiri snob as Ana Sofia, Martine didn't care for the frozen concoctions.

After that, Martine didn't know what to say. A beautiful woman, totally her type—sexy, available, and not local—and she had nothing to say. Her banter skills felt so undercused after almost a year off the market. She hadn't known she was off the market while she was sleeping with Elliot, but it felt like that.

"Do you dance?" Dianne nodded toward the floor.

Martine shrugged. "Not really."

Dianne leaned in and said, "Do you want to go somewhere quiet and talk?"

Martine pushed away her drink and nodded. They wandered through the crowds with no destination in mind. Martine spotted some empty spaces along the concrete planters looking over the marina and took Dianne there. She didn't pay attention to their conversation, mostly on autopilot until Dianne stopped.

"Am I boring you?"

Guilt spiked through her. "I'm sorry. I'm not good company tonight." Or really, any night this week.

Dianne exhaled. "Oh, good. I thought it was me."

Martine touched her hand. "No, you're perfect." And she was perfect. Perfectly uncomplicated.

"I was so surprised that you hit on me last spring. You threw me for a loop."

Martine smiled. "What? No one's ever tried to seduce you out of a ticket?"

"That doesn't happen as often as you think. Especially in Glades County." Her face fell. "Oh, was that what it was?"

"Oh hell, no. There was no amount of flirting that was going to get me out of that ticket. I thought you were…are hot."

Dianne blushed, actually blushed. "Then I missed your court date. I came down here on a whim. Thought if I ran into you, I might get a do-over."

Tenderness welled up. "Oh, Dianne."

She nodded. "I missed my chance, didn't I?"

"I'm so sorry." Were those the only words she knew anymore?

"Is there even a chance?"

Not even remotely. Not after Elliot. Who else in Martine's life would she have agreed to move in with so quickly? Who else in her life would she have slept with almost without question? And while she didn't know if she loved Elliot, she definitely knew that she couldn't replace her.

Her silence answered for her. Dianne didn't seem too upset, and Martine had to give her credit for trying. But how had this kind of hookup ever sustained her before Elliot?

CHAPTER THIRTY-TWO

Two weeks in Miami and Elliot already hated it. Grace knew it and asked for another week before she sent her back. To what, Elliot had no idea. She hadn't spoken to Martine since she'd left. No texts. No calls.

She strapped her boarding gear on and looked around at the three fresh-faced seamen facing her. *Here goes.* She squared her shoulders and shoved all extraneous thought aside, pulling a litany of procedures to the forefront. She walked along the deck, inspecting their gear and giving them an encouraging nod here and there. Poulson needed a buckle tightened. Greer had everything correct, but Elliot straightened her helmet anyway. Nelson had his hand wrapped so tightly around his gun that she needed to move it to check the safety.

They pulled up portside to the container ship registered out of Panama and owned by Tropical Shipping. A legitimate shipping business, Tropical moved cargo throughout the Caribbean. The captain had radioed the manifest over, and Elliot had already picked a couple of containers to inspect. They were the perfect practice boarding for her new recruits. She didn't mind routine; it kept her mind busy and her feelings at bay.

"Look sharp, people."

Elliot followed Lieutenant Chen aboard and greeted the captain but kept an eye on the crew's movements while Chen spoke with him. The captain led them to the first container and swung it open.

Elliot stepped inside, followed by Nelson, and they flipped their helmet lights on. Dark and humid, the container smelled of the wood and tar stacked on pallets throughout. "Wood and tar. Want me to open any of the barrels?"

"Yeah. Pick one."

Elliot held out her hand, and Nelson fumbled for a crowbar. He dropped it twice before handing it over. She suppressed a sigh. If he'd shown any interest in being prepared for this mission, she would have had more sympathy, but he'd spent his downtime goofing off. So she only offered him a stern, "Steady, Seaman."

Sweat dripped into her eyes and down her back under all the extra gear while she wrenched the top off a barrel and caught a whiff of the foul-smelling liquid. Glancing around, she spotted a long-handled broom and dropped it inside the barrel, sweeping it back and forth and all around. Nothing. Properly sealed, both guns and drugs could hide in these barrels, but the risk of ruining it with leakage made it unlikely.

"Want another one?"

"No. Let's head to the next one."

Elliot relished the sea breeze outside the container and felt the sweat dry along the edge of her hairline. Out of the corner of her eye, she caught Nelson pointing with his gun at something along the deck. "Nelson, keep your weapon down."

She didn't bother to see if he paid attention. Her voice alone should have been enough. In the next container, she followed Greer in and let her take the lead. Bananas and coconuts. Elliot's light cast spidery shadows along the back wall while she watched Greer work. One of those shadows moved, and Elliot grabbed Greer's hands. "Careful."

A large black tarantula sauntered up the banana crate.

Greer shuddered. "Ew."

She called back, "We've got a spider in here. Can I get a plastic bucket or something?"

"We're going to catch it?" Greer's voice squeaked on the last syllable.

"We can't have it coming to shore. If customs finds out we left it here, there will be words." Elliot cupped it in her hand, glad to be wearing gloves. Spiders didn't freak her out as much as snakes did, but holding a big one in her hand while projecting calm took all her bravado.

"Do we have to? Who's going to know?"

Elliot knew she was speaking from fear. "I am. And so are you." She handed the spider over and watched Greer suppress her revulsion and trap it in her hands.

"Coming in." Nelson's boots echoed on the steel floor, and his shadow danced along the walls as he weaved through the tight aisles of crates. He held out a bucket, and Greer practically threw it in. Nelson yelped. "What the fuck? That's huge!"

"And it's yours now."

Nelson carried it out off to the side, as far from his body as his arm could get. His gun hung at his side, banging against the crates, and then it caught on the slats. Elliot saw the flash of light, heard the retort, and shouted, "Look out," in the span of time it took to yank Greer to the deck. The bullet ricocheted off the metal walls and pinged a few times before it stopped.

Several lights appeared in the container, and Lieutenant Chen shouted, "Tillman, you okay?"

Elliot pushed to her feet, her ears still ringing and her stomach roiling with her anger. "Yes, sir." Seething at Nelson's incompetence, she glanced down at Greer. "You okay?"

Greer didn't move, and Elliot dropped to her feet. Blood pooled around Greer's head. "Shit. Medic!"

Martine hurried through the streets, weaving in and out of the crowds. A Cat 1 hurricane barreled toward the Keys, but that didn't seem to deter the tourists or the locals. Cat 2 and below often got brushed aside as no big deal, but Martine wasn't taking any chances with her inventory. And she wasn't alone. A few stores had already been shuttered with corrugated metal or plywood. Key West was only a mile and a half wide and four miles long; the eye of a hurricane could be twenty to forty miles. If it was coming toward them, it would be hitting them. Seventy- to ninety-mile-per-hour winds could still do some damage if things weren't tied down.

She hadn't heard from Elliot in two weeks. Maybe she had been pulled back to Key West for hurricane duty. Maybe she'd be at home tonight. And what would Martine say to her? That brief glimmer of hope flickered and faded.

She opened the door and started to work. A few hours later, she'd burned out all thoughts of Elliot until Ana Sofia closed the door to her office and leaned against it. "What's going on?"

"What do you mean?"

"You're in a foul mood today."

"Am I? There's a hurricane coming." She'd been too preoccupied with getting everything stored and stowed.

"And?" Ana Sofia folded her arms and raised her eyebrows. Apparently, something had showed.

Letting some of her sadness surface, Martine rubbed her face with her hands and sighed. "I haven't been sleeping."

Ana Sofia came in and sat, concern in her tone. "What's wrong?"

"Elliot and I had a fight. I think." Was it a fight? They hadn't yelled or said hurtful things to each other, but she still felt bruised and beaten.

"You think?"

She exhaled. "Well, she left."

"Left? As in, moved out?" Ana Sofia's voice took on a sharp tone.

Confused, Martine looked up. "No. Not yet."

"Then where is she?"

"Miami. Temporary assignment."

Ana Sofia pointed at her. "You need to fix this."

"I don't think I can." She could fix a fight, but this…she didn't know where to begin.

Ana Sofia crossed her arms and shook her head. "Well, you better because she's in love with you, you moron."

"Did she tell you that?" Was that what they were talking about at Cass's going-away party?

Ana Sofia frowned. "She didn't have to."

Martine looked up and saw the pain of Cass's leaving on Ana Sofia's face. Her vehemence made sense. If Ana Sofia couldn't have love, she'd make sure someone else did. "I'm sorry about Cass."

Ana Sofia dismissed her with a gesture. "We're not talking about me. Start at the beginning, and tell me everything that happened. And then we'll see how you can fix this."

And so she did. Every little detail that led up to her leaving excluding the more graphic parts.

"Well, there's only one question. Do you love her?"

"I…I maybe."

Ana Sofia threw up her hands. "You can't even say it."

Why couldn't she say it? She loved Ana Sofia, she loved Cass, but that was easy. They were family. But love with Elliot meant something different. A level of trust and commitment that scared her. Love with Elliot meant changing the way she lived and the way she viewed herself. She didn't want to change. She liked her life as it was.

"I just want it to be the way it was."

"When you were friends, or when you were sleeping together?"

"Can't I have both?"

"No, not anymore."

"Why not?" she snapped. Why did those three words change everything?

"Don't get pissed at me. What did you think would happen?"

"The same thing that always does." But nothing about Elliot had been the same. As a roommate, as a friend, as a lover. Martine had ignored the differences because she'd craved the closeness.

Ana Sofia looked at the ceiling and sighed. "I wish Cass was here. They'd know how to say this to you."

Martine braced herself and said, "Go ahead."

"I watched you live this life of half commitments and never said anything because it worked for you. But, honey, these last few years have been hard to watch. Even before Elliot. It's not working for you anymore."

Her words hit the mark. Would Martine have chosen to live with Elliot so easily or jumped into her bed so quickly if she hadn't already been looking for something different? She voiced the fear that lived close to her heart. "What if I lose her?"

"If you don't talk to her, you already have."

CHAPTER THIRTY-THREE

Elliot left Miami after dealing with the aftermath of Greer's shooting. Grace had been right. Miami was a mistake. Nelson's ricochet had absorbed some of the velocity, making the shot less deadly but still damaging. Lodging in Greer's upper chest, the bullet had splintered her collarbone, so she'd be in pain and out of commission for a while. The responsibility of her injury weighed on Elliot. If she'd been more focused, if she hadn't taken the job, if she'd pulled Nelson off earlier, if, if, if.

Grace had shown up at the temporary barracks and had listened to her unload before she'd finally said, "You should go home."

"But the operation..." The boarding party had been a routine part of Elliot's temporary position at the station and wasn't related to the work she was doing with Grace.

"I should never have let you come. Your heart's just not in it."

"I know it's my fault, Greer—"

Grace had held up her hand. "Oh no. That's not what I'm saying. Shit happens. Nelson's superiors knew he wasn't up for it. And Greer is going to be fine. You need to go home and deal with your personal life."

"But I made a commitment to you."

"If you still want this after a year, I'll get you on my team. But for now, your CO needs you back in the Keys. That storm's coming. Be safe." Grace had clapped her shoulder on the way out.

She'd packed up and left. She breezed south on a mostly

deserted Overseas Highway, all of the traffic headed north. She made good time, only coming across more cars as she drove in and out of towns where people scrambled to get last-minute supplies. Dark gray clouds amassed on the southern horizon as she finally pulled into the station's parking lot.

She earned a few confused looks as she headed up to Harriman's office. He glanced up and smiled. "Oh, good, you're back."

And she went to work. Portia had stalled over Cuba and had been downgraded to a tropical storm. Turning northwest, the edges of the storm clipped the Keys from Islamorada to Key West. As the storm hit and the night wore on, bands of rain and bursts of wind buffeted the island. Two calls came in, but another crew answered them. Finally, the day broke, and Harriman rotated Elliot out with another group. "Go home, but be ready to come back."

She ran to her truck between breaks in the rain and drove home. All the feelings she'd avoided in Miami surged inside her when she pulled up in front of the house. Was Martine home? Would she be asleep? When had it all become so fraught? Instead of gaining perspective, two weeks had solidified her feelings. She wanted more. And if Martine didn't want that? Elliot's chest hurt thinking about it. She screwed up her courage and rushed up the stairs two at time. Once inside, she closed the door and padded into her room.

Wired and tired, she then headed into the kitchen to make coffee. The place felt different and yet the same. All around, she saw their life together—the table, the couch, the TV, the pool. Each one brought a memory, sometimes loving, sometimes funny, sometimes serious, but all precious. Martine loved her. Who cared if she didn't say it? They could go back to the way it was before. Friends with benefits. She could do that. If it meant keeping Martine close.

She poured a cup and sat at the table, rehearsing what she'd say.

Martine padded into the kitchen and froze.

Elliot smiled and lifted her cup. "Good morning." She loved the way Martine looked in the morning. The way her hair stood out at all angles, her sleepy shuffle, and her slight grumpiness that she didn't try to hide.

"What are you doing here?"

Elliot tried not to read too much into her distant tone. "Coffee?"

Martine nodded and collapsed in a chair opposite her.

Elliot jumped up and fixed her a cup.

Martine wrapped her hands around the mug, closed her eyes, and took a tiny sip. She threw her head back and hummed her pleasure. "I missed this."

Elliot stared at her neck, remembering the way Martine's pulse moved under her lips, the way her skin felt, the way her throat vibrated as she spoke Elliot's name. She looked away and backed off before she picked Martine up and lay her across the table.

"Don't look at me that way." Martine spoke with a husky undertone.

Elliot was sure her voice sounded the same. "What way?"

Martine stood. "I'm going to take a shower, and then we'll talk."

She watched Martine walk away, itching to grab her from behind and spin her around. Shit. This was never going to work. Just like before, she wanted her, but now she yearned for a deeper connection. She wanted the whole package.

❖

Martine made it into her room before her knees gave out. Elliot had looked at her like she wanted to consume her, and she'd barely controlled the urge to give in. If she did, nothing would change. And Ana Sofia was right. Her old way of life had stopped working, and she hadn't noticed until Elliot had walked in. She'd been immune to Martine's defenses, barriers she'd built as an adult. But Elliot had been her childhood friend and known her before the walls went up.

But Martine didn't want to jump into bed with her again. She wanted to do this right. She started to strip out of her clothes when her phone rang. Ana Sofia. She never called this early. "What's wrong?"

Ana Sofia's voice came over the phone cracked and broken. "The barrel room. You need to come in."

Panic seized her, and she hung up without saying good-bye. She threw on clothes and stumbled into the kitchen, banging into the table as she sidestepped Elliot.

Elliot reached out. "What's wrong? What's happened?"

"I don't know. I have to go to work." She fumbled with her keys, dropping them on the floor.

Elliot scooped them up. "I'll take you."

All sorts of scenarios spiraled through her brain. As they pulled out of their street, Elliot laid a hand on her knee. Martine grabbed hold and didn't let go until they arrived.

She hopped out before Elliot switched off the car and ran to the back entrance. With a gasp, she covered her mouth when she saw that a section of the roof had peeled back like a tin can. Right above her barrels.

She rushed inside and found an even bigger mess. The room reeked of wet wood and rum. Water had come in and flooded past the bottom shelf, coming up six inches over half the barrels on the first shelves. In the back, roofing material had smashed into three barrels, all of which had poured their contents onto the floor.

"Oh shit," Elliot said behind her.

Martine splashed through the room, touching barrel after barrel, cataloguing the losses in her head. About a third of her inventory gone. She'd need years to replenish her aged rums. All that work gone. At least the rum she'd distilled with Elliot had survived.

"Martine?"

She hurried past and searched the rest of the building for damage. Ana Sofia met her in the tasting room, looking as shocked and devastated as she felt. "Is there anything else?"

Ana Sofia shook her head. "How much do you think we lost?"

"A lot of the Cochin, and I'm not sure how much Crèvecoeur. I don't even know where to begin." Short-term, they'd have product, but the next few years, they'd have to buy their rum from other sources to keep those two expressions running.

Elliot came up behind her and said, "Have you contacted your insurance agent?"

Ana Sofia shook her head. "Let me find her number."

"Let's take some pictures and see if we can stop some of those leaks."

Martine turned around and faced her. "You don't have to do this."

Elliot moved closer. "I know. But I can't leave you like this. No matter what else happens, I'm still your friend."

The loss of Cass, the loss of Elliot, now the loss of her rum. She couldn't take any more. If Elliot was here to just leave again, she couldn't do it. She needed more from her and for herself. "What if I don't want that?"

Elliot's face crumbled, and she started to step back. "Oh."

Martine grabbed her before she could move away. Everything she had worked for lay wrecked in the next room, and she was damn sure she wasn't going to let her relationship with Elliot fall into ruin. "I mean, what if I want something more?"

Elliot smiled, kind and understanding but not jubilant. "You've had a shock. You're not thinking clearly. Let's not talk about this right now."

"No, you can't believe me one minute and not the next." Why was it so hard to say this? She'd made up her mind. It should be easy from here on out.

"Then what are you saying?"

Martine took a deep breath. No going back. Time to put it all on the table. "No one knows me like you do, and I like that. I feel like myself when I'm with you."

"What does that mean?" Elliot moved closer.

"Come home. With me." Martine reached out and held her hands. "To me."

Elliot pulled her closer, keeping her far enough away so she could look her in the face. "Are you sure?"

Martine had been living in stasis all her life. She didn't want to do this alone anymore. "Yes."

CHAPTER THIRTY-FOUR

Elliot adjusted the place settings one last time. Ana Sofia leaned in and said, "It's perfect."

Elliot laughed at herself. "I didn't realize how nervous I'd be."

"Martine says you made a turkey last week for practice."

Her face grew hot, slightly embarrassed. She hadn't stopped at the turkey. She'd also made stuffing, gravy, and mashed potatoes. Just in case.

Martine came up behind her and hugged her. "You'll do fine."

Elliot leaned into the hug, holding the hands around her waist. She'd thought the last year had been the best of her life, but it had nothing on the last three weeks. Nothing had changed, but everything felt different. Before, they'd been two separate people with these pockets of connection: deep, intense, but ultimately fleeting. A new foundation had formed underneath them, and everything flowed from it.

While Martine had dealt with the fallout of her collapsed roof, Elliot's promotion papers had come through. She'd invited Martine on base for the ceremony, showing her around and introducing her to the crew. Weiss had given her the once-over and had extended her hand. "A pleasure to meet you."

Martine had charmed them all before and after the ceremony, surprising Elliot with tears in her eyes as she pinned the stripes on her.

Coming home from dinner, Martine had turned to her and said,

"I didn't expect that to be so moving. Is it weird to say I'm proud of you?"

Her heart had swelled, and she'd leaned in to kiss her. "Not weird at all."

A few days later, Weiss had come up to her and said, "I see why you turned me down."

She'd just smiled, and they'd gone back to work. She hadn't bothered to say that she and Martine hadn't been a thing when Weiss had first hit on her. She'd finally had a talk with Weiss and had gotten her to ease up. Best to leave that alone.

After Martine had canceled Thanksgiving with her mother, citing the need to stick close to the distillery, Elliot had suggested an alternative. "Why don't we host it instead?"

Martine had been confused at first. "You'd do that? My stepfather can be a little…much."

"Of course." That was how families were. But she didn't say it.

Pilar showed up first, with Angelica and Ernesto right behind her. Then Aunt Elise and her kids, followed by a few more Pinders and a couple of Robertses as well. Her mother came last and hugged her. "I remember you. Look how big you are."

Martine's eyes almost popped out of her head, and she caught Ana Sofia's surprised look. Not sure what had happened, Elliot waited to ask. But she didn't get a chance until much later.

Martine put the last dish in the dishwasher and said, "I can't believe my mother hugged you."

"Why?" Elliot rinsed the soap off the sheet pan and set it on the drying rack. She didn't want to let the dishes rest overnight. She had plans for brunch tomorrow and wanted a clean kitchen.

"She doesn't hug."

"Maybe it was peer pressure." All of Martine's family had hugged her. She emptied the sink and wiped down the counters.

"Is there any of that pecan pie left?"

Elliot groaned and held her stomach. "How can you still be hungry?" On top of her turkey dinner, everyone had brought enough food for a second meal. No one had left without leftovers.

Martine sauntered over. "I'm insatiable."

"Is that so?" Elliot pulled her close and kissed her. All her nervous energy from earlier uncoiled into a languid kiss, slow and searching gradually becoming more intense as Martine opened her mouth. Inside Martine's mouth, she teased her way in and then out. Martine grew more insistent, clutching at her shoulders and pushing her against the counter. Elliot arched toward her, and Martine pushed back.

"Is that the best you can do?" Martine bit her earlobe.

Elliot gasped, startled from her hazy arousal, and stared. "Is there something you want?"

"Stop being so timid and fuck me."

Elliot didn't think she was timid, just going slow. But thinking back on the last few weeks, Martine had taken the lead when they'd had sex. She'd fallen into the submissive role without thinking because she knew it was something Martine liked. Not wanting to upset their new equilibrium, she'd avoided taking control. But Martine had challenged her every move, almost as if she was daring her to possess her. Elliot finally understood what she wanted. "Go into my bedroom while I lock up."

Martine started to protest, and Elliot silenced her with a look. "Now."

She took her time turning off the lights and checking the locks. She wanted Martine to stew for a little bit. Imagine all sorts of scenarios while she wandered the house. She walked into her bedroom and found Martine lying naked with her hands between her legs.

"I see you've started without me."

Martine shrugged. "I couldn't wait anymore."

Elliot slipped off her pants and started unbuttoning her shirt while Martine watched. Nodding toward her open legs, Elliot said, "Don't stop on my account. Continue."

Martine continued stroking herself, her face flushed, whether from embarrassment or arousal, Elliot didn't know, nor did she care. Either way, she looked hot.

"I didn't know if you'd punish me."

Elliot stilled. Something tickled the back of her mind. Was

Martine deliberately goading her into spanking her again? "I thought you didn't like that."

Martine stopped touching herself and dropped eye contact. Interesting.

"Is there something you want to say to me?" When Martine mumbled, Elliot smiled. "Speak up."

"I did." Her hands clutched at the sheets.

She did what? Oh. She'd liked it after all. Elliot could work with that. She smiled. "I see. Is that something you want now?"

Martine shrugged, another side of her emerging. "It's up to you."

Aware of Martine's stare, Elliot let that hang between them while she finished getting undressed and sat next to her. She ran a hand along Martine's torso, smooth strokes toward her center. "And what else do you like that you haven't shared?"

The words spilled from her lips as she played with Martine's folds, slowly building her up and then letting her go while Martine confessed her desires. Touched and turned-on by all that she'd said, Elliot leaned in and kissed her with all the love she felt inside. "Thank you."

Martine clutched her face. "I love you."

Elliot smiled, hearing those words for the first time but already knowing in her heart how Martine had always felt. "I know."

EPILOGUE

One year later

Martine and Ana Sofia landed at Heathrow two days before the Annual International Wine and Spirits Competition. Neither of them had been on vacation recently, so they spent the two days sightseeing. Everything reminded Martine of Elliot. A coffee shop here and a boat there. Elliot's work schedule and the six-hour time difference made checking in so much harder.

Ana Sofia had ordered custom tuxes for the two of them. Neither wanted to wear a dress, and Ana Sofia had liked the statement made by wearing men's clothes to an award ceremony traditionally dominated by men.

"You look amazing. This color looks good on you." Ana Sofia turned her around and fixed her bowtie.

Martine smoothed her hand down the vest, a rich iridescent green. She'd modeled it for Elliot before she'd left, and the reaction had been intense and pleasurable. "Back at you, my friend."

Ana Sofia had chosen an amber color for her vest and bowtie that matched the soft brown tones in her hair. She held out her arm. "Ready to go?"

With Ana Sofia beside her, she relaxed at the high level of glamour and glitz at Guildhall. Passing through the wooden doors, she entered the reception area and the quiet buzz of conversation from several hundred people. Once again, she wished Elliot had come. Not out of need, but because Elliot grounded her. Then she saw Jean-Claude and heard his big booming laugh.

"You made it." He wrapped her up in a massive bear hug and set her down. He winked. "Come on. Let's meet your competition."

Ana Sofia had already joined another conversation with two blond, blue-eyed men. Martine mixed and mingled until dinner and then sat through the awards ceremony, dutifully clapping with each new announcement. Until they got to her category.

"This year's rum comes from a relative newcomer in the field. While most of the distilleries honored tonight have generations behind their brand, this duo started their distillery only twelve years ago. But they have built upon tradition while developing a distinct style that has earned them a bronze star for this year's white rum category. Cejas y Roberts and their unaged expression, *Cubalaya*."

Ana Sofia gasped and grabbed her arm. Martine sat for half a second as the entire room turned toward her table and applauded. She stood and slowly followed Ana Sofia onstage. Hands reached out to congratulate her, and she stepped up on stage to accept the award.

Ana Sofia hugged her and then spoke to the crowd. Martine didn't hear a word, feeling the weight of the bronze medallion in her hand. This expression represented the culmination of several years' work. She'd struggled to find the missing piece for the last two years, until that breakfast with Elliot and those beautiful crepes. Velvety chocolate and tangy mango. And then she'd known. Each step of the way, she'd hit a wall, and each time, Elliot would be there. They'd go somewhere, do something, eat something. All of those experiences poured together and blended with that final distillation that day in the distillery.

For years, Martine had strived to make something so transcendent, and always, she'd come up short. Now she knew the missing ingredient had been love. Not just love of the work or the product or the process or the place or the community, but love of and with another person. Love without barriers and boundaries, love between equals, and love between friends. Love with Elliot.

She'd been a fool to think that she didn't need love like that in her life. That vulnerability didn't hurt her. It made her stronger, more complete. It gave her purpose, deep purpose, and it showed in the most honest expression of herself, her rum.

She stumbled through a thank-you and followed Ana Sofia offstage.

She spent the next few hours networking and enjoying the accolades, but every once in a while, she'd reach for Elliot and remember she wasn't there. Elliot had tried but hadn't been able to get off in time, and although they'd been disappointed, Martine understood. They'd held their own celebration before she'd left.

Ana Sofia had a driver waiting to take them back to their hotel. Bidding her good night at her room, Martine opened the door and kicked off her shoes. She put the bag with her award and other party swag on the ground and dug out her phone to call Elliot.

She froze as a phone rang in her adjoining room. Was that… She ran in and hit the light switch.

Elliot stood, holding her phone up. "Should I get it?"

"No, it's probably your girlfriend. You wouldn't want her to know that you're with me."

Elliot tossed it aside and said, "You're probably right."

Martine jumped into her arms. "What are you doing here?"

"I switched shifts. Sorry I missed the ceremony. This was the earliest I could come." She pulled back. "How'd you do?"

"I won bronze. Wanna see?" Martine went over and grabbed the bag.

Elliot grinned. "That's awesome."

"It is." She hefted the medal, then set it on the nightstand. "How'd you get in the room?"

Elliot sat on the edge of the bed and pulled Martine between her legs. "Ana Sofia helped me out."

Martine rested her arms across Elliot's shoulders and laced her fingers behind her head. "She did, did she?"

Elliot tugged her bowtie loose and used the ends to pull her close. "Did anyone tell you how hot you look in this tux?"

Martine leaned in and teased her with a kiss. "Maybe. Why?"

Elliot nipped her lips in response. "Should I be jealous?"

"I don't know."

"I have ways of making you talk." She unbuttoned Martine's collar, moving down her shirt, kissing the skin that she revealed.

Martine moaned. "Like what?"

Elliot yanked her shirt up and undid the last buttons. She pushed it down, pinning Martine in place. "I brought a whole bag of toys with me. Care to find out?"

Martine would have loved to have seen the look on the customs agent's face as Elliot handed over her bag.

Elliot slapped her ass, not hard and barely noticeable through her pants, but the intention was clear. "I asked you a question."

Once, Martine would have struggled to keep some semblance of control, so afraid of losing herself in someone else that she'd shut off the things that turned her on, but now she looked at Elliot and smiled. "I'm afraid you're going to have to work to make me talk."

Elliot leaned into her and purred in her ear. "I can do that. Take off your clothes."

About the Author

Leigh wrote her first story in a spiral notebook at the age of five and she never stopped pretending. She grew up in three of the four corners of the US before heading to college. Despite the warnings that doing so would make her a lesbian, she went to a women's college.

She lives and works in upstate New York with her wife, son, and two Siamese cats, Percival and Galahad. When she's not writing, reading, or parenting, she's tabletop gaming with a crew of like-minded nerds.

Books Available From Bold Strokes Books

A Cutting Deceit by Cathy Dunnell. Undercover cop Athena takes a job at Valeria's hair salon to gather evidence to prove her husband's connections to organized crime. What starts as a tentative friendship quickly turns into a dangerous affair. (978-1-63679-208-8)

As Seen on TV! by CF Frizzell. Despite their objections, TV hosts Ronnie Sharp, a laid-back chef, and paranormal investigator Peyton Stanford have to work together. The public is watching. But joining forces is risky, contemptuous, unnerving, provocative—and ridiculously perfect. (978-1-63679-272-9)

Blood Memory by Sandra Barret. Can vampire Jade Murphy protect her friend from a human stalker and keep her dates with the gorgeous Beth Jenssen without revealing her secrets? (978-1-63679-307-8)

Foolproof by Leigh Hays. For Martine Roberts and Elliot Tillman, friends with benefits isn't a foolproof way to hide from the truth at the heart of an affair. (978-1-63679-184-5)

Glass and Stone by Renee Roman. Jordan must accept that she can't control everything that happens in life, and that includes her wayward heart. (978-1-63679-162-3)

Hard Pressed by Aurora Rey. When rivals Mira Lavigne and Dylan Miller are tapped to co-chair Finger Lakes Cider Week, competition gives way to compromise. But will their sexual chemistry lead to love? (978-1-63679-210-1)

The Laws of Magic by M. Ullrich. Nothing is ever what it seems, especially not in the small town of Bender, Massachusetts, where a witch lives to save lives and avoid love. (978-1-63679-222-4)

The Lonely Hearts Rescue by Morgan Lee Miller, Nell Stark & Missouri Vaun. In this novella collection, a hurricane hits the Gulf Coast, and the animals at the Lonely Hearts Rescue Shelter need love—and so do the humans who adopt them. (978-1-63679-231-6)

The Mage and the Monster by Barbara Ann Wright. Two powerful mages, one committed to magic and one controlled by it, strive to free each other and be together while the countries they serve descend into war. (978-1-63679-190-6)

Truly Wanted by J.J. Hale. Sam must decide if she's willing to risk losing her found family to find her happily ever after. (978-1-63679-333-7)

A Good Chance by Ali Vali. Harry, Desi, and Desi's sister Rachel are so close to getting everything they've ever wanted, but Desi's ex-husband is coming back to get his revenge and rip apart their chance at happiness. (978-1-63679-023-7)

A Perfect Fifth by Jaycie Morrison. Streetwise pianist Zara Keller and Lady Jillian Stansfield couldn't be more different, yet their connection brings a new awareness of who they are and what they truly want in their lives—including each other. (978-1-63679-132-6)

Catching Feelings by Ana Hartnett Reichardt. Andrea Foster expected to catch a lot of pitches from the Alder Lions' star pitcher, Maya, but she didn't expect to catch feelings. (978-1-63679-227-9)

Defiant Hearts by Lee Lynch. In these stories, you'll find your lovers, friends, and lesbians you wish you knew—maybe even yourself. (978-1-63679-237-8)

Love and Duty by Catherine Young. All Princess Roseli wants is to marry her three lovers, but with war looming, she must instead marry Princess Lucia to establish a military alliance between their planets. (978-1-63679-256-9)

Serendipity by Kris Bryant. Serendipity brings jingle writer Annie Foster and celebrity pop star Bristol Baines together, and their undeniable attraction keeps them close, but will their different paths drive them apart? (978-1-63679-224-8)

The Haunted Heart by Jane Kolven. A ghost, a ring, and a quest to find a missing psychic—it's a spell for love. (978-1-63679-245-3)

The Rules of Forever by Nan Campbell. After reconnecting at their high school reunion, Cara and Lauren agree to embark on a textbook definition friends-with-benefits relationship, but trying to keep it uncomplicated is harder than it seems. (978-1-63679-248-4)